Given to the
room   Oct. 31st

Alex Crosby – member of
Barnwell W.I.

BARNWELL

By the same Author

Novels
Lying-in
A Fleshly School
Linsey-Woolsey
Paradise
A Pillar of Cloud
The Golden Veil

Biography
Gerard Manley Hopkins
A Most Unsettling Person: Patrick Geddes (1854–1932)

Guidebook
Poets' London

Wendy Davies, Chairman of Banwen W.I. pouring tea at an 'open day' at Banwell Manor, 1991

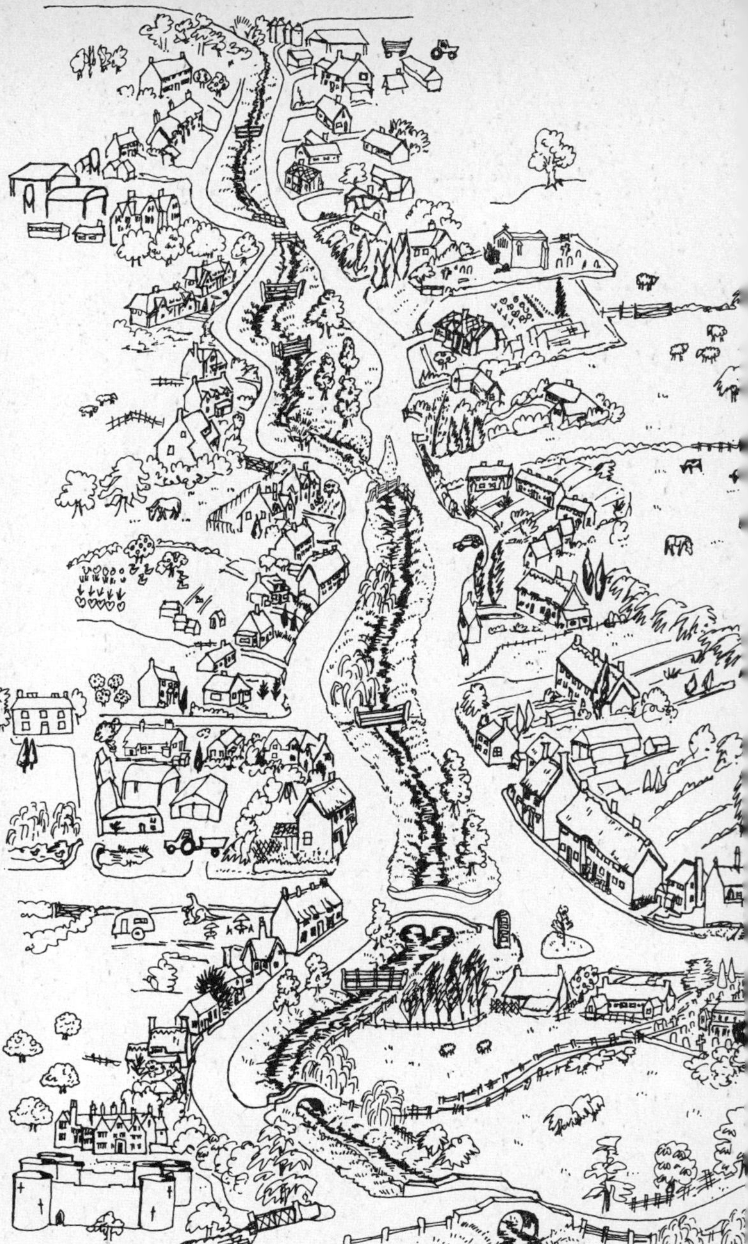

BARNWELL

Paddy Kitchen

Illustrated by Carry Akroyd

Hamish Hamilton · London

First published in Great Britain 1985
by Hamish Hamilton Ltd
Garden House 57–59 Long Acre London WC2E 9JZ

Copyright © 1985 by Paddy Kitchen

British Library Cataloguing in Publication Data
Kitchen, Paddy
   Barnwell.
   1. Barnwell (Northamptonshire)—Social life
and customs
   I. Title
   942.5'54   DA690.B26/
ISBN 0-241-11520-5

Typeset by Rowland Phototypesetting Ltd
Printed in Great Britain by
St Edmundsbury Press, Bury St Edmunds, Suffolk

CONTENTS

	Foreword	1
1	The Shop and the Post Office	7
2	The Playgroup Entertains the Friendly Club	18
3	Dry Harvest	26
4	No Through Road	35
	West Side	36
	East Side	49
5	Next-Door Neighbours	61
	The Garratts	61
	Emma Babb and Bob Scotney	65
	The Kirks	68
	The Lillymans	71
6	The Chancel	74
7	Parish News	83
8	The End of the Year	98
9	The Dinosaur's Lair	111
10	The Wren and the Butterfly	124
11	'Queen of Months'	136
12	One Red Rose	148
13	Songs of Praise	160
	Postscripts	171
	Index	177

FOREWORD

I have wanted to write about Barnwell for a long time. But how can I squeeze a whole village into a book? What literary equivalent is there for the intricate folds that enable a three-dimensional pop-up village scene to lie flat between two covers? Also, how soon do I 'come out' and admit to the village what I want to try to do?

One morning in June 1983, I wake at half-past five and, most untypically, get up and go for a walk. Later, I self-consciously make notes of what I saw and heard in the fields above Castle Farm. Description will, presumably, be an ingredient of any such book, and what better place to start than the cart-track up to the ridge, surrounded by acres of thigh-high green corn, with rabbits lolloping ahead and the occasional startled partridge whirring up like a Jack-in-the-box? When I'm abroad I write notes about what I've seen. But it does feel odd, doing it to Barnwell.

Back in London, I face up to the fact that I will have to find out how the people of the village feel about the idea of a book. If I sense objection, I won't do it. I ponder the advisability of anonymity. The authors of three recent village books changed the names of both the places and the people. But I feel uncomfortable at that prospect. Barnwell is Barnwell. Also, how can I possibly find suitable new names for the Allens and

Akroyds and Bustins and Blunts and Burrowses and Batleys and Babbs and Browns and de Bocks and Burnses and Berridges and Blacks – well, the Blacks have left the village now, but I couldn't write a book about Barnwell and leave them out, and the thought of having to select different but suitable Christian names for Richard and Michael and Geoffrey is tedious. Still, I'd better be prepared to do it. Though I'm not sure how one chooses pseudonyms for members of the Royal Family, and Princess Alice and the Duke and Duchess of Gloucester live at Barnwell Manor.

I don't have any hesitation about whom to sound out first: Peter Bustin, the Rector, who came to the village thirteen years ago. One of the advantages of taking this first step from London, is that I can write to him; I would have felt embarrassed, springing the idea on him face-to-face. Since I am not a participating member of his Church, I feel a little guilty about availing myself of his guidance: am I similar to those people who go to church only when they marry? Perhaps not. Anyway, to plan a book about Barnwell if he had grave misgivings would seem ill-advised; the Church and the Rectory are focal points for so much that goes on. Also I know that Peter has closely studied the parish records, and there is a possibility that either he or Tom Litchfield, Barnwell's native local historian, might be writing a history of the village, and I don't wish to trespass on their projects. So I write to him setting out my idea, indicating that I'm prepared for a negative response, and asking if I may call the next time I'm down.

Two weeks later, I'm back in Barnwell and arrange to go up to the Rectory in the morning. The weather is remarkably hot, and as I walk through the village it feels as though the sun is firing a further few centuries of survival into the stones of the old cottages. There are tall patches of comfrey in flower along the banks of the brook; it is said that the Crusaders first brought the plant to England after they had discovered from the Saracens that it could heal wounds and set bones. The Church clock says half-past-ten as I approach the open Rectory gate, and when I step out of the sun through the front door into the cool, tiled hall, Anne Bustin comes forward and unexpectedly gives me a welcoming hug. She says Peter will be back in five minutes, and that she thinks the book is a wonderful idea.

Anne always reminds me of Natalie Wood, pretty and mercurial, much more like the art student her father would not permit her to be than any image conjured up by the phrase 'vicar's wife'. I sit in the blue-and-white kitchen drinking coffee, while she talks and finishes making strawberry jam, a plastic Cinzano apron over her cornflower sundress. I remind myself, before I become too lulled, that Peter might quite easily not share her enthusiasm for the book. He has the organizer's necessary gift for anticipating consequences; Anne is pure impulse. When he comes in, he has a few carefully-considered questions to ask. They are proffered with hesitation but conviction. Only one surprises me: am I considering a novel or non-fiction? Yet it is a perfectly sensible question, since I write novels, and one of them was based on the lives of real people. He looks relieved when I say 'non-fiction'. He is generous and helpful over the historical aspects and positive about the idea as a whole.

When I walk away down the short drive, I feel rather like a young man who has been given a father's blessing to court his daughter. But as I continue down the hill, past the Church and School and the stone archway to the Almshouses, and reach the familiar green with its huge lime trees and stone bridge over the brook to the Pub, the village suddenly seems to draw back behind its calendar looks—a beautiful daughter who has no wish to be wooed.

Anne and Peter are only two citizens. What will the other three hundred and forty-two feel?

*

I fully intend that the next person I consult will be Mrs Norah Blunt. She is Chairman of the Parish Council, Chairman of the Women's Institute, and runs the Girls' Brigade. She lives in one of the terrace of eleven council houses across the brook opposite our cottage. The terrace was built in 1956, seven years before I first came to Barnwell, and friends tend to say, as they look out of our front window for the first time and glimpse the fields behind the council houses: 'What a pity they built those. They quite ruin what must once have been a lovely view.' I've seen an old photograph of the Pump Field on which they are built, and I wouldn't exchange them for it; not because they are very attractive, they're just plain rural council houses quite imaginatively landscaped, but because so much of my relationship with the village has developed from being within view of a rich selection of neighbours.

Most early mornings, Norah Blunt walks her sheltie down the path from her house and emerges through the bushes onto the grass verge, where she briefly surveys the scene. If I am up, and sitting at the table by the window with a mug of coffee, her erect bearing and firm step give me a positive nudge into the beginning of the day. Her brother, Trevor Marriott, lives at Lower Farm at the end of the village, as did their father, Percy, who, when he was well into his eighties, with thick white hair and a Roman emperor profile, used to ride through the village on a bone-shaker of a tractor up to the Post Office to collect his pension. Like his daughter, he was Chairman of the Parish Council.

Circumstances prevent me seeing Norah on the same day that I went to the Rectory, and by the time we do meet I have had to tell several other people about the book, including one of her oldest friends, so of course she knows. I explain that I had meant to see her and Peter Bustin before anyone else. 'As representatives of old and new Barnwell?' she asks, looking at me squarely. 'Well, more the religious and the secular.' She nods. Her assumption is understandable; we all have a sense of 'old' and 'new' in Barnwell, the time boundaries varying from each individual's arrival in the village. Sometimes this habit can be divisive rather than merely descriptive, though not deeply so. I would not be writing this book if the village didn't have a healthy capacity for absorbing its newcomers rather than keeping them at arm's length.

Norah proffers no doubts about the book. Rather, I faintly sense that it is simply an appropriate thing for me to do. After all, if a writer has half-lived in the village for twenty years, isn't it time that this was made apparent in his work? Not that she says anything that remotely hints at this, but her pride in Barnwell comes across. She lends me three thick books of photos and press cuttings to take home.

I walk back over the white footbridge, hugging the heavy albums. There is a plop in the sluggish summer water, and a movement in the grass at the edge. Probably a water vole. I only discovered the other day that water voles and water rats are one and the same, and that the former, despite Ratty in *The Wind in the Willows*, is the name most commonly used. In one of the albums there is a group photograph of the village school taken in 1932 when Norah was eight. Although it's black-and-white, her blue eyes are unmistakeable, and I realize that one of the arresting things about her is that her eyes are still as bright now as they were then.

No one has raised the question of anonymity and name-changing. I have a feeling that if I'd suggested the possibility, it would have met with a baffled response. Why should Barnwell be disguised? Do we have something to hide?

I did say, both to the Bustins and Norah Blunt, that although I want the book to be a detailed portrait, I will avoid gossip. Scandals occur, of course they do, it would be an eviscerated village if they didn't, but I have no wish to ferret out details of wayward loves and jealousies and injustices. So I have tried to keep aspects of private lives mentioned to what the people concerned have told me and what I have personally observed. Only when writing about those who have left the village or have died have I wittingly broken this rule.

June 1983–October 1984

ONE

The Shop and the Post Office

It is easy to miss Barnwell, to drive straight past the sign pointing east just after the Roman section of the Thrapston to Oundle road that runs parallel to the River Nene.

Once, the village's outpost was its railway station, and anyone taking the turning was immediately checked by a level crossing. But that crossing was removed when the line was axed in 1964, and the pretty little wooden station—after first being briefly decorated in an uncomfortable combination of yellow and green for a television paint commercial – was transported away one dawn to become the booking office of the Nene Valley Steam Railway Preservation Society.

The station house still remains, and Norman and Miriam Elcock have lived in it since 1937. 'I'm still a retired railwayman, you know,' he says. 'I felt as if I'd lost something when they closed the station.' The last engine that went through was draped in black flags.

Just beyond the Elcocks' house, the road forks beside two enormous horse chestnuts, and on the corner of the right-hand turning a sign in old-fashioned serif capitals says 'BARNWELL'. The main village is still invisible at this point, and the road enters a short tunnel of trees.

When I first walked through that tunnel with warm rain dripping from the leaves in mid-June 1963, I'd no idea what I was going to find. I felt nervous, the way one does coming into strange territory with no fully justifiable mission.

I had put an advertisement in *Exchange & Mart* saying, 'Writer wants to rent very cheap rural cottage', and had received a reply about a small cottage for sale in Barnwell. The asking price was £400. I hadn't got £400, but it seemed so cheap I couldn't resist taking a day off to investigate.

I was twenty-nine, with a year-old son, a husband who had just left art school, a full-time job, and a first novel doing the publishers' round. The impulse behind my advertisement sprang from a feeling that I didn't want our son to grow up entirely in London, and the fact that I knew someone who rented a Dorset cottage for ten shillings a week and wondered whether I could find something similar.

I didn't know Northamptonshire at all, and have only recently discovered a phrase which conveys what happened to me in the weeks after that first visit. It was written by Arthur Mee in his guide to Northamptonshire: 'Barnwell. It comes into our dreams once we have seen it.' *Comes into our dreams* . . .

*

I rejected the very small, rot-smelling cottage, sandwiched in a row of three, the first time I peered through its letterbox. The neighbours who kept the key were out, and I could not get inside. It was Barnwell itself that sent me back for a second look. Instead of returning up the road to the station, I had a faint impulse to explore the rest of the village and followed the brook along the road past the Pub. At this point the rain petered out, and a line of sapling weeping willows planted along the bank caught the light of a watery sun in their leaves. A crook-backed limestone footbridge crossed the brook between the last two trees, leading to a path which sloped up through a meadow to the Church, its lovely Early English spire outlined clearly against the diminishing clouds.

The bridge had obviously been built centuries before to enable the occupants of the Manor House, which rose sideways to the road on the opposite side, to go to worship. Over the Manor's boundary wall could be seen, through flowering shrubbery and trees, a bastion of a ruined castle. But it was the sun on the bright willows, the old bridge, the brook, and the meadow path, rather more than the historic buildings, which made me stand still and think, 'This is beautiful. I want to stay.'

I turned, and walked back to take another look at the deserted cottage.

By the first week in July, in that summer when the black railway engines still steamed noisily between the fields of corn, the keys of No. 22, Barnwell, were mine. Its owner, who did not live in the village, proposed the most generous, and quite unprompted, terms of payment: £200 down, £150 paid off interest free at £2 per week, and two small paintings by my husband, Frank Bowling. If the phrase 'irresistible offer' hadn't already existed, I would have coined it.

*

Any stranger usually needs two things: goods and information. The most obvious purveyor of these in a village is the shop – which is often also the post office. Barnwell is fortunate; it has a shop, and a separate post office which is a shop too. They are usually referred to respectively as 'David's' and 'Ron's' – or 'Ron-'n-Pat's'.

The Post Office is one of the first houses in the village after the road emerges from the short tunnel of trees. It is modern, and Ron and Pat Rutterford were young when they came to Barnwell twelve years ago, but their style is timeless. Pat is gentle, smiles and blushes easily, yet is fierce in her beliefs. Ron is watchful, a fen farmworker's son making sense of the world – he loves to learn, to tease. Voice a practical problem within his hearing, and he goes quiet for a few seconds while he considers carefully whether he can help to solve it. If he can, he will.

Opposite the Post Office is the Rectory, its high garden wall dipping to the low adjoining churchyard wall whose gate faces the entrance to the School. Past the School is the courtyard wall and archway to the Almshouses. All these old walls – the Rectory, Church, School and Almshouses – are local limestone, lightly colonized by ivy-leaved toadflax and yellow corydalis. The road is sloping by now, and within seconds one is down onto the village green with its massive lime trees. There are right-hand turns past cottages both immediately before and immediately after the old road bridge over the brook, but they are marked No Through Road. The left-hand turn in front of the Montagu Arms on the other side of the bridge leads to the Manor and Castle, but they are not visible. A passing motorist might well carry straight on to the next village, thinking he has seen all there is to see of Barnwell.

The Shop is one of a group of stone and thatched cottages that faces the bridge at the beginning of the first No Through Road. David Brown has run it for nine years, but still wears a slightly bemused expression when people actually buy things. 'I remember my first Christmas, I was overwhelmed one day when Lewis Burrows came in and spent eight pounds on Christmas things. I thought it was fantastic. I was ever so pleased. It still is exciting – I don't suppose it should be really – when you sell things to people.' Originally he'd wanted to be a doctor. 'But I'm realistic. I'm not quite clever enough, so I went to college to do biology, but for no better reason that it was my best subject at school. Afterwards I started to train as a public health inspector. That sounds good on paper, but it was a bit slow and boring.' His wife, Judith, went to London University to study Spanish – her best subject – but, 'We only did two days work a week, and it seemed rather a waste of time, so since I was into social work I decided to do a social studies diploma.'

They'd intended, in the first place, to turn it into a crafts shop. David had been running a lock-up crafts shop while they lived in a children's home where they worked as houseparents. 'I suppose we had visions of employing local old age pensioners making things by hand and us selling them, that sort of thing.' They'd left the children's home because Judith was expecting their first child. That job had been based on a social ideal too. 'We felt,' she said, 'that if there are children nobody cares about, we'd look after them. But we found out they never accept you as their parents. And I didn't think I could cope with seven children plus my own.' So they were looking for a

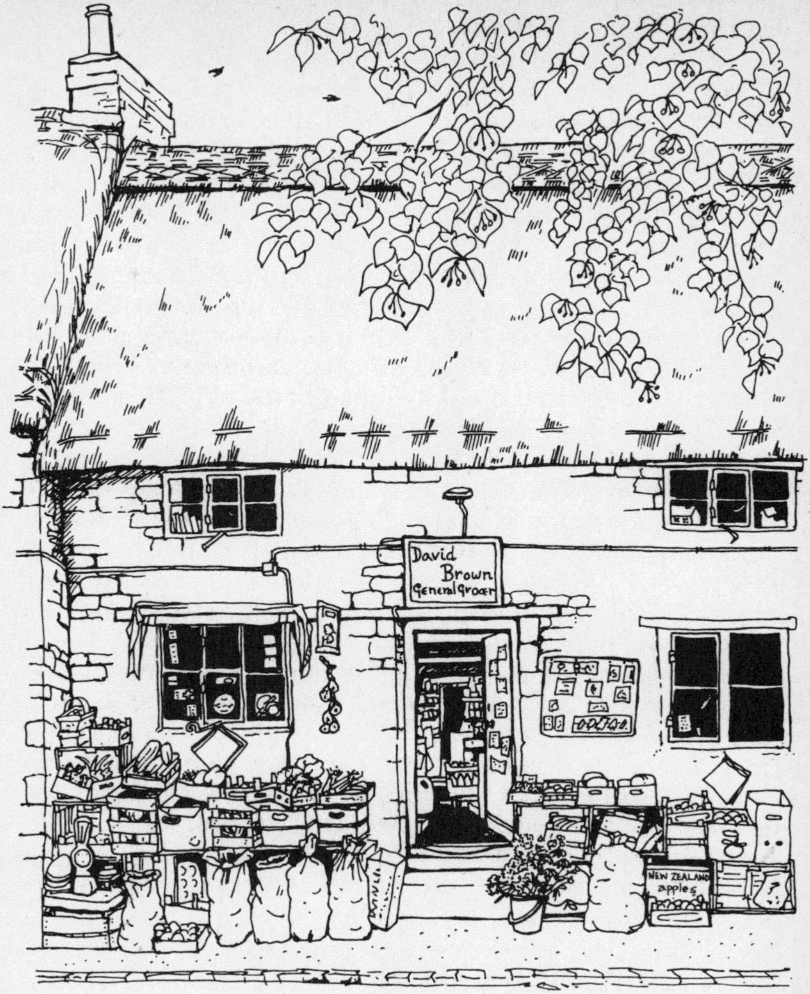
David Brown General Grocer
NEW ZEALAND apples

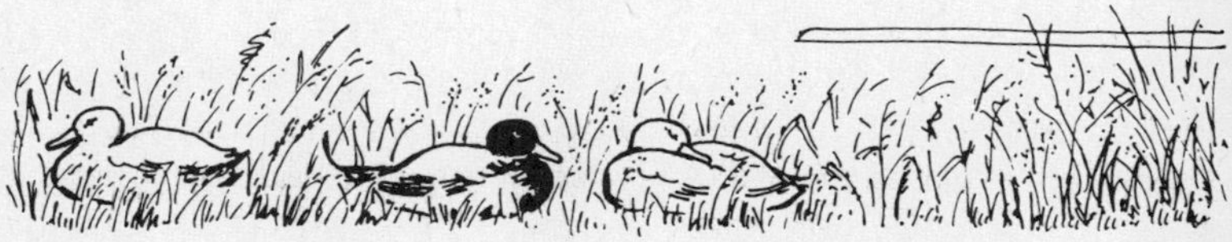

potential crafts shop with living accommodation at just the time Dolly Cole had reluctantly decided to retire and sell the Barnwell Shop. 'It was Dolly who persuaded us to keep it as a general store,' said Judith. 'We thought that she possibly would not sell to us if we didn't carry on the business, because she said it had been in the family for a hundred years.'

Dolly herself had owned it for twenty-one of those years, and it took quite a while to remember to stop referring to it as 'Dolly's'. It seemed strange at first to be greeted by a diffident young man with no particular accent, rather than a fragile-looking woman with a porcelain complexion, ice-white hair, and a fluent, slightly anxious, stream of remarks spoken in the warm local inflexion. Now, though, there are lots of people for whom it's never been anything other than 'David's'.

'I think,' he said, 'it was a pretty mad thing to do, really. Of course when we came, we had to stocktake. That was quite an experience. We spent a long time on it because Dolly'd have to explain who had this, and who bought that regularly. She sold us everything, and there were some very old-fashioned things — including some amazing old cards with sort of bathing beauties on.'

Dolly carried on working in the Shop for a fortnight after they arrived so they could finish decorating the living quarters, and David did the orders with her. 'She helped us a lot. But we've made mistakes over the years — mainly just in things we stocked. To start with, we'd get anything anyone would ask for. Not many do ask, but a few forthright people say, "Why haven't you got this, this and this?" So you get it in — and you have to buy a dozen — and then only that one person might buy one every six months.'

Their first daughter, Emma, was born two months after they moved in, and, as Judith said, 'Financially it wasn't very good. Things were tight, and we got behind with our weekly national insurance payments. A nasty man came to see us, Emma couldn't have been very old, and he told David he shouldn't have a child. It really upset us. We arranged to pay by direct debit immediately, and I said I never want a man like that in my house ever again. He was very left wing, and didn't approve of people being self-employed. I don't think we were irresponsible. I mean nothing ventured nothing gained — nothing would ever have been discovered in the world, nobody would ever have done anything.'

David altered the premises, re-jigging the public and private spaces so they no longer had to walk through the shop every time they needed to get to the kitchen. There are three small display areas to walk around now, and on the shelves in one of them are a few pieces of local craft pottery. Outside on the pavement are vegetables and fruit, brooms and buckets, houseplants and footballs. In spring there is a demand for skipping ropes and butterfly nets – as there must have been a century ago. But, as Judith said, 'The turning point for us was when we got the off-licence.' Now they can afford to employ some help, and a neighbour from over the brook, Mrs Pat Shacklock, takes over on the afternoons when David goes to Cash & Carry and when they have a holiday. 'We were four years without a holiday, and then we decided we'd just have to go away.' They have a second daughter now, Rachel, and 'When you've got a young family you don't, you can't, idealize quite so much. I don't sit and think out what life's all about so often as I used to. You just get on with the business of living.'

Yet . . . 'Sometimes,' David said, 'you have a morning in the shop, and you think, it's really gone well today. Everyone sort of stood and *talked* to each other. And you've managed to talk to them.' 'Yes,' said Judith, 'sometimes I think it really does seem like the centre of a community.'

Having a rival shop does not bother them. It tends to mean that more people do the bulk of their shopping in the village. They don't know Ron and Pat all that well: 'It's always been that we've led our separate lives.'

Pat Rutterford confirms that two shops are better than one. 'People don't just come in because they've forgotten something from the supermarket, they actually come and do proper shopping.' 'And they'll use both shops,' said Ron, 'they're very loyal. If they get something from David's, they'll come up to the Post Office and get something from us.' 'Fifty fifty,' Pat agreed.

Both shops will deliver. 'People trust you,' said Ron. 'Some houses, you go in, and they're out. So what you do, you put the fats in the fridge, the frozen things in the freezer, and then leave the rest. And you know where the key is. It's very trusting. It's nice that you can be trusted. And you don't look at cost-effective when you're in a village.'

When they came to Barnwell, Ron had been working at Perkins Engineering, and Pat looking after their baby son, James – now man-size at thirteen. They had decided they wanted to become involved in a small community, and for James to grow up in the country, so taking on the Post Office seemed ideal. Pat became the post-mistress and to begin with Ron took on extra evening farming work to make ends meet, and was also caretaker of the outside of the School. He'd left school at fifteen, and followed his father onto the land. But one day, when they were both labouring in an inhospitable sugar-beet field in mud that sucked the boots from their feet, he suddenly vowed it would be the last time he worked out on the fens. The first job he found for himself was in Woolworths. 'I always liked playing at shops when I was a boy!'

He values the sense of continuity in Barnwell. There is a spinney across the road which stretches between the Rectory gate and Stone Cottage – which was built around 1828 as Barnwell's original Post House and continued as its Post Office until 1938. One day an old man from Thrapston came in and told Ron that as a boy he'd worked at the Rectory, and used to have to sweep a path through the trees every morning. A few years later Ron was helping to clear the spinney and found the path. 'It had become buried. It's still there, the stones are still there, and the track, the cinder track. You can imagine the ladies in their wide dresses going along the path, because the road was very narrow then, and they used to go along the path to save getting splashed by the carts.'

Donald and Sheila Akroyd came from West Yorkshire to live in Stone Cottage over thirty years ago, and for Carry, their daughter, the spinney with its huge horsechestnuts was a childhood den of privacy and splendour. There is another spinney opposite, and in the spring they have daffodils, hyacinths, primroses, violets, celandines and bluebells under the trees, and in autumn, conkers and acorns spatter on the road. But best of all, when it has been winter for a long time, yet well before the daffodils, the dark ground is pierced by thick clumps of green and alabaster snowdrops and a sprinkling of aconites that look like yellow marbles set on green ruffs.

When I first came to Barnwell, the Post Office was in a house right down the village, and Dolly's was the first premises I entered, signalled by a familiar Lyons ice-cream-cone sign. She lives now, with her husband Fred Cole, in an immaculately neat cottage facing David's across the brook.

The old Lyons sign was not easily acquired. When Dolly took over the business in 1954, the icecream vans came round regularly, and the vanmen warned the manufacturers that if village shops were leased freezers, the vans would lose trade. 'So I said to them I said, you won't stop me from trying. And a year and a half after that, you see, I bought meself a fridge out and out, I didn't ask to rent one, and they couldn't refuse to sell to me. David's still got it there, that's the same fridge in the corner, and it's still running. I never had any trouble with it.'

Dolly, who was born in Oundle seventy years ago, first saw the Shop in 1932, when she was being courted by Tom Wells, the adopted son of Walter and Annie Pask. Annie's family were called Kisbee, and it was they who founded the business. 'They'd only got the one room. They started it at a table, and they used to have their breakfast on that table, and the fire used to be burning at the back of them.' When Annie's mother died in 1894, Annie, who was twelve, started serving in the Shop and was still helping Dolly in the 1960s. She used to sit in her kitchen at the back, plump and very upright, with a shawl and black velvet choker, and would invite the smaller children to go and see her. Sweets would be handed out and a few kindly words spoken. After she died, Dolly was clearing her things and found stacks and stacks of blue sugar bags, reminding her of the days when 'Sugar came in sacks, and you had these old scoops to weigh half pounds, pounds, two pounds. And you used to have to twist newspaper for sweet bags – make a cornet – and lard was come in a big seven pound box and you used to have to cut it up in quarters and halves and weigh it, and we had all these reams of greaseproof paper.'

Thomas Wells died in 1940, only three months after he and Dolly married. 'My only regret was that I didn't marry him when he asked me the first time. You see I was a bit younger than him, and I felt I weren't ready, and I put it off, and I regretted that. He was one of the happiest chaps around. If you saw a group of people and you heard them laughing, you would know he was in the middle of them. It altered my life completely. It struck the nerves in my head. I couldn't cry, and they couldn't make me cry. I've never felt the heat since. It was a very hot summer that summer, after it happened, and I used to sit outside with a big blanket round me.' It was during those months that her hair began to turn white.

After the war, she remarried and lived in the Cotswolds, but when Mrs Pask became ill with shingles in 1954, she took a day off to come and see her. 'I put me car under the trees where I always put it, and she didn't know I was coming, and I just walked in, and her eyes filled up with tears when she saw me, and that's a thing she never did.' It ended with Dolly buying the business, and coming to live there with her second husband, Bill. He had been very severely injured in an accident before they married, and he died a few years later. His brother Fred, who with great patience had taught him to walk again after the accident, became Dolly's third husband.

She used to take all her customers very seriously, including the children. 'When I first took over, and they was all so little a lot of them, the mothers was picking everything for them. The children could never see what they wanted, they used to have to lift them up. So in the end I made a low stall right along the back of the counter, and put all their bits and bobs on it, and let them come round a few at a time so that they could see what they was buying.' She also let them deposit their pocket money with her, writing the amounts down on a special sheet. This enabled the children to create a grand effect on visitors by sweeping into the shop, asking for sweets, and ostensibly not having to pay for them.

A few years ago, the bus service between Oundle and Thrapston, which stopped at Barnwell, was severely reduced. This has made the Shop and the Post Office – or 'Brown's of Barnwell' and 'Rutterford, Barnwell P.O.' to use the official names on their prices stickers just for once – even more indispensable. They respond so well to needs and trends and vague requests, that one becomes spoiled and willing to forgo even the traditional visit to Oundle on Thursday, market day, so much is on the doorstep.

Drycleaning, beansprouts, brie, knitting wool, coley for the cats, coal for the fire, cheese bread, apricot chutney, buttercup cough mixture, cherryade, campari, Walker's crisps, wine boxes, clove drops, cold meats, birthday cards, garden chairs, balloons, nappy pins, pizzas, seeds, hairnets, damsons, spring greens, avocados, tobacco, Danish pastries, doughnuts, dinner-money envelopes, paperbacks, poacher's pie, Thrapston fudge, free advice, free delivery ... David Brown was even approached to see if he would become an outlet for a video library firm, but he looked at the list of preponderantly dubious titles and said 'No'.

Newspaper reports on how the village shop is dying always make me think of the high stone step up into David's, and the old, jangly bell on the door; and of the flower-lined path up to Ron's, with the seat by the post box where the children sit with their ice-creams. Surely the factors that make them die will not converge here?

TWO

The Playgroup Entertains the Friendly Club

The morning after I had spoken to the Bustins about this book, Anne came down to our cottage to invite me to a strawberry tea at the Rectory that afternoon. It was being organized by the Playgroup for the Friendly Club (the over-60s), and she thought it might be the sort of thing I'd like to witness. Her thoughtfulness had the salutary effect of making me take the final plunge. Being neither over-60 nor the mother of a pre-school child, I would have to explain why I was there to partake of the strawberries.

I was glad that our neighbour, Rene Kirk, was passing the gate just as I was leaving – she was an easy person to explain to. The Kirks have always been our neighbours; their two younger daughters, Pat and Pauline, playing with my son Dan when he was a baby, and Bert Kirk stopping work in his vegetable plot to have a chat when I'm at the top of our garden.

Rene had already told me that being recently retired meant she was kept really busy, there was so much going on in the village. For the past twenty-one years she'd worked at the Manor, mainly looking after the quarters of the outdoor male staff, whose numbers had shrunk drastically during that time. As we walked along, she said we'd call for Dolly since they always went to things together. I thought how contrasted they were: Dolly dainty (even in a Marks & Spencer size 10 dress, she said, she needed a padded bra) and slightly anxious because she'd fallen asleep after lunch and wasn't quite together, and Rene robust and calming, but walking with just a little difficulty as we went slowly up the hill.

The Rectory has a lovely cushiony lawn facing the west entrance to the Church, and the wide semi-circle of chairs set out in the sun was already filling up with members of the Friendly Club. There are over forty altogether, and a fair proportion were there. Between them they have getting on for three thousand years' experience of life, many of which must have been in harsh contrast to the Club's amiable programme of concerts, games, slide-shows and coachtrips.

The Playgroup were taking their host-role seriously. Four-year-old Steven Allen plodded solemnly towards the laps of the seated guests with a plate of sticky cake held at an extremely dangerous tilt. He looked like a man determined to do his duty, while not thinking too highly of the order. Other children proffered slices of currant bread-and-butter and gingerbread. Their mothers handed round cups of tea. The elderly people talked to one another and watched. Not everyone would be familiar to them, for in the last fifteen years several young couples have come to live in the village, bringing small children and producing more. Most people are glad, but it can be bewildering, not to be able to put names to faces. Dolly remembers remarking to Mrs Pask, 'Look, if we don't get some young people soon, Barnwell is going to be a village of all old people with no growth of youngsters.' Then, just before Mrs Pask died, one or two newcomers arrived, 'And now we've got a wonderful village of nice young children. I don't know them, they don't know me – and I used to know every child in the village – but it's what Barnwell needed.'

Without any fuss, casually and naturally, Marilyn Burrows organized most of the children, some of them tiny, into a performance of singing games. She was one of the mothers who welcomed the start of the Playgroup in the 1970s when her elder children, Andrew and Trina, were small. Now that her youngest, Donna – whose fierce, dark-eyed stare jogs the memory back to another generation of Burrowses when young – is school age, she is uncertain what best to do in the future. 'I left school, got married at seventeen, and now I keep looking and thinking, I'd like to do this and I'd like to do that, but it's not easy. You read the adverts in the paper and it's all people aged eighteen to thirty-five they want. Well, I'm only thirty, but by the time I've trained to do something, I shall be old. I've thought about going to teacher training college, but there's that many teachers around nowadays, it seems a bit silly.' The toddlers on the lawn gazed at her, concentrating hard in their efforts to follow her simple movements, while the four-year-olds sang the familiar words and tunes with brimming confidence, their voices clear in the summer air.

After the strawberries had been eaten, the children rushed off to the glade at the end of the garden where they could play as robustly as they liked. There were no scenes: several mothers kept a watchful eye, teacups were refilled, and Liz Allen's baby daughter was admired. It was Liz, prompted by Anne Bustin, who sorted out the formalities needed to set up the Playgroup in the first place. She's a PE teacher, and has returned to part-time work after having each of her four children. 'I was lucky. The person who kept my job open for me is a career woman who's had children herself. I teach all the primary schools swimming in the King's Cliffe area where the Rural Schools project has really got going. And then I teach tennis another day at Prince William School in Oundle.' Her fitness and energy are striking, but they're not accompanied by any daunting competitiveness. Dark-haired and deeply tanned, she stood back from the pram and let us peer at sleeping Frankie.

Among the older people chatting in small groups was Dora Robinson, known by some as the Flower Lady because of her close attention to the flowers in Church. Born in Barnwell in 1899, she still walks around the village with a firm step, taking an interest in all that goes on. 'I love doing the flowers, particularly when we've got a lot. If you look after them, top them up with a drop of water, you keep them. But if you're just going to stick them in and leave them, which I think is a downright shame, they'll die in a few days. I like to hang on to them. It's nearly my daily job. And it makes somewhere to go, just to walk out. You feel you've got something to do.'

If she'd been told sixty years ago she would one day sit on that lawn wearing a straw hat and a patterned dress and be handed tea by the Rector's wife, Dora would probably have given one of her inimitable laughs and told the speaker to talk sense. For then she was the cook at the Rectory, working with three maids and a gardener to care for Rector William Baillie and his wife. 'He was a semi-invalid, and you had to be a bit careful. Of course he'd been in the Cambridge boat, and we used to have to talk about that. Mrs Baillie went to India alternate years, shooting. She'd got all sorts of heads and things – there was a lion in the hall. When she came home she always visited all round the village, house to house. She was great fun, she really was. She'd giggle, you know.'

Dora's mother, Rhoda Kisbee, worked for a previous rector before her marriage to William Robinson, kitchen gardener at the Manor. Dora still has the certificate presented to Rhoda on July 27, 1898, 'For ten years faithful discharge of duties in the employment of Reverend G. W. Huntingford'. She praised the Bustins for making the Rectory available for so many village functions. 'Anything and everything, they'll have it. They just offer the house and that's it.'

For parishioners to be able to use a spacious house that was rebuilt in the Regency era is a boon. When the Bustins first came to live in it, Anne felt the weight of historical responsibility. 'I really hungered to learn more about the past. I loved hearing stories from various people, like Dora. I almost wanted it to be again as it was years ago.' Looking after such a big house and garden on a shoestring though, as well as a young family and pastoral duties, had really been too much, and in those early years she was sometimes still decorating the walls at two in the morning. But now, with a few modern improvements, and the children grown up, things were a bit easier.

The sun had shone throughout the strawberry tea. The roses against the churchyard wall were in full bloom, and Anne surveyed the scene with pleasure. The guests were in no hurry to leave their chairs, and the children were running races up from the glade. It was important, she thought, that the generations should meet; that children, however young, should learn to be hospitable. For a few seconds she relaxed. Then she noticed some mothers were beginning to carry the washing-up indoors, and she dashed away to help them.

*

During that week, the July meeting of the Parish Council was held. Due to start at 7.30, people arrived quietly at the Reading Room in ones and twos after hurried suppers, children's bathtimes, and a very hot working day.

The Reading Room is a rectangular stone building just past the Pub on the way to the Manor. It was built a century ago by the Duke of Buccleuch, who then owned Barnwell Estate, and set up as 'The Barnwell Working Men's Club and Reading Room, to provide rational social intercourse, mental improvement and recreation.' Now it houses the Women's Institute, the Playgroup, the Youth Club, the Barnwell Entertainers, the Friendly Club, the Whist Drives, the Wine Circle, the Barnwell Broiderers, the Keep Fit classes, jumble sales, and various celebrations. Its waist-high panelling and inside doors are painted canary yellow, the walls are generously endowed with electric heaters, and only the few rows of books in deep-hued bindings darkened with age recall the days when access to newspapers and books and visiting speakers could be a lifesaver to underpaid people who worked with their hands all day but had thoughts going round in their minds which they needed to explore and develop.

Liz Fox is Clerk to the Council, her economical name suiting her adroit way of doing things, and the trace of Newcastle in her voice lending precision to the inevitably imprecise matters that often have to be discussed. Her husband, Ian, is a member of the PC, and he occasionally quietly puts forward a neat professional suggestion to help solve some of the more diffuse money matters. His work as an accountant with a large concern in Peterborough brought them to this area several years ago, and it was with some trepidation that Liz agreed to become Parish Clerk as the post tends to suggest lifelong experience of local custom and practice.

Norah Blunt, however, the PC's Chairman, can provide that. Mostly she allows the committee to have its head, but will contribute an occasional down-to-earth comment – like over the planks on one of the footbridges which had become unsafe, despite having been repaired in the not too distant past. 'They never fitted,' she said. 'It was never a woman's job – nice and neat and tidy.' Then she seemed to look Walter Woolman straight in the eye, no doubt anticipating a challenge. Mr Woolman challenges most things.

That look of Norah's can be a little intimidating. When I'd gone to see her, it was the first time I'd been right inside her home and I'd felt rather nervous. What made me quickly at ease was the fact that her living-room was so delightfully cluttered. If I'd thought about it, I would have expected it to be strictly orderly, and seeing her surrounded by the materials and products of her craft hobbies, plus the hundreds of

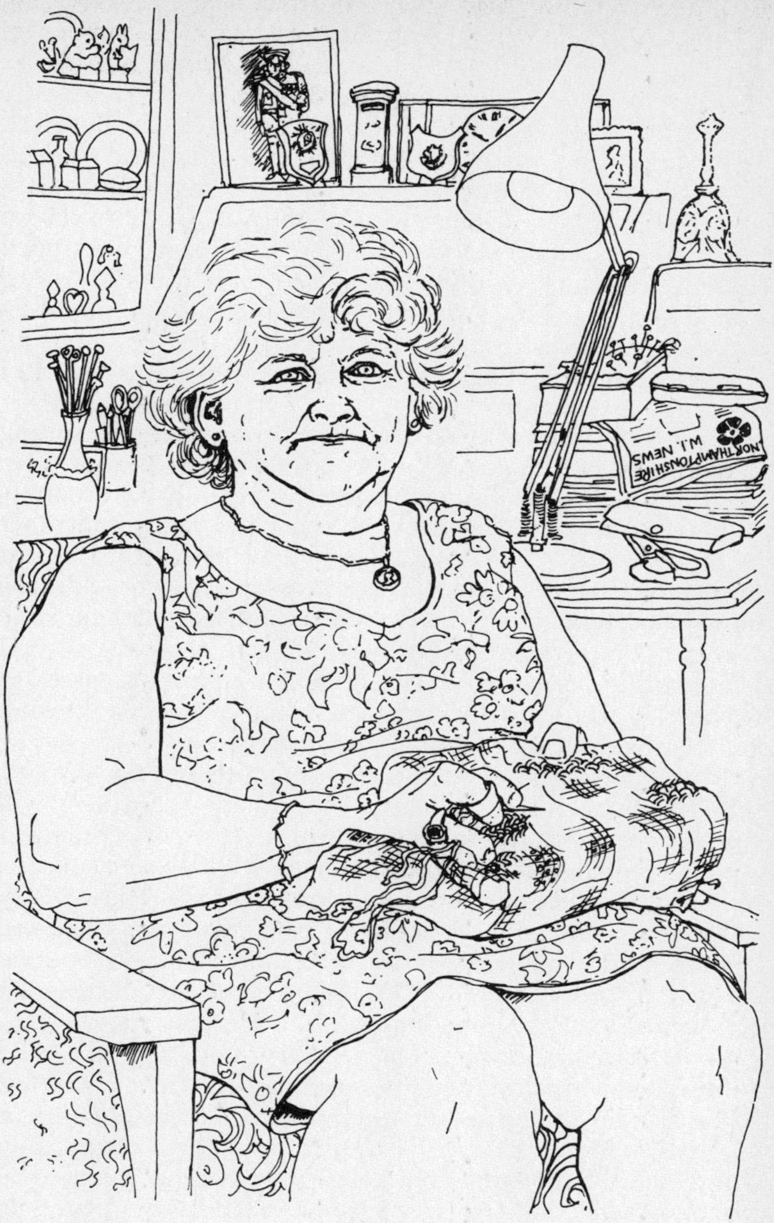
NORTHAMPTONSHIRE
W.I. NEWS

mementoes and treasures she's collected over the years, was somehow reassuring.

She and Liz Fox sat at a table facing the other members of the PC, who occupied the first of three short rows of chairs. That evening the members present were Walter Woolman (the Vice-chairman), Gerry Allen (Liz's husband), Graham Wise, Ian Fox and Joan Crump. Behind sat four interested parishioners: Rene Kirk, Dolly Cole, Pam Stratton and Peter Scopes.

Liz opened the meeting with reports on various items: the bill for renovating the parish notice board; an estimate for mending the seat on the bank below All Saints' Chancel; the fact that the District Council had offered a donation of trees; that the leak in the ground by Montagu Terrace was in hand; and the date of the next PC meeting in two months' time.

Walter Woolman protested that meetings were not held often enough – they used to be monthly. He is mistrustful of quick decisions and expediences; a retired Oundle policeman who is virtually a one-man watch committee for what he believes are Barnwell's best interests. It's not good enough, he said, for planning permissions to be shoved through members' letterboxes for automatic signatures. Others, however, pointed out that some planning issues were fully debated, though in any case the Parish Council has no powers to withhold or approve permissions – it can only express an opinion. Everyone feels that that is not very satisfactory.

Then came the matter of the Wigsthorpe bridleway. Someone – who, it was not said – had complained that the bridleway, which has a sign pointing to it down the entry between the School and the Almshouses, is not open. There is no way a horse and rider can get from there to Wigsthorpe – a hamlet 1½ miles across the fields – and the first obstacles are the stiles through Ken and Barbara Preston's field. The complainant felt strongly that she should be able to ride her horse on an officially signposted bridleway.

One or two people said they thought that it had been wrongly designated, and later I discovered it does not exist at all on my 1954 (reprinted with corrections 1960) map, though it does make an appearance as a footpath on my 1955 (reprinted with minor changes 1966) map. Quite when the District Council's green 'Bridleway to Wigsthorpe' sign by the

Almshouses was erected no one at the meeting could remember, but a few agreed it was not there twenty years ago. Dolly, anyway, was adamant that no bridlepath existed fifty years ago when she and Tom Wells were courting, because then at either end of what is now the Prestons' field there were kissing gates – narrow gates that are hung so only one person at a time can sidle through. Privately, I thought there was no way a person could even walk without difficulty across the fields from the Wigsthorpe end, because I tried to once and there were no paths or linking gates, and the fields were under plough; but that was several years ago, so I kept quiet.

It was nine o'clock, and Norah, looking resplendent in a dark dress whose white trim positively shone, had to leave for a reception. In the road outside, Dolly reiterated about the kissing gates, and how new people didn't – couldn't – understand all the complicated ins-and-outs of rights of way in Barnwell, and that was partly why she came to parish meetings, because she knew a lot of the facts.

THREE

Dry Harvest

Early August was hot and windy, and the air became filmy with the dust blowing over from the fields where they were harvesting.

One afternoon I met three children, Hanneke and Basje (pronounced Bashie) de Bock and Amanda Davies, coming out of the side lane from Castle Farm with a plastic bag of corn they had gleaned – a process rather different from the days remembered in a booklet* by Dora Robinson's cousin when, at the beginning of this century, she 'went gleaning with my Mother, and had a small calico bag tied around my waist' as soon as the stooks of corn had been carted away. Hanneke explained that when the newly-threshed wheat was backed into the barn, the trailer went over a bump and spilled some, 'So we asked Simon Berridge if we could pick it up, and he said, "Go on, I'll be glad to get rid of it, because the birds only eat it." They can't use it, 'cos it's full of dust and everything, and they need perfectly clean corn. It's good, because we use it for our bantams, and it costs about 70p a bag to buy.' It was to feed their hens that Dora's cousin and her mother used to glean too, just as her grandmother 'in her print patterned sun bonnet, still in my possession' had done well over a hundred years ago.

Hanneke, whose parents come from Holland, was eleven this summer, very slight, with dark hair and serious eyes, and a wonderful appetite for conversation. She loves the country ''Cos in the town everything seems so squashed together, and if a fire ever broke out then it could seep along all the houses', and seems to come to terms with the less pleasant aspects by talking about them. 'Buttons, our cat, caught a wood pigeon. She broke its claw off so we had to kill it. She's rabbiting at the

---

*Barnwell in Northamptonshire by Laura Stokes, edited by A. R. Traylen (Spiegl Press, Stamford, 1984)

moment and spewed up yesterday, all rabbit hairs. I've saved about three rabbits, because she just holds them by the scruff of the neck and doesn't really hurt them until she starts eating them. And I yell at her, "BUTTONS!" and she drops them, and they're too scared to move, so I pick them up and take them all the way back to the fields. Once she ate the head and all the fur, but left the meat and intestines. She's horrible, because she left the heart and liver and everything right on the doorstep where you stand on it.'

The side lane from Castle Farm comes out just up the road from our cottage, and epitomizes a problem we have with names for locations in the village. I've only ever known it as 'the lane', but Ron recently referred to it as Horseradish Lane and was surprised I didn't call it that. 'It's got horseradish growing up it; not very good, but it's got it.' That name doesn't appear on the electors' register in the addresses of people who live up the lane, but what does appear are names for Barnwell's two chief streets, which I thought were anonymous. The old cottages are all numbered, newer houses have names, and most people's addresses are simply a number or name followed by Barnwell. But a few who live along the sides of the brook have added 'Brookside', 'Brook Lane', 'Main Road' or 'Main Street'; and others living up by the Church also have four alternatives: Church Street, Church Hill, Church Lane and Church Road. What are invariably referred to as 'The Almshouses' (now a housing association for the over-50s) are, I see, correctly called Latham Cottages after their founder, Nicholas Latham, who built them in 1601. However at least the names of the two 20th-century rows of houses are constant: Montagu Terrace and Chancel Terrace.

Two days after meeting the children, I went to the window and observed the tail-end of a great commotion over at Montagu Terrace. There was a fire engine, knots of people, and a fast-disappearing pall of smoke. Since everywhere looked intact, I assumed it was a chimney fire – a not uncommon occurrence, though it seemed a hot day to light a fire. But the house in question appeared to be Bill Groom's, where anything might happen. Later, I learned he had set the shed in his back garden alight with his flame gun.

Bill, who's in his mid-70s, has lived alone since his wife died fifteen years ago, and it's as though his floricultural dreams have gradually taken precedence over real life. A tall, rangy man, beginning to stoop, obsessively sucking at an absent cigarette in the corner of his mouth, he will impart an unstoppable stream of details as how best to grow strelitzas, cinerarias, agapanthus, helleborus, meconopsis, zantedeschias – unlike the rest of us, he always knows the official names off pat. However, his own garden and greenhouse have gradually become more and more neglected, with nettles rearing high, while indoors the packs of unplanted exotic seeds that he orders yearly from the catalogues are gathering dust and mounting into toppling piles. Sometimes he does not appear at all during the day, and his foil-covered meals-on-wheels dinners grow cold on the doorstep; then suddenly he will emerge at midnight, and chop wood in his back yard. He came from Northolt in 1933 to marry Gwendoline Norwood; he was a haulage contractor and she (like Eileen Woolman, Walter's wife) was one of the Barnwell blacksmith's daughters. Now the smithy is just a barn, though William Norwood's ironwork still adorns the Church porch and gateway.

Montagu Terrace, with its eleven houses separated into four blocks, is a very far cry from the crowded terraces of a town, but nevertheless fear that a fire could 'seep along all the houses' might have been momentarily aroused by the flaming shed. Marilyn and Nigel Burrows live on one side of Bill (though separated by a gap) and Marilyn admitted she did have the occasional anxiety. 'When I went in there a couple of years ago, when he was bad, he'd got a big pile of newspapers on the settee – it must have been a year's supply. Some had fallen off, and they'd spread all over the floor and were creeping up the hearth. And the ashes were coming out of the hearth, but they must have been cold because the paper wasn't on fire. I picked all the papers up, but as I picked them up a lot more fell off. Why he didn't have the house on fire, I haven't got a clue!' But she was adamant there was no simple solution for the safety of independent old people. 'I don't think it's very nice, putting people into homes.'

They are an easy-going couple; Judith Brown had told me, 'I was talking to Marilyn, and she said she was going to see you, and I said we were a little bit apprehensive about what we were going to be asked, because we really didn't know what it was going to involve, and she said, "Oh, I'm not a bit worried, I think life in Barnwell is fantastic anyway."' Marilyn is one of the people who has benefited from newcomers: 'When I first came here from Oundle I used to feel like a fish out of water because everybody was old, compared to me, then all these younger people started coming and from my point of view there's a much better social life because of all the things they've brought with them. There's loads and loads to do if you want to join in, you couldn't possibly do everything.' She's learned to drive so that she can do a part-time job as a waitress in Oundle, and before Donna started school she went to English classes in Corby and passed her 'O' level. Enjoying that made her consider the idea of going to college. She'd recently cut her involvement with the Playgroup from three mornings a week to one: 'I just couldn't fit it all in, I was ill, and I decided it was just because I was doing too much. I was rushing around, really rushing, not just working at a steady pace, until seven or eight o'clock at night. The Playgroup had become a chore, I hadn't got the energy. I'm starting to enjoy it again now, it's a lovely feeling when you walk in and they all come running over to you.' On Friday evenings she helps with the Youth Club. 'We usually get at least fifteen a week. We go swimming, iceskating, rollerskating, ten pin bowling; we went to Oundle Marina a couple of weeks ago, that was very good. We've got a disco next week, and a barge trip coming up.'

Nigel has worked for the past ten years as a boatbuilder at Oundle Marina. 'They gave me a month's trial, when I started, just showing you how to do everything. If you do all right you're all right, if not they get rid of you. It's not a bad job.' He's lived in the same house in Montagu Terrace all his life, bringing Marilyn to live with his parents and brothers and sister when he married at eighteen. (Since then, the rest of the family have moved to different homes.) He's not so enthusiastic about the changes in village life. 'I don't know a lot of the people now, and I used to know everybody.' 'That's only because he doesn't mix,' Marilyn said matter-of-factly. He builds hulls for ocean-going boats that sell for as much as £75,000: 'Most of them go abroad, they don't pay VAT then.' Orders are received at the London Boat Show, but he's never been to it – cricket's more his line, and he's Treasurer of the Barnwell Cricket Club.

Sidney and Kathleen Batley live next door in the end house.

'I always know that if I want anything,' said Marilyn, 'Kath's there. When I first came here, there was a nice atmosphere along this terrace. A friendly atmosphere.' The Batleys are one of the families who implanted that atmosphere, for they occupied their house when it was first built.

Their six children were born while they lived in Kath's parents' house on the opposite side of the brook. 'We had to wait till these houses were finished for one of our own.' Her father, Walter Tough, used to work for Barnwell Estate as a woodman, and Kath was working in the dairy at Berridge's farm when she met Sid. 'Milkmaid met milkman,' he said. He came from Norfolk with a farmer who moved his complete stock to Thorpe, not far from Barnwell. 'The trains were running then, and we brought sixty cows – Friesian – implements, horses, everything.' 'We used to fetch milk from his farm, to bottle,' said Kath. She was nineteen when they married in 1939, and now twelve grandchildren are among the family who regularly visit at weekends. 'The five girls have all got married here, and had their children christened here.' Some of them 'would dearly love to live in Barnwell' but property has become too expensive.

When the Norfolk farmer sold his herd and went arable, Sid changed jobs and worked for a builder. 'I could have stopped at the farm, but the money was a lot less as a labourer than it was as a cowman.' In forty years he never had a day off work, but a few years ago he developed severe cataracts and blood pressure and had to retire. 'One eye was completely gone, and I couldn't see the television or read the paper.' He had two operations, and now can see with the aid of very powerful glasses. 'I didn't mind the operations. I didn't want to be blind. They done a good job. I can't see without the glasses, I can't see you, I can't even tell it's Kathleen, but I know her voice.' He appears to enjoy domesticity, taking charge of some of the household chores in a striped butcher's apron, and tending his regulated rows of vegetables and dazzling summer flowers.

Kath can often be seen on her bicycle, perhaps going up to the Church to clean the brass, or to the shops, or to visit an old person. When Mrs Muriel Russell, who was in her nineties, was still in the village, living on her own in a cottage on the green, Kath used to visit her first thing in the morning, then in the winter go and lock the back door when it got dark, and return again at ten 'To see that she was in bed. She sometimes was asleep in her chair. She'd leave her wireless on, and by mistake move it to a foreign station, and of course there'd be all this jabbering going on, and she'd say, "These people are in my house again, they're all up in that corner." She had a second son, Harold, who got killed in the war. Before she was taken ill the last time, she used to talk to me about him. She showed me some tables and things he had made, when he was at school. When I told her other son about it, he said, "That subject was always taboo. We never ever said anything about Harold." Funny, isn't it, how they go like that? All of a sudden it all comes out.'

For years Kath was in the Church choir, and usually sings when she is out on her bicycle or walking along the street. The snatches of hymns and light opera seem to reflect her wish to be positive about life, and perhaps help to camouflage an involuntary layer of anxiety. 'I can't stand politics and arguments about politics. I always vote, but I don't like arguments. They cause an awful lot of upstir.' Norah Blunt is a life-long friend. 'She's one of those people who doesn't let anything worry her. She went to camp, and there was some helicopters there, and she went up. She doesn't let things worry her, whereas I do. Whatever she's got to say, she'll say it. I wish I was like that.' She worried sometimes about Bill Groom. 'Last summer, we hadn't seen anything of him, and I said to Marilyn, "Have you seen Bill?" "Well, no," she said, "now you come to say, I haven't." Well, I walked up and down that side, and I said to Marilyn, "It's no good, we'll have to do something." "I'll go and tell Nigel," she said, and Nigel hammered on the door. We didn't get any reply, and then all of a sudden the bedroom window opened, and Bill said, "Hello. What's the matter? What's the time?" He shuts himself up in the house, and you think, now, is he all right?'

It isn't so many years since Bill used to call round to see if our old neighbour, Eric Garratt, was all right. If he got the chance, he'd buttonhole me and tell me what I ought to be doing with our little magnolia tree that will never grow as big as the one in front of his house, planted in the days when he was up to nursing it with all the right feeds and composts.

That August, our garden would not have excited him much. Only the tawny black-eyed susans seemed to enjoy the weather, while the dark seedheads buried in feathery dried leaves of the love-in-a-mist recalled its other name – devil-in-a-fog. All weekend, a tractor with a royal blue trailer laden with corn had been passing our window at intervals and returning empty. In the early evening, I bicycled up the Thurning road where over the hedgerows the rumpled straw disgorged from the combines lay across stubble awaiting the fires. A young man was just beginning to shave the edges of one almost over-ripe field, and a cloud of thick dust flurried around his machine as it husked the corn.

On the road, the occasional squashed rabbit or bird had quickly dried in the sun and wind. A shallow depression in the verge was overflowing with the small, smooth lozenges of a shattered windscreen. From the field under harvest, I heard the plaintive, repeated high peep of a bird, and was glad I can't recognize most bird cries. It sounded in distress, and I recalled Hanneke saying, 'My brother and my dad went to watch them combining and there were several rabbits being chopped up because they weren't fast enough.'

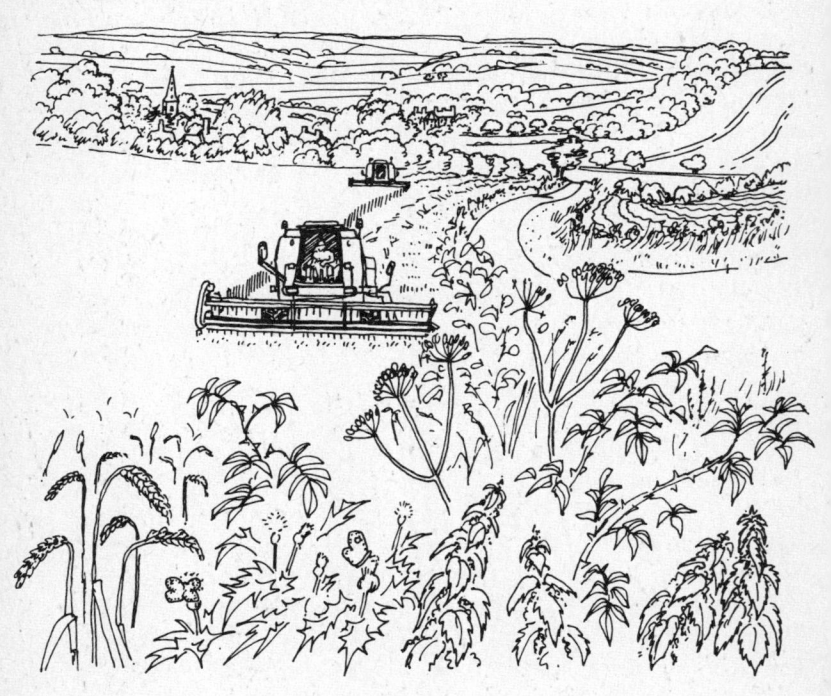

After the bleached harvest fields, it was almost a shock to see, past North Lodge Farm, two that were chocolate-brown, newly ploughed. Suddenly the season seemed to have changed, and even the sky above had lost its high, dry blue and acquired a little grey. But when I turned to go back, and was facing the sun, it was pure, late summer – the kind that goes on for ever.

Tom Litchfield used to farm North Lodge, and it was his observations of fragments turning up under the plough that led to the excavation of a Roman villa site there in 1973. Now he lives in a modern house near the Post Office, surrounded by records and relics of Barnwell's history. Like all passionate historians, he talks about the past as though he'd been there. Knowledgeable on buildings and artefacts as he is, it is the people who matter most. His ability to wander back in time has led him to feel that there is only 'a thin veil between history and the supernatural'. Being able to raid his knowledge, lift facts from his pamphlets, and repeat his stories, makes me realize what an invaluable asset a resident historian is for a village. So often people said, 'Tommy Litchfield'll know about that. Have you talked to him?'

Ann, his vigilant, cordial wife, shares his present difficult burden of nurturing his energies. Whilst still at the farm, he contracted Parkinson's disease: disastrous for a farmer, and also for a researcher and writer because of the harm it does to the eyes and control of the pen. When Tom lent me his volume of poems and Barnwell history by Thomas Bell – *The Rural Album* printed in 1853 – I noticed that these lines from 'The Village Schoolmaster' had been marked with a pencil. I thought perhaps he had made the mark privately:

> Ere his harvest had been gather'd,
>   Storms arose to cloud the sky,
> Leaving him with prospects blighted,
>   Here to weep and here to die.

Publicly, he is cheerful, and an excellent mimic. The late Prince Henry, Duke of Gloucester, asked him to write a potted history of Barnwell Manor and the ruined castle in its grounds, which could be hung on the wall for curious house guests to consult. Tom submitted a draft, and it was returned with an entry concerning one of the Buccleuch ancestors (Princess Alice, Duchess of Gloucester's family) struck out. Tom enquired the reason, and the Duke replied: 'Don't want everyone to know what a bloody fool he was!'

His remark about the 'thin veil' between history and the supernatural was not made lightly. There are several contemporary ghost stories floating around Barnwell, and the most famous is Tom's experience at the Castle.

When he was a young man, he and a friend consulted an ouija board to try to discover secrets about the reputed Castle ghost. Answers to their questions led them to attempt to spend a freezing December night in the Castle's ruined north-east tower. There they experimented with another ouija session which revealed that monks used the Castle as a courthouse and used to execute people there. Then suddenly they heard a loud crack, as of a whiplash. Both were terrified, and sprang to the narrow doorway. Tom got out first, but his friend turned and saw the head and shoulders of a monk brandishing a thonged whip. A year later, Tom by chance discovered, on a brass floor plate in Sawtry Parish Church, the family crest of the Le Moine family who built the Castle: it was the head and body of a faceless monk brandishing a scourge.

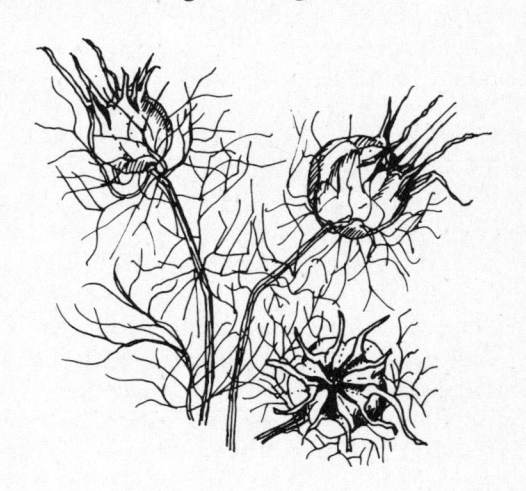

FOUR

No Through Road

The fact that the main street is a cul-de-sac contributes a lot to the cohesion of the village. People can't steal in and out of the lower end, but are bound to come up to the main bridge at the centre. In the evening, I like to walk up and down its length, zig-zagging across the brook by the footbridges and fords. When the limetrees are in flower, the whole brookside seems to reverberate very gently with the hum of bees, like a golden-green cathedral where the organist is perpetually holding a faint chord.

A simplified plan of Barnwell resembles a printed 4 with an elongated tail. The Manor is at the top, the old station house at the point, the Pub is on the crossroads, and the No Through Road makes up the tail. This road is almost half a mile long, and choosing where to stop along it now is difficult – or, rather, choosing where *not* to stop is hard. Every household has its own particular claim.

I shall have to curb my habit of piling pieces of random information on top of one another. It only needs a visitor to look out of our window and say, 'Who's that girl working in the garden over there?', for me to reply with this kind of tangle: 'Oh, that's Marion. Marion Leesons. Well, Marion Carter as was. Gary's elder sister. He lives in Oundle now, but he stays with her some weekends. Her father, John, lives in Chancel Terrace. Works at Berridge's. He said hello to us in the Pub last night. And her grandfather lives just down the road. Next to Graham and Juliet Wise. You remember, you met them just now. The ones with the bassets. And three little girls. Juliet was making jokes about all the disasters on their holiday, and Graham didn't say anything but winked. He's a widower – Jim Waite, that is. Marion's grandfather. Her mother's father. That's her daughter helping her in the garden – Lizzie. Her grandmother – that's her father's mother, not Jim's wife – gave us the most wonderful sweet williams one year I remember.

Called them sweet willies. Said they needed lots of rain to make them stand up, then gave a splendidly dirty laugh. But that's ages ago. Marion had a heart operation at Papworth. Had one of her valves replaced by a pig's. Says it makes her feel a bit odd when she thinks about it.'

Marion's a reflective, independent woman, who even as a schoolgirl had an air of gravity. She lived for a while in another village where the well-off people and the not so well-off didn't mix. 'But in Barnwell,' she said, 'the whole lot mix together. You've still got the base of all the older people who were here, and the newer ones have built on top of that. Obviously people talk, like in any other village, but usually it's quite harmless. You listen, you nod your head, and then I usually just forget it.'

West Side

There's a wall topped by a small flowerbed fitted into an angle of the cottage next to David's shop. Sandra and Roger Wilkins recently came to live there, and have managed to infiltrate an alpine or a creeper into every cranny of the wall and crampack the flowerbed so that in summer it fizzes over like a garden cocktail.

Next to them is Tudor House, built in 1604. Despite its imposing name, it is cottage-scale, though stone mullions and an arched doorway distinguish it from neighbours. It was Barnwell's first school, paid for by Rector Nicholas Latham, and used as such for over a quarter of a century. It has been the Strattons' home for a long time, but since William Stratton died, his widow, Millicent, and Pam, have decided to move to a bungalow and so it is up for sale.

Next door is a cottage and a joiner's yard, in which one man might be polishing a hearse, another feeding a family of ducks, and a woman entreating a semi-wild cat to emerge from under the woodpile. This is Crowsons, funeral directors and joiners, now owned by Derek and Eileen Gunn, animal lovers extraordinary.

They used to live and work in King's Cliffe, a larger village about twelve miles away, where Derek taught woodwork and metalwork at the senior school, and Eileen was school secretary. Then there were educational changes in the county, the school became a middle school, and Derek decided to set up in business on his own. At the time, Crowsons was owned by Arthur Malster, and Derek started to do a lot of work for him. 'I've always had an interest in the funeral business. When I was an apprentice lad we used to make some coffins. Once I got to know Arthur Malster we used to talk a lot, and he showed me different things. Then he said he was thinking of retiring early. That was how we became interested in Crowsons.'

'At first,' said Eileen, 'I was horrified. I had never seen anyone dead. I used to lie awake in bed at night, and I must have said a million times, Are we doing the right thing?'

Certainly if there is a received image of funeral directors, the Gunns don't fit. Fair, comfortable, friendly, good listeners and good chucklers, they are much more the type of people you would choose to go to in trouble, rather than the professionals that death makes necessary. Very professional they have to be, however, for there are no funeral directors in either Thrapston or Oundle, and Crowsons covers a wide area. Arthur Malster was anxious that the business should not become just an offshoot of a big company – 'He and Mrs Malster went out of their way to help us come here' – and while clients may come from many miles away, they are not treated impersonally. 'When people come to visit the chapel to see their loved ones,' Eileen said, 'I like to think that they are going to come in here to the sitting-room, sit in here, have a cup of tea, and have a little chat afterwards. It's more of a sort of homely atmosphere. We like to think that when they're dealing with us it's not just a job.'

Having the joinery and the funeral business on the same premises has presented problems. 'We've got people who've come perhaps to arrange a funeral, they don't always use the front door, which is what we would prefer, they go round the back, and there's no telling who is in the workshop, or what the conversation is at the time.' As John Jeffs, one of their assistants, said, local people come to the workshop to be cheered up. 'One chap came in, looking dreadful. He felt dreadful. Didn't want anything, just cheering up. Knew he'd get a laugh here. Doctor'd done bugger all for 'im. Left after a couple of hours, talking to me and Roly, having split 'is sides!' The workshop is about to be moved to some buildings half a mile away, and I shall rather miss it – even John's dreadful jokes like, 'They're all dying to see us.' Though, given the predicaments the Gunns can be faced with, it is both sensible and sensitive.

'You never know,' said Eileen, 'when someone rings the door bell, what you will be faced with. Not long ago, a fairly young man came and said, "My daughter has committed suicide in London." You just have that said at the door. You must never show people you're floundering.'

Dora Robinson lives a couple of doors down, in the middle of a line of small thatched cottages set back from the road. She'll call out to John Jeffs when she passes, 'I expect I'll be the next.' Like the rest of the village, she takes the presence of an undertakers for granted. 'I've always been used to funerals going away from here. I don't take any notice. I wonder who it is sometimes, but it doesn't worry me a bit.'

Her living-room still has an old-fashioned black range, with an open fire burning at the centre, and a kettle standing on either side. Two comfy chairs face the hearth, and the room is crammed with pictures, photographs, pot plants, treasures. The cushions have bright crochet covers bought in a charity sale by her niece, and the bookshelves contain Mrs Henry Wood, Charlotte M. Yonge, and Jane Austen.

Dora left Barnwell School at fourteen, and would have liked to go on to high school. 'They wanted me to stay on, and I didn't want to leave. But my people just couldn't afford it. I got a certificate for two years' unbroken attendance. Not many got those.' She went to live with her aunt who ran the post office in Cotterstock. 'I had to deliver telegrams to Tansor, Fotheringhay and Southwick, on the bicycle. No matter what the weather, I had to go pedalling around on this old bicycle. They hadn't got telephones then, and an auctioneer lived at Fotheringhay, and you'd perhaps get there and deliver one and get back and there'd be another one waiting. And at shooting time, at Southwick Hall, they used to have a lot of telegrams.'

She came back to Barnwell and worked at the Rectory, and, when Rector Baillie retired, she lived with him and his wife in Hastings until he died. 'I was very sorry really when I had to come home. But my mother got ill, and my sister too, and then she died, and it was a case – well, my work was at home then. I sort of did bits of daily work and things, and I brought my two nieces up more or less.'

She was employed as fourth housemaid at the Manor. 'I did the men's rooms, the indoor servants. I used to go every morning. And I used to do a bit up in the nursery too. I was very happy there.' Among her photographs is one taken in the 1940s of a group of servants standing with the Duchess of Gloucester. I remarked that, although they are about the same age, Dora then looked much the younger. 'Well, I hadn't had such funny sorts of jobs to do as she had. She's always had to look serious, I expect.'

The old smithy stands at the edge of the road a little further along. I never knew it used as such, but memories of other smithies, with their smell of singed hoof and the hiss of red-hot horseshoes being plunged into a bucket of water, makes me a little regretful for things past. Particularly as two ponies, Chunky and Freckles, sometimes graze the small adjacent paddock, coming up to the fence to accept handfuls of clovery grass pulled from the brookside, and leaving a warm smell and light grey film on one's fingers after being stroked.

Mick and Susan Burns live in the second of a handsome pair

of thatched cottages with long front gardens. It was renovating the cottage that changed Mick from a joiner working for a firm into an all-round, freelance builder. 'I think it's the best way to learn. I enjoy work more now. In a joiner's shop or with building carpentry it tends to be very repetitious. I found I could do a job for two or three years, then I was getting itchy feet. Now I don't know what I'll be doing from one day to the next. And it certainly keeps me on me toes.'

Mick grew up in Thrapston, and met Sue when she was working at a local restaurant and he was called in to do some carpentry. 'Broke me heart. I must have spent thousands going to pubs and dances at night and chasing the girls, and then I meet me wife at work. The first time I see her I think she was scrubbing the grill room floor. So I knew she was a worker! I certainly couldn't have done the cottage on me own.' It took them about two years, working in the evenings and at weekends, with help from Sue's family who live at Montagu Terrace, and even from their then very small daughter, Emma. 'She spent a whole weekend with me once, when I concreted the floor. With her little green barrow, she loaded the cement mixer with her bucket and spade from the seaside. She tended to do what I did, and done it properly.'

Mick and Sue have a unique perspective on the 'old' and the 'new' in Barnwell. When they were first married, they rented their present cottage before buying a house and moving to Thrapston. Sue's family had been settled in Barnwell since she was a child, and her grandparents had once lived in the cottage, so she was undoubtedly a Barnwellian. But Mick found that it was the leaving and coming back that turned him into one. 'Nobody really ignored me before, but there was more of a tendency when we moved back for people on the other side of the brook to speak to me because they knew me. I was more accepted as a Barnwell person.' By then many more young couples had come to the village, and the older people were becoming slightly bewildered by so many strange faces. 'Of course, for those that moved in while we were away, we were complete newcomers, and for a long time they couldn't make me out. We were known by all the older ones, the establishment accepted us, and there we were, working away on the cottage, in the muck.'

Sue, who looks pretty and neat even when she's wheeling

barrowloads of rubble down to a skip, thought that in many ways the influx was good for the village, particularly the School. Her mother, Mrs Joan Crump, is caretaker at the School, and their two families are very close. When Norah Blunt asked Mick whether he would be willing to stand for election to the Parish Council, he said he had too many other commitments, but wondered if Joan would. She said she'd have a go.

'To me,' she explained, 'it's Barnwell, not money, that should be discussed. It's about the environment, not bank books. You see I get so boiled up inside about it, I don't know, there's so many things that you know you could do. The Council's a place for thrashing things out but not for losing your temper and arguing about it. Because I don't like arguing with people.' Both Joan and Sue have a natural diffidence combined with deep feelings that one sees might not always be easily expressed in the context of committee meetings with their dry procedure rituals and formalities of language.

Mick pointed out that nowadays more people in Barnwell have, or have had, jobs concerned with administration. 'You get two or three of them together, and they could waffle on all night about the consitution of a meeting,' he said smiling. 'In general, we try to steer a middle course. In a village, you get a lot of little feuds going on. Perhaps Sue sees them more than I do, at the School and things. People will talk to you every morning for a month, and then they'll stop and look right through you. Things like that goes on. It's a happy village, but with being a village I think you get to know about all the scandals and tragedies. Bad news travels fast.'

Joan represents Barnwell on Oundle's After Care committee. 'If you've been ill, and you need help, like if you needed a wheelchair or something, then they do their best to get what you want.' She organized some whist drives to raise funds for After Care, and then Mick took them over on a more frequent basis. 'Joan was doing one a year, and you'd get a dozen or so people there, and then there were three or four who'd like to have come but didn't know about it, and the dozen or so that came perhaps didn't all fit in with any of the other activities of the village, people don't like to join in on some things, but a game of cards is very easy going, so I thought, well, I'll give it a try. And it built up to fifteen, sixteen people, and it's gone on from there. Two whist drives a year are still for After Care. It's just a nice, easy going night. I did say if ever it got too serious, which cards can get, I'd pack it up.'

As long as Maggie Head continues to go to them, there's little chance of that. She and her husband, Charles, live in Montagu Terrace, next door to Marion Leesons. 'If there's any strange people there,' she said, referring to the whist drives, 'we're quiet for a bit. But of course, if they start, we start. Mick told me he's going to ban me last week. I'd got a pink jumper on, and I'd got me slacks on, and a thick cardigan. And he'd got all the heaters on. I'd taken me coat off, and of course I was flirting, then I took me cardi off, and they said, "Watch out, Maggie's stripping!" I said, "Yes, if it gets too hot, me jumper's coming off. And I've got no tit-bags on!"' At that, the budgerigar in her sitting-room shrieked loudly. 'The children bought me a budgie when John got married, as company, being in the house on me own. He was getting so he was talking and answering me back, and doing a little bit of swearing, when a cat got it. So, of course, I sobbed and sobbed. It was like a child to me. Then John took me to Oundle to get this one, he's only a baby.'

Maggie originally came from Sandringham, and went into domestic service when she left school just before the war. 'Then, when all the young ones were joining up, I got the urge to go. There was no room in the Air Force or the Navy, and I had to go in the Army. I feel old when me oldest granddaughter comes, because she's joined the cadets, and she says, "If I can't get a job, Nan, when I'm eighteen, I'll join the Army." She looks at it, If Nan can do it, I can do it. But she doesn't realize it was a jolly sight harder then. You had to rough it, you see.'

Charles – often known as Charlie, and called Charl by his wife – is a keeper's son, and was once 'the youngest shepherd round here'. He was a groom at the Manor before the war, and now that he's semi-retired, his list of jobs seems to grow. 'I can't keep him at home, he won't stop here,' Maggie said.

One of the most familiar sights in the village is Charles, ruddy-faced, swathed in gardening implements, riding his bicycle on his way to various gardens or one of the churchyards. He cuts several lawns, 'And I've got three gardens up the Almshouses what I dig and set. Then last year I took that one of Pam Stratton's on, and that's fifteen yards wide and a chain long. Then there's two down this end of the village. One old girl, I generally go and mow her orchard and rake it up and cut her hedge. She's got all michaelmas daisies and golden rod, and I go and put them up so as they don't come all over the path so she get wet through. Then the other one, I generally have about a fortnight down there when I'm on holiday.'

The 'holiday' is from Oundle School where Charles works in the mornings during term-time. 'I clean all the things up from the floor like, clothes and that, see as they got soap, toilet rolls and all such as that, sweep places up. Just cleaning like. Some on the boys, they're rough and ready. They come across one place and smoke. It's worse than what it's like with an ordinary fire.' 'You're telling tales,' said Maggie very firmly, 'you shouldn't split on 'em, having a crafty smoke.' 'Oh, I never interfere with them.' Earlier, she had said: 'I smoke wicked, I do. I try to pack it in, but the boys come in, because one smokes a pipe, the other one rolls his own, another one smokes cigarettes, and then Charl smokes a pipe, and that's it. Once you smell the smoke, you've got to start.'

Norah Blunt and her husband Jack live next door to the Heads. 'Somebody very sarcastically said to me, "What are you doing now you're retired?",' Norah remarked, surrounded by the fruits of her patchwork, carpentry, tapestry and embroidery, not to mention folders of committee papers, library books, scrapbooks and diaries. 'So I told them, "I knit all morning, and drink gin all the afternoon!"' The retirement is from working in the Oundle Bookshop. 'Since I've retired, I've said ever so many times that I'd like to do 'O' Level needlework. They do it at Oundle, but I don't think they do it for older students. Having pushed three daughters through exams, I feel I'd like to do something too. They say they're starting an 'O' Level English course at Oundle for mature students. I might do that.'

She met Jack Blunt in the late 1960s at a cadet training camp which he went to annually as RSM. Her first husband, Sandy Morrison, had died of cancer, and she felt uncertain when friends in the WRVS asked her to join a team of their members who cooked for the camp. However they persuaded her that a change would do her good. 'A lot of them had been before, but there were three of us new, and evidently Jack turned to his friend when we all walked in the sergeants' mess the first night, and said, "Oh well, they're pretty much the same as usual, but I quite fancy the one in navy blue!"' Jack, who used to be in the Marines, walks with what can only be described as a strict military bearing that has a restraining effect on scruffs like myself, and at first it seemed insubordinate even to think of him at a bar making such comments. However, I was reassured when, on another occasion, Norah mentioned that her daughter had given him a poster of a nude with miniature tanks and armoured cars positioned up and down 'its hills and hollers' for his office.

Below the end of Montagu Terrace there is a ford and a footbridge. The ford is frequently dry, but after rains it is an excellent place for children to rear their bikes dangerously into splashy wheelies, or to potter with nets and sticks and pails. When the brook is fairly high, and I am on my way over the footbridge to the tiny letter-box buried in the hawthorn hedge, I sometimes stand for a few seconds and listen to the rushing water. Often, though, the brook is low and still, its turbid surface clogged with weed.

After the ford, the village feels different. The banks are wider, the trees dense and old, and the buildings are set higher above the narrowing roads. Many of the houses are larger, several new, and they have more ground and foliage around them. But the difference lies deeper. For once this was a separate parish and had its own church and manor. The latter has completely disappeared, apart from depressions and banks tracing its site in the meadows, but the chancel of the church remains, and it imbues this rather private end of Barnwell with an atmosphere that some find very special.

The church is called All Saints – the main one is St Andrew – and until 1821 the parishes were known as Barnwell All Saints and Barnwell St Andrew. Then, because All Saints Church had fallen into such a bad state of disrepair, it was dismantled, except for its chancel, and the parishes were joined. It is now known simply as the Chancel, and gives its name to the terrace of houses opposite. The roadside bank below the peaceful graveyard is thick with daffodils in April, and was once the site of two wells, which, according to Thomas Bell, in the age of ignorance and superstition were widely famed for the miraculous cures they performed in the diseases of children, who were dipped on the Eve of St John the Baptist's Day, and it is said that at length sacred veneration was paid to them, and that pilgrims from distant parts resorted hither. From these wells, including perhaps a fine spring in the adjoining parish of Barnwell St Andrew, called Cross well or Holy well, and which still gives its name to the field in which it rises, may have derived the name of these parishes, Bernewell or Bairnwell . . .

An alternative origin is Beorna-Wielle, old English for Warrior's Spring, and Leland reported that young men 'on the Eve of John the Baptist's day practised wrestling and other youthful sports' by the wells. There is a traditional saying in the village, which each generation of children repeats, that no one is a true Barnwellian until they have fallen into the brook.

Miss Agnes Broome, who lives in a bungalow near the end of the village, has a photograph of one of the old wells below the Chancel. She took it herself on a snowy day many decades ago, and Ernest Crowson is standing by the well. 'I used to lodge with the Crowsons, they were friends of ours when my father was stationmaster here, before the First World War. Then when I was working in Oundle during the war I lodged with them, and in the evening I'd got nothing else to do so I used to help paint the carts and wagons and things that came in. And I gradually improved, of course, and got to putting the fancy lining on. There wasn't so much undertaking done then, it was more a wheelwright's, and we used to shoe the wheels with iron tyres – heavy work but interesting. Then, as the wheel-wrighting died out, Mr Crowson took up decorating, and Mr Malster came to us as a boy, and then he took over the business. He had the decorating for a short time, but the undertaking was getting so busy for him he dropped the decorating and I took it on myself. I used to go all round the district – I had an old autocycle. I used to borrow Arthur Malster's truck to take my plank and trestles about, and then used to go to work on the autocycle.'

Agnes is Barnwell's oldest inhabitant. She was born on All Saints' Day 1887 and it's unfortunate that, apart from arthritis, her main trouble is deafness, since she's such an interesting person to talk to. 'It's the thing I'm most sorry about, my hearing. Because it's a strain on other people when they come to see me. That's the one thing that worries me more than anything.'

She was ten when her father came to Barnwell as stationmaster. 'I had two years at the school here, and then I got a scholarship to Wellingborough. I liked it up to a point, but you were rather looked down on in those days by the people that paid. That was the worse part. Maths I always liked. But sport, mainly. I played hockey for the 2nd eleven, kept goal. And I was the only girl in the Barnwell boys' cricket eleven.'

Cricket is her passion. She saw Jack Hobbs and Herbert Sutcliffe play at the Oval, and has very definite views on the parlous state of English cricket today. 'They ask for trouble. They don't get on top of the ball like the old cricketers used to do.' When there's cricket on television, she won't be persuaded out for a run in a car by anyone. 'It's the first time I've seen it in colour this season, and it makes such a difference. As soon as I saw the maroon and the tudor rose, I thought, Oh! that's Northamptonshire.' During the 1914–18 War she was the first female booking clerk on the branch railway line that ran between Northampton and Peterborough, working first at Oundle and then – 'Because the man came back from the war who's job I took' – at Wellingborough. From the latter, she used to be able to go up to the County Cricket ground to watch the final couple of hours play after work was over.

'I've got wonderful neighbours all round,' she said, explaining how they enable her to keep going in the home that her parents built in 1932 – indeed, she herself helped to build it. 'I did putting all the windows in and that sort of thing.' Mary Marriott, from Lower Farm, is one of these neighbours, coming in every morning and encouraging her to have a private cuss when it's particularly difficult to get her arthritic joints moving. But Agnes doesn't believe in moaning to others. 'You can moan and groan when you're on your own.'

'Good philosophy that,' agrees Mary. She took over from Agnes the job of reporting on items of Barnwell news for the weekly local newspaper, and between them they have a fund of information and memories. Mary believes that at one time the wider acquisition of private motor cars almost caused a breakdown in close-knit village life, though recent developments have helped to bring people together again, if in a different, more casual, way. Both she and Agnes are pleased that newcomers next door were willing for Agnes's emergency bell to remain wired to their bungalow. 'They've only been here four months, but it seems as though you've known them all your life,' Mary said. That end of the village has always had its own community spirit, she feels, and she's anxious it should continue.

Lower Farm is the only farm in the village which is both family-run and family-owned. It has the silvery silos of recent years, but in its yard and old outbuildings are many relics of past practices. Percy Marriott took it over just after the First World War, and his son, Trevor, now approaching sixty, remembers how 'We used to grow all our own food for the animals, such as mangles and oats, and do all the grinding work.'

'Grandad milked by hand when I first came here,' said Mary. 'And we had all the hen roosts in the fields, and went every afternoon with the little children with the buckets to collect the eggs. I can just remember stooking the corn, and seeing them stack and weave the thatch on the stack. The hay was loose then, whereas now it's baled. I'd never skinned a rabbit or dressed a chicken, but I've done a good many since. I can remember being up nearly all night when it was Christmas, doing chickens and turkeys for the milk round.'

Norah had said that when she was growing up on the farm, 'I used to help with the sheep and that, but I would never learn to milk a cow because I found out at a very early age that they had to be milked twice a day. It was the same with driving a car. I would never learn to drive when I was at home because you'd always have to go and fetch the bit that broke on the tractor or the binder or whatever. I'd drive a tractor, I used to enjoy it. And I can remember having a pig, I don't quite know what was wrong with it, but it laid there, and the vet said he didn't think it'd live, and I used to feed it with a great big wooden spoon with warm milk and gruel. It survived.'

The milking herd remained until Percy retired in 1968 aged eighty-one. 'Nobody is as tolerant today as he was,' said Mary. 'The stupidest little things they seem to get het up about. Even when he was eighty, he'd got a lot of time for young people.' A few years after he died, Trevor became ill. 'I had a cold, or that's what I thought. Of course I was on me own, so I took all sorts of tablets. Then I got so I used to go out and do about half hour's work and have to come and lay down on the mat until I revived again enough. It went on through January, February, and I went to see the doctor, and found I had double pneumonia. I can't do much work at all now; me lungs fill up all the time.'

His two elder sons, Robert and John, took on the farm, which is now mainly devoted to cereal crops. 'The yield's more than doubled in my lifetime. When I was a boy, we used very few fertilisers, apart from farmyard manure. It was 90% hit or miss. Apart from a few big bugs who could afford it, you never had a soil sample taken. Now every two or three years we take samples, and know what the soil is deficient in.' With better crop control, and little daily animal husbandry, the farm is no longer a full-time, round-the-year job for a whole family. Robert and John do other work during slack months, and David, their youngest son, is preparing for college.

The EEC elections were taking place that week. 'I'm one of them that don't let it bother me,' Trevor said. 'If you're into politics, one side or the other, you're either arguing for one side or arguing for the other. If you're like me, happy go lucky in between, you just take it as it comes. You can have one person will come one day, and he'll say to you, Look, if we hadn't have gone in, it'd probably have done this. Well, who knows whether we should have been any the better off if we hadn't've been in, we might have been worser. And the next one'll come and say, It's a good job we went in, because this has happened and that's happened. Well, I mean, it's always the same, isn't it? Who knows what you don't have, whether it would have been right. It's like growing a thing. You can have a wonderful harvest on one small crop, and you say, Well, if I'd put half the farm in, we could have made a fortune. But the trouble is, if you had put half the farm in, it might have been a bad year. I'm afraid I don't let it worry me that much. My father always used to say, What you lose on the swings you gain on the roundabouts.'

East Side

Across the brook, the road dwindles to a track which leads past Foot Hill Spinney and a steep field called Toot Hill that makes a good toboggan run when it snows. One can follow the track a long way, between hawthorn and blackthorn, looking over acres of smooth, cultivated fields to the trees of Barnwell Wold. Having this beautiful landscape right on her doorstep is a permanent joy and solace which Mary Marriott values beyond price. Young Jane Fox, who is growing up at Orchard End, the last house on the east side, has one of her favourite play places just outside her home: a dip where water gathers, and very small boats can be sailed. Walking back towards the centre of Barnwell, past a pretty group of thatched cottages and Mrs Moira Shepherd's verdant garden at Long Meadow, one comes to Friars Close Farm which has a huge conker tree that Jane loves.

It's seldom called Friars Close; usually people say 'Cooks' or 'the turkey farm': a generous, late Victorian house, with a complex set of outbuildings that contain a highly technical modern industry.

Eighteen years ago, when Phil and Norah Cook came from Barton Seagrave where Phil's family had farmed for generations, things were very different. Friars Close was a run-down mixed farm belonging to the Dyott Estate which owns several farms around Barnwell. They had tried to auction it, but the fairly low reserve price wasn't reached. 'We couldn't raise the money for the reserve,' said Norah, 'which was a crying shame when you think what we could have bought it for. So the estate let us rent it.'

Gradually they built up a turkey farm, keeping abreast of changes in methods and marketing, and moving away from concentration on the Christmas market to emphasis on fertilized eggs, chicks, and poults. Stacks of rotating shelves inside the vast metal containers in the incubating sheds can take thousands of eggs at a time. The regulated heating and humidity creates a permanent hum, and control panels indicate the minute-by-minute conditions in each container. If one of them begins to overheat, an alarm rings immediately in the house. As Phil Cook quietly demonstrated the various processes that lead up to a colossal hatch, I was reminded of a sturdy sea captain in charge of a well-loved but demanding ship. Indeed, supplying fertilized eggs and baby chicks in tip-top condition to markets all over Britain and Europe requires the equivalent of naval precision.

He and Norah have three lively daughters who are all interested in the poultry business. 'It's very rewarding for me,' said Norah, 'because I used to fight constant battles with my conscience, because we couldn't go out at weekends, and didn't do the sort of things I did when young, but they all finish up settling themselves with seven-day-a-week jobs and I think, Oh, well, it can't have been that bad then.'

Heather met a Norwegian poultry farmer at college, and they are now married and live in Norway. A red gymkhana rosette won by Jennifer, their youngest daughter, lay on the hall table; she's a weekly boarder, studying for 'A' levels before going to poultry college. Hazel, who did a business management course, was working late in the office – recently a stable – where a computer is now installed. She is married to her childhood friend, Geoff Shacklock, now the farm's sales administrator.

By the time the turkey farm had become a viable enterprise, the circumstances of the Dyott Estate had changed and they no longer wished to sell Friars Close. However the Cooks have been able to buy land in Thurning, two miles away, and expand into a second site, Home Farm, where Geoff and Hazel live. At the busiest time of the year, the two sites employ up to fifty people; a long way from the time when the Cooks first started to keep hens in Barton Seagrave and, said Norah, 'We couldn't afford one deep litter house.'

It's not the first time Friars Close has been a poultry farm. In the 1930s it was still part of the Barnwell Castle Estate, then owned by Major Colin Cooper who was connected with the International Stores. He initiated an ambitious chicken farm there, accounts of which vary. The most enthusiastic I heard was from Bert Kirk. 'That was when Barnwell was a different place. There were hostels up there for chaps and girls, all beautiful buildings, and a billiard hall, you never saw anything like it in your life, and a dance hall. I used to come home Friday evening special to come to these dances. And they had a football team, they called them the Barnwell Roosters.'

It's difficult now to imagine this quiet end of the village thronging with groups of mainly Northern young men and women. At that time there was a shop in what is now the Watsons' home, and its trade increased enormously in the brief boom before the poultry farm went into liquidation. Dreams of what might have been can be imagined from part of the 'Chairman's Message' in the farm's social club's magazine, *The Rooster*:

> If we take the building of the Club steadily we shall accomplish all those things mentioned at the last general meeting, swimming pool, fully equipped sports field, the external and internal beautifying of the club rooms, and the building of separate billiard room and gymnasium rooms –

tremendous things to do, but it can and will be done if we all pull together.

Chancel Terrace, the group of houses next to Friars Close, was built for employees of the poultry farm, and now mainly houses people who work on farms belonging to the Dyott Estate. Brian Sharman and John Carter, who work at Castle Farm, both have houses here, and for years the Gliszczynskis – known throughout the village as 'the Gees' – were at No. 1. Vans belonging to Rory Shepherd's tennis-court construction business would zoop up this section of unmade road as the Gee boys grew up and started work. Their father, Jan, who came from Poland, died nine years ago, and Jean has remarried and is about to move from the Terrace.

In the early 1970s, three quite large building plots were sold by Chancel Terrace, and now three families, each with two children, live in the three distinct houses. The one that excited most comment as it took shape was the De Bocks', designed, and to a large extent built, by themselves. Werner is a landscape architect, and he and Jeanne travelled backwards and forwards from their home in Northampton to build the house at weekends. 'Then,' said Hanneke, 'we decided to move in to finish the rest 'cos it would be easier than driving up and down all the time. We hadn't finished the bedrooms and things, so we all slept in the living room in camp beds.' Opinions on the final result varied from 'It's nothing but a huge roof' to 'The only aesthetically-pleasing modern building in the village'. The 'huge roof', an olympic slope of pan-tiles broken by the window that lights the big kitchen, shelters a home with high beams, natural finishes, and an air of peace. Werner has his office there, and coffee time round the wide kitchen table, where Jeanne likes to sit and read long, literary novels, is very tempting to a skiving writer.

After the new homes, just by the ford are four semi-detached stone houses, built for Barnwell Castle Estate in 1900. At that time most of the village belonged to the Estate, which its owner, the Earl of Dalkeith (later 7th Duke of Buccleuch), had leased to Colonel and Lady Etheldreda Wickham. Their lease ended in 1910, and the Earl, probably fearing the direct Land Tax proposed by Lloyd George, sold the complete estate to a wealthy Pole, Horace Czarnikow. Ten years later, in July

1920, the village suddenly learned that the four-thousand-acre estate was to be broken into ninety-one lots and sold by auction. Czarnikow, so it was said, had lost his fortune as a result of the Russian Revolution.

The auction catalogue, writes Laura Stokes, 'Spelled out dismay to many of Barnwell's population — for therein was listed every farm, field, holding and cottage, all awaiting the highest bidder, and the knowledge that "The Estate" was to be broken up, and the livelihood of many of its workers placed in jeopardy. No longer would keepers, carpenters, bricklayers, painters, etc., work together, and this unit of village life would be disrupted for ever.'

The estate attached to the Manor was reduced to about five hundred acres, and was sold first to Major and Mrs McGrath, then to Major Colin Cooper, and finally to the Duke of Gloucester in 1938. Princess Alice, Duchess of Gloucester, is the daughter of the 7th Duke of Buccleuch, and was nine years old when her father sold the Barnwell Estate. She had never seen it, but when a friend told her and the Duke of Gloucester that it was up for sale the coincidence seemed timely, for they had been having difficulty finding a suitable country house for family weekends. After 'dithering' a little over the price, they bought it, and the elaborate wrought-iron gates installed by Major Cooper at the drive entrance were removed and replaced by simple wooden ones. From then on, Barnwell Castle became known as Barnwell Manor.

When I asked Dora Robinson which year she came to live in her present cottage, her reply demonstrated the upheavals caused during the frequent changes of ownership of the Manor. 'Now, which sale was it? One of them! We went where Gordon Allen used to stop, after we got out. When we moved from that cottage, we moved over there. It was still the Estate, you see, so they put us over there, which was quite nice. Well, then the Estate was sold again, and my father was under the impression that some of the Manor people had taken it over, but it wasn't so. An uncle that went to the sale came back and said our cottage was sold, that one over there, to the farmer round that side, so that's when we had to move. And this was the only house in the village. We didn't care very much for it at first. It was awful. I mean, my father was, well, very upset about it. Because he'd enquired, you see, and someone had said, Oh, it's all right . . . But you get used to it.'

Times have changed. The four semi-detached stone houses remained part of the Barnwell Manor Estate until fairly recently, often referred to as 'The Duke's row'. Three have now been sold as staff at the Manor were reduced, but the fourth remains rented to Jim Waite, a retired estate worker, for as long as he needs it. His wife died several years ago, but the house is as trim inside as his tall row of beans and lines of lettuces and greens are in the front garden. Though he left school aged eleven to work on the land in the First World War, Jim has moved with the times as easily as a bird in a thermal current, and sits in his upright chair, with his lunch cooking on the stove, in front of a bronzed *Sun* calendar pin-up girl who beams down from the wall behind him.

The story of this century's developments in medicine could almost be encapsulated in his history. He was born in the small cottage – 1½-up, 1½-down – Dora lives in now. 'There were seven of us. Well, there were thirteen, but only seven lived. My father was on the Estate. He used to do hedge laying and that sort of thing.' The bone in one of his elbows sticks out at an awkward angle. 'When I broke that arm, I was only four years old. In that field, at the back where Marion lives, that's where I broke it. There was an old big elm tree blown down. And of course the thin end used to go up and down, and of course there were two of us swinging on it, and of course I went down as it come up and shot me right off.' He was taken into Oundle by horse and cart, and the doctor strapped his arm to his chest for seventeen weeks. 'It ain't straight now, but it's straight from what it would have been because the old dad, he knocked some here nails in this here old big beam (I don't know whether they're still in it, I bet they took a bit of pulling out), and made a swing. They used to make me swing on it, and that pulled it straight to what it is now.'

After he was married, he lived for thirty-three years in Armston, a mile away, working as a cowman. Then he got severe lung disease, which took some time to diagnose. It turned out to be caused by dust from mouldy hay. 'I had to leave off milking, they told me I mustn't go in the cowshed, so I got a job at the Duke's out in the open on the land. I was there five or six year before I retired at seventy, and then they said this house was empty and if I liked to move down here we could. Still worked for him like, for a while, but not regular. Potatering and that sort of thing.' Since then, he's had two experiences of hospital. 'I went in for prostate gland, and I went on one of these scanners. It comes on the telly at the side on you. He's just running this thing over your stomach, and you could see everything on the blooming thing. He kept telling me which was which, but I was no nearer when he was finished! But he did tell me what things were.' Then, 'A few weeks back, I went and had me eye done. They stitched a contact lens in it somehow, and you can't tell much difference, can you? I can see as well with that as I can with the other one. I hadn't seen a thing out of it for twelve month. I lay in bed the next morning, and the nurse came and took the pad off, she just got it undone, and I sat up and I could see right across Peterborough with it. And I thought, well, that's all right.'

By the footbridge opposite Horseradish Lane there is a giant weeping willow, and in summer its branches make a green canopy under which groups of children can play at house or shelter from the rain. It was planted by Walter Woolman, whose bungalow it faces. His wife, Eileen, is often in the garden, kneeling and patiently weeding despite joints severely swollen with rheumatism. To her, as to me, the fiddly side of gardening is inexpressibly satisfying. A bit of her path-side veronica she gave me years ago has increased into several large mats dotted around our garden. In July they have hundreds of deep-blue miniature spires which the bees love.

Next is Gordon Allen's yard with a large workshed and several trailers standing outside. It has been strangely quiet for a few months, and often the shed doors have been shut. The sound of an electric saw, or the clanking of equipment from the yard, has always been part of the familiar background noises along this part of the village. But Gordon has been ill, and the last time I saw him, scything the brookside, he was very thin and his dark eyes looked strained.

Next to the yard is a long, roadside cottage, the home of Gerry and Liz Allen – no relation to Gordon. Their cottage is two old farmworkers' dwellings, merged and extended; a handsome building that has metamorphosed since Gerry first saw it. He's a chartered surveyor and has worked for the argicultural division of the firm in Kettering that manages the Dyott Estate since he left college. 'I was sent over here in the late 1960s because we'd had a report that Barnwell village had been flooded, and there was this family in one of the estate cottages in great distress. I came in here, and the wife was at the cooker, with about three inches of water on the floor, and about five kids, and the water was coming through the roof, and in through the back door and in through the front – it was dreadful. I went back and said, We must do something about this.' The family moved, and since the next-door cottage was already vacant, the pair were put up for sale. 'It was during a very depressed period in the house market, and we couldn't sell them. We kept advertising, and the man I worked for kept saying to me, Why don't you buy it? But I wasn't interested in property then.' However he showed it to Liz – this was before they married, while she was still at college – who liked it, and finally he asked how much the estate wanted for it.

'As soon as I said that, they said, If you want to buy it, we can have nothing to do with it and must get an independent valuation. In the meantime, someone offered £700, but the independent report valued it at about twice that. I thought it was far too much, but they said I'd be silly to miss it, so I said, All right, I'll have it. The other chap then offered £850, but I had to tell him it was already sold. He asked how much it went for, and I said, In excess of £1,000. The fellow must be mad, he said, He must have taken leave of his senses. I didn't like to tell him it was me and that I'd paid a good deal more than £1,000.'

They started doing it up themselves at weekends, and Emma Owen, who was an irrepressible old lady, used to put her head through the glassless windows as they were digging out the floors and say, 'Are you looking for treasure? There's nobody ever lived here as had any money.' Then she'd go to the shop and say, 'They must be mad down at that cottage, they must be mad. The place will fall down. It floods as it is now, but they're lowering the floor, they must be mad.' Several years later, when Liz was expecting their first child, the telephone rang at five one April Sunday morning — Mothering Sunday, in fact. 'It was Pam Stratton from over the way,' said Gerry, 'saying, Did you know that the stream's broken its banks and it's up to your door? And I said, Oh, don't worry, Pam, it's all sorted out, I've got a flood board on. So Liz said, Well, we'd better go and have a look. We came downstairs, and there was our wedding photograph album, bobbing up and down, and my slippers floating across the room. And Liz said, Oh god, there's nothing we can do, and she went off back to bed!'

Six years later, again on an April Sunday, when there'd been gales and heavy snow, the brook started to rise and the electricity was cut off. 'I'd got sandbags up at the back, and I thought, we're all right now, we're safe.' They had three children by then, and Ellen, who helps look after them, had to be carried back through the flood by a fireman after she'd been out. 'It was all a big joke. We were sitting round the fire, having a drink, and when I got up and walked across the room the whole carpet seemed to go up and down under my feet. The water hadn't come through either door, it came up through the floor. And we had a proper damp-proof membrane and everything.'

'It's amazing when you do get flooded in this village,' Liz said, 'how many people come and help. The village seems to come to life.'

That particular weekend was exciting all round. The flood cut the main street off completely from ordinary traffic, and when Margaret Marriott started to have her baby, she had to be driven part of the way to hospital by John on a tractor. A dam had just been built across the brook beyond Lower Farm, and it has a control gate that was supposed to regulate the water when it got dangerously high. 'I'd persuaded the farmers and the estate to allow the water authority to put it in,' said Gerry, 'so of course, when they discovered I'd been flooded, they said, There you are, you silly bugger, I told you it wouldn't work.' In fact, the gate wasn't quite completed then, though even with the controls on maximum it is still problematic whether a really speedy rise in the water can be controlled sufficiently to stop the water building up by the low arch of the stone bridge and being forced out onto the road.

No one enjoys being flooded, but each time the brook rises and brims its banks, flood stories abound and are told, particularly by those with the longest memories, with some relish. Details as to which front doors were penetrated in the distant past are circulated and contradicted, and so are tales of boats being rowed up the brook. A *History of Northamptonshire* published in 1849 has this account, which has probably formed the basis of one or two of the more dramatic anecdotes:

> On the 17th of June, 1721, a heavy rain, accompanied with thunder and lightning, inundated the village, the water rising to the height of 5 or 6 feet in the houses, drowned several sheep, and in subsiding, carried a waggon laden with wood along with it for 200 yards.

Dolly said Mrs Pask remembered the shop being flooded once, but it wasn't because of the brook. 'Them fields at the back couldn't take any more rain, and it came in the back way and out the front. Right through the house.'

Gordon and Winnie Allen's cottage adjoins Dolly's, and sometimes from the road one can see Win working at the kitchen window. If she looks up she gives a shy, sweet smile – a trait she's passed on to their two pretty daughters. Marilyn, who's fifteen, may be walking along having a robust altercation with a friend, but if you pass, she'll stop in mid-tirade, her voice will soften into a cheery 'Hello', and that same enchanting smile will follow. Chunky used to be her pony, but she grew too tall for him and began to teach Georgie, Liz and Gerry's daughter, to ride him. 'She's very attached to that pony,' said Gerry, 'and she didn't want to lose him. So she thought if she could persuade Georgie to persuade me to buy him...' It worked, and Chunky, a solid little Welsh grey, still canters along the brookside past our window, while Marilyn rides Freckles, the larger pony which used to be her sister Thelma's.

Thelma is nineteen, with a cloud of pale hair and a slightly withdrawn, dreamy expression. She drives a car and goes to work in a family supermarket in Oundle, looking rather like a girl who's stepped into this modern era from another age. When I asked some of the older girls if they thought they'd ever seen a ghost in Barnwell – they hadn't – Thelma told me this story which she'd heard from her grandmother, who used to live in the double cottage next to Dora. 'She called the ghost the Green Lady. I think she was dressed in green. She often used to appear round the back of her cottage. But Grandmother took no notice of her. Then one day her sister-in-law saw the woman, and she was with a little girl. She said, "Who's that walking up there?" And Grandmother told her it was a ghost. Then when the workmen was digging up the road for the drains, just by her entrance, they found a skeleton of a child and a woman. Grandmother never saw the woman again after that.'

In the spring after her grandmother died, I passed Gordon looking across at her garden. 'See that old almond tree?' he said. 'It's the first time it's flowered for twenty years. Mother would have liked to see it.' In the tangle of the neglected garden – Mrs Allen wouldn't let the birds' nesting places be disturbed – the unpruned black twigs were covered in shell-pink blossom.

Now the cottage has been rethatched with thick reed, renovations made, and Mrs Allen's daughter and her husband will live in it when they retire.

There are hardly any cottages left with the old brick floors, narrow pantries, and twisty wooden stairs leading to a landing-bedroom. The No Through Road has, in estate agents' parlance, vastly improved in recent years, and the children who are growing up along it, in this era of good plumbing, duvets, and restored open fireplaces, will find our tales – that are not so very old – of bucket privies, damp blankets and poky 'modern' fireplaces very primitive indeed.

FIVE

Next-Door Neighbours

The Garratts

Before I ever set eyes on Trevor and Mary Marriott I knew of their existence, for we had their children's cot. The first night Dan, my son, slept in Barnwell was his first in a bed, and he was up half the night. As soon as Eric Garratt, our immediate neighbour, heard of this in the morning, he promised to find a cot for us. At midday he brought one to our door. 'It's Marriotts',' he said, 'and they don't want nothing for it. You can keep it.' Throughout the following night Dan barely stirred, and I blessed the Marriotts whoever they were. Soon I gathered that Eric worked on their farm.

Eric and Agnes Garratt are both dead now, but not many days go by in Barnwell without our mentioning them. They lived in No. 21, a 1½-up, 1½-down dwelling like No. 22, and our various rights of way were inextricably meshed. (No. 23, where the Kirks live, though joined on, is separated off at the back by outbuildings and a stone wall.) Neither the Garratts nor we had a front door – the cottages rise straight from the road, and the communal gate at the side of No. 21 led first to their back yard and then to ours. Eric had to cross our yard to get to his coalhouse, which was one of the middle brick sheds of four, the other three being our decrepit wash-house, coal shed and bucket privy (which the council emptied weekly). The garden was divided by an invisible line, but a strip at the top of ours belonged to Eric, enabling him to get to one of a long-collapsed pair of pigsties. Until the Second World War, the cottagers would each have kept a pig, its lard and heavily salted meat being a staple part of their nutrition through the winter. Eric had hutches up there containing large black-and-white rabbits which he fattened for the pot.

The Garratts were an incongruous pair. Eric was like an old jockey, wiry, wily, with pale blue watery eyes and a battered pink face; he would talk to anyone. Agnes hung back, peering around the door of their tacked-on plank-and-corrugated-iron scullery, her face and neck heavily made up, a sparkling brooch at the low neck line of her dress. She was plump and henna-haired, with dark, brooding eyes. When I met them, he was sixty-nine and she was seventy-one.

I was alone the first weekend that I spent in Barnwell, wrestling with the crumbling, dank, rot-smelling interior of No. 22 (not in any expert way, just scrubbing brush and white emulsion). On Sunday, when I'd been working for several hours, I heard from upstairs the sound of the latch on the outside door. I stood, paintbrush in hand, listening to footsteps downstairs and a voice chanting quietly but rather desperately, 'I'm *going* in, I'm *going* in, I'm *going* in,' as though someone were trying to build up their courage. I went down, and there was Mrs Garratt, dark eyes very apprehensive, with a blue patterned plate piled with proper Sunday lunch: roast beef, Yorkshire pudding, potatoes, cabbage and gravy. I could not have been more surprised – or grateful; I was starving. She told me to bring my plate back when I'd finished and collect my rhubarb tart.

Later I was to realise she had been brave, coming in herself when Eric could have done it easily, for she suffered from what must have been agoraphobia and never walked out in the street or talked with strangers. She would go out in the car though, and Eric was determined to keep their old Ford Prefect, which lived in a makeshift shed by our gate, on the road. Bert Kirk remembers once after 'He'd had a slight tip up, Eric heard from his insurance people, and he were that worked up. He came round here, and he said, "The wuss thing that's happened is that I've lost me no bone claimus!"'

Whenever I was in Barnwell on my own or with just Dan, the Garratts always brought round a complete Sunday dinner; and, if there were more of us, they would bring a plate of Yorkshire pudding and gravy to be shared.

The one person Agnes – Aggie, Eric always called her – would walk to see was her neighbour on the other side, Emma Babb. There was an orchard in between them (the Lillymans' house is built there now), with a filled-in well which had once provided water for our cottages. (The Garratts told me that the reason the one tap in No. 22 was four inches from the ground, and hidden under the stairs, was because when water was piped to the village, Florence Swingler – who had last lived in the cottage – was so afraid people would steal her water, she had ordered the tap to be placed out of sight of the window. Used water had to be emptied away in the yard outside, from where it drained straight into the brook.)

Eric had put a special gate through his hedge into the orchard so Aggie could go across unobserved to visit Mrs Babb. Emma remembers one day when 'Eric didn't come home to lunch at the proper time, and she was worried he was laying hurt in a hedge somewhere.' He'd been doing some hedging and ditching, with a viciously-sharp billhook among his tools. '"I know he's laying there bleeding, he's dying somewhere," she said. She went into panics. I was just getting me wellingtons on to go and see if I could see him, when he come. His watch had stopped! He used to come and say to me, "She wants you to go round and talk to her." I didn't mind talking to her, but the horrible, oh, horrible smell in there!'

It was true; No. 21 wasn't at all clean. Aggie never liked living there, she missed the much bigger cottage they used to rent higher up the village which she had polished and scrubbed, and where her sister had lived next door. She used to read a lot, quite widely, and was devoted to their elderly dog, Tinker. When he growled, she'd say, 'He's not using language, you know, he's not using language,' meaning that he wasn't swearing at me. She loved to watch the painted lady butterflies that flew into her bedroom and congregated on the ceiling.

When she became very, very ill with stomach cancer, we realised she had probably been feeling dreadful for a long time. She died in June 1970, and we were allowed to see her during the days when she was suffering appallingly. Eric nursed her, and coped. He would not let her be taken to hospital, and she was very grateful to him. They'd had one child, a daughter, who had died of meningitis when she was three. It was to my mother that Aggie spoke about her, and we worked out she would have been exactly the same age as I.

Eric lived for seven more years, and he made the best of them. He joined the Friendly Club, went to the pub (where one evening he danced on a table to show the young ones how he could still cut a caper), did odd jobs – including grave digging, and went out logging with Bill Groom. Once, they went down to London to the Chelsea Flower Show together. Eric hadn't been to London since he crossed it to join his regiment in the First World War. They took their two terriers, parked Bill's van at Shepherd's Bush, fed and watered the dogs, then left them in the van while they made their way over to Chelsea. The flower displays must have seemed like heaven to Bill. Eric was really more of a vegetable man, but he adored outings.

When our writer friends borrowed No. 22 to work in solitude for a while, Eric would usually look after them in the way he continued to look after us: coal buckets sometimes filled, objects mended, handfuls of fresh cabbage, shallots, tomatoes, brought to the door. Joyce Marlow, who met him in the last year of his life, wrote down her recollections of him.

> It was among his vegetables that I met Eric who looked like a weathered garden gnome, but with a pair of the neatest, most dapper feet I had seen, twinkling even as he dug over the rich soil. Whenever I was in Barnwell, he appeared with my Sunday dinner which he left me to eat in solitary enjoyment. His Yorkshire pudding was delicious, light and crispy on the outside, satisfying but not heavy inside. Later in the afternoon I would return the washed plate to his cottage, averting my eyes as I passed through his scullery with its jumble of greasy pans and blackened primus stove in and on which he cooked our Sunday dinners, to the disarray of his single downstairs room.
>
> In front of the roaring fire I would sit for an hour or so each Sunday, and once a week, though on no set day, Eric would make the return visit, whereupon I would stop typing for an hour or so, while the smoke from our cigarettes filled the room and he chattered like a starling. I had not been wrong about those dapper feet. Once, they had apparently twinkled to a considerable effect, and from time to time he would jump up to demonstrate how he had sashayed around countless ballrooms. From the winks and nudges, I also gathered that he had been something of a Lothario.
>
> But *the* subject was the 1914–18 war, as it had been for my own dead father, the war that had astonishingly transported millions of young men who had wandered little further than the back streets of Manchester (as my father) or the quiet lanes of Northamptonshire (as Eric) to live in

unbelievable conditions and to die in unbelievable numbers in Flanders' muddy fields. Having found a willing and not unknowledgeable listener, Eric held forth at length. His most insistent memory was of the Indian troops who for some time had been in a support trench behind his platoon's. Proper darkies they were, according to Eric, with turbans on their heads, always huddled over fires, trying to cook their food. Curry, he now reckoned it to have been, but it didn't half pong. It was funny to think of them Indians such a long way from home and they must have felt the cold something terrible, poor devils.

At the end of September 1977, Paddy telephoned to say that he died. We travelled to Northamptonshire for his funeral. It was the most glorious of autumn days, the sky bright blue, the sun golden, the leaves deepening to auburn and russet. Throughout the service the high piping voices of the children, rehearsing for their Harvest Festival in the school across the road, were clearly audible. The juxtaposition of the young voices and the cadences of the old burial service were heartrending. When we stood by the freshly dug grave in the churchyard, the sun was burnishing the limestone buildings, the school, the cottages, the almshouses, the distant chimneys of the manor house and the church itself, to a mellow bronze. No wind disturbed the trees, no clouds the blue brightness of the sky, and the only sounds in the peaceful air were the continuing thump of the schoolroom piano and the children's singing.

Emma Babb and Bob Scotney

Before I had time to realise how much I should miss Eric for practical as well as personal reasons, Emma Babb called round and said shyly, If it would help, could she and her brother Bob do any odd thing for us, like Eric used, though she didn't want to push in. Things like cut the grass, light a fire when someone was coming. Please, I said.

In the late 1960s, when Frank and I had divorced and I was married to Dulan Barber, my mother had helped me to buy No. 21. It had been sold cheaply, on condition the Garratts were undisturbed, and now, with Eric gone, there was suddenly much more garden to look after.

Bob Scotney is Emma's youngest brother, whom she helped to bring up when their mother died, and they live in a steeply red-tiled stone house that Emma and her late husband bought nearly thirty years ago. They keep hens and ducks, grow and freeze vegetables, and Emma can chit nearly any flower in the seed catalogue. The inside of their house is permanently in flower with fuchsias, geraniums, busy lizzies and African violets, and during the spring and early summer she has trays and trays of seedlings waiting to be planted out in our gardens. Most years she tries something new, so that penstemon, arctotis or mimulus appear with the flowers such as asters, snapdragons, marigolds and pansies that we have every year. I claim that she and Dulan colluded to edge out my vegetable patch. For years I grew pole beans and courgettes and broccoli and lettuces, but once we had Eric's garden as well as our own, Dulan – who hates vegetable gardening – saw a chance to grow unlimited flowers. Not any of those labour-saving ground cover plants, permanently in leaf, but bright, fleeting flowers. Since Emma raises things I have a particular passion for – auriculas, helichrysums, Iceland poppies – as well as everything else, and Bob's vegetables are always available and much better than mine, I capitulated.

Between them Bob and Emma erased Eric's Steptoe-and-Son-like collection of old wooden and plastic sheds, dismantled his tacked-on scullery, turned the collapsed pigsties into a rockery (brickery), and helped us create a garden that to an expert would seem a dreadful muddle and a dead loss half the year, but in midsummer is a luxuriant paradise. 'People keep telling me it's the best garden in Barnwell,' said Emma, 'but I think that's because they get just that glimpse over the gate. When you stand there and look up, you can see all the pretty colours together.' If there's one thing Emma can't abide, it's a bed or vase of flowers that are all one colour, or a piece of material without a pattern. Her aprons have huge, pastel dragonflies on them, her wallpaper has multicoloured flowers, and her favourite tulips are bright yellow splashed with scarlet. She likes people to be cheerful too, and has a laugh that travels easily from her garden across the Lillymans' to ours.

Bob, who is a solid, deliberative man in his fifties, spends a lot of time on is own tending the poultry and doing the garden, and usually has his transistor with him. He's not a great talker,

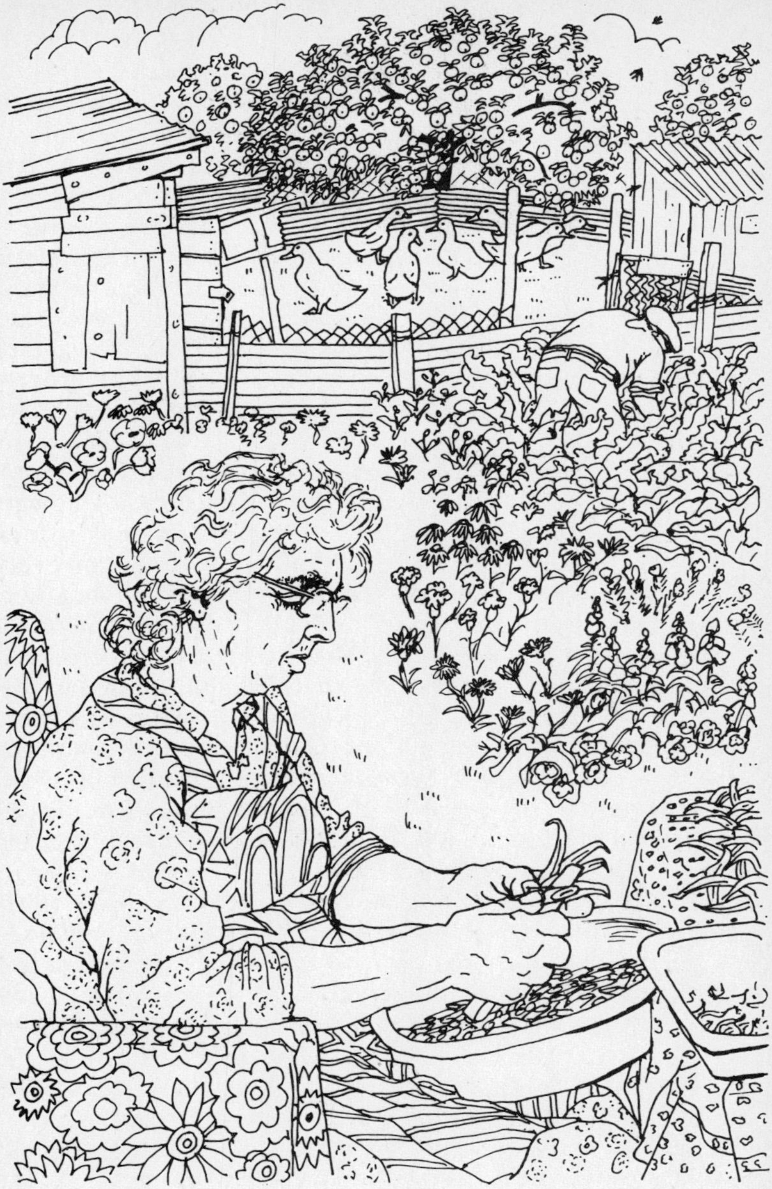

but every now and then will pass on the latest information about a strike or international crisis that he has heard, and he always knows the most recent weather forecast. He learned about poultry some years ago when he worked at Friars Close. 'I'd always been on the land. I've never been with hens, with poultry, before. I was doing potatoes and sugar beet. I learned about killing and feeding, and this here AI. Another worker who'd been there quite a while before me, he showed me the knack of killing. You've got to have a clean break. It felt a bit queer at first, but you get used to it.'

'It's the same with dressing the birds,' said Emma. 'I mean it seems an 'orrible job. But you get used to it. And we've always got a dinner, a meal. I mean, if you've got an egg and you've got a chicken, you're all right, aren't you?' Particularly if you can add fresh peas, carrots, new potatoes and a jug of July roses.

The Kirks

It's always stuck in my mind that Bert Kirk told me years ago he'd never been in either Dolly's shop or the Post Office. There was no need: Rene or the three girls – Helen, Pat and Pauline – did all that sort of thing.

He is a carpenter joiner, retired from full-time work now, though he frequently helps the Gunns as a bearer and gravedigger. 'If things had gone as they should have done, I would have been the village undertaker. I was going to be apprenticed with Ernie Crowson when I left school. In those days, instead of getting a wage, your parents had got to pay a sum of money for you to earn a trade. Well, I suppose it was a matter of the highest bidder. My father was going to pay . . . I think it was fifty-something pounds. But Arthur Malster's father paid a sum of money bigger than that.' So, when Bert left school, he went to work and train with his uncle in Bradford, then moved down to a job in Kent.

'I bought myself a new bicycle, and I thought – I'll cycle home! I set off at seven o'clock at night, from Orpington, and I cycled across London – that was the time when they had trams. I got across, but then I was beat. I hadn't been used to cycling like that. My hands had gone all set with exhaustion, and me legs were aching. I thought, I'm never going to make it. I got to Barnet, and I saw this policeman, so I had a word with him. I told him what I was doing, and he said, "Well, you've taken something on, lad. Look, that house is still open," – it was a pub – "go in there, and get yourself a drop of whisky." I'd never drunk whisky ever in my life. But I bought a little tiny flat bottle, and had some, and do you know, I could feel it working? When I got out on the bike I come up the A1 and I could hear the music in the spokes. I landed up here four o'clock in the morning. My dad stuck his head out the window, and he said, "What's the matter now? Have you been turned out of your lodgings?"'

Bert first saw Rene in 1946 at the wedding of Jack Ashby who used to work at Barnwell Station. 'I met her in the September and we were married in the April. We didn't spend long courting.' She was working at Oundle School then, in the same house where Helen, their eldest daughter, is now the head cook. The day their youngest daughter, Pauline, started at the village school, Rene began her job at the manor.

I came to Barnwell about three years later, and Pat and Pauline used to come and play with Dan, and would take him back to watch children's programmes on their television. Their friends, Marion and Christine Batley, Hazel Burnham, Margaret Gilbert, and Karen Burrows came round too, and we began to learn who was who in the village. I liked talking to them, and rediscovering what long summers are like for country girls old enough to roam around, and young enough to enjoy jacks and plantain-bashing and singing games. Pauline and Hazel were particular friends, rather quiet and serious, and when they were about nine they talked of sharing a flat in London and wearing exotic clothes. Pauline's forgotten about that ambition, but said, 'I know we got it in our heads once we were going to join the army. But it all worked out different.' Hazel's a teacher now, married and living in Scotland, while Pauline, who's twenty-nine, lives at home and has worked for a small boot and shoe factory in Oundle since the Monday after she left school. 'I make boots. You know where the eyelets are, where the laces go through, well I join the front to the back, the row of stitching round the eyelets. That's my proper job, but when it's not there to do, I have to do a bit on anything. I do like it, but then I've not known anything else. I sometimes think I'd like a change.' This is said with a gentle smile. The boots, rather ironically, are army boots.

When Joyce Marlow and I came down for Eric's funeral, Rene called to see if we'd like to go round and have some tea before walking up to the Church. I don't remember now what we talked about, but I recall that the gesture, bridging the gap between the other worlds we'd come from, and the ceremony at the Church, was welcomed. We probably lightened the occasion by mentioning some of Eric's more eccentric characteristics: the way he'd suddenly pole vault over the brook to save walking along to a footbridge, or entertain some children by stalking along the road on perilously tall stilts; the buckled ladies' shoes he bought in jumble sales for his neat feet; the gun he'd produce from nowhere and point virtually over one's shoulder while talking in the yard in order to shoot a pigeon off the top of the tree at the end of the garden.

Only recently Bert told me that Eric came round to him twenty odd years ago roaring with laughter because he'd shot a bird off our roof and it had rolled down into Dan's pram. 'And near frit him to death.' Eric never let on to us about that, but it explains why Dan was so terrified of touching birds when he was small. 'Yes,' said Bert, 'he used to shoot rats too, you know. And he used to bring them round here to show me. He had some funny ways, Eric. He'd bring the rat round, and he'd say, "Oo! I got a socker today. Look at this!"'

We were drinking a glass of wine, strong and lovely, made from the Kirks' Beauty of Bath apples. Over the years, they've often handed across the wall a lettuce, or a cabbage, or some sweet peas from the garden. The other day Bert wanted to show us a baby toad that had appeared in his greenhouse, but it was hiding. He has a very genial smile when things amuse him, and he takes particular pleasure in the slightly curious or odd facets of nature, both human and otherwise.

The Lillymans

When Kath Batley took two of her granddaughters who don't live in the village up to a fundraising 'do' at the School, she asked them if there was anyone there they recognized. 'Oh, yes,' they replied, 'Miss Decorum.'

They were referring to John Lillyman, whose fame as a pantomime dame has gone well beyond the parish boundary. But I think that if anyone had told me before the founding of the Barnwell Entertainers three years ago that John would perform, and be very good at, a drag part, I'd have said they were daft. I wouldn't have been able to visualize the tall, somewhat unwilling figure behind the weekend lawnmower, camping it up in a frock.

He and Ann, his wife, bought the plot of land that linked the Garratts to the Babbs fifteen years go. When they saw it advertised, they thought the house was already built, though in fact it had only reached planning permission stage. 'We'd wanted to live in the country for some time,' Ann said. 'We both wanted to get out of the housing estate in Barton Seagrave, it was very hemmed in.' They called their new home Aosta, because the builders started work on it in August, and they had stayed in a pretty Italian town called Aosta, which seemed near enough to the Italian for August – Agosto – but not so harsh. Both their children, Mark and Sarah, were born after they came here.

A year ago, after 'I'd taken three or four years whittling and worrying whether I should do it or not', John decided to go into business on his own. He'd been working for a firm of steel-suppliers based in Birmingham, and managed to achieve that elusive objective: spotting a gap in the market. 'I was getting enquiries from farmer friends around this part of the country, for bits and pieces of steel, and of course the company I worked for just wasn't interested. It was just too small, too small fry. Two or three of the farmers said, "Well, where do we get it from?" So I thought, if there's a few like that there must be more, and I will supply the small user. It's building up very nicely indeed, and it's almost got to the stage where it can support us.'

To tide things over when he started, he undertook some regular delivery work for Friars Close. 'I take 20,000 fertilised eggs to Aylesbury every Saturday morning at the moment. For shipping to Italy.' 'Funnily enough,' said Ann, who does invoices and accounts in the farm's office, 'the customs place they have to go through is Aosta.' Mark, who is thirteen, does an after-school job at the farm collecting eggs. 'He's such a willing worker,' said John, 'he really likes to work.' 'Andrew Burrows and Mark are doing it between them,' Ann explained. 'Andrew's got mumps, so Mark did the whole seven days, and Andrew's done it for Mark while he's been on holiday. If they're going to disco, or the Youth Club, they'll go up and help one another so they can both go out. It's quite hard work, and responsible. You have to push all the birds off the nests, three flocks, collect the eggs, and then you have to clean them all and put them in the fumigator.'

I remember once going round to Ann, before we had a telephone, because a pipe had burst. I spent a frustrating ten minutes on her phone, failing to rouse a plumber, and Mark, who was about eight, suggested I talk to the council plumber who was working over at Montagu Terrace. I said I didn't think he'd be allowed to come and help me, and Mark gave me the sort of bewildered look that people do when they find your stupidity unfathomable. He left the house without saying anything, and within five minutes had approached the plumber and persuaded him to come and mend my pipe immediately. He watched while the man was working, asking questions from time to time, and I had the feeling that when another pipe burst, Mark would be quite capable of mending it himself. The plumber was delighted by him, and adamantly refused any payment.

The Barnwell Entertainers were conceived, John said, when 'The Browns and the Parkes had an evening together, and I think Anne Parkes threw into the boiling pot, "Wouldn't it be rather nice if we put on a pantomime in the village?"' Anne is the wife of John Parkes, headmaster of the School. So John Lillyman became first the mother in *Jack and the Beanstalk*, and then Miss Decorum, governess to the princess in *Puss in Boots*. He's also been a successful Ali Baba, Lucien Tomb and Augustus Sidebottom, but Miss Decorum's impact seems to have been particularly indelible.

Perhaps the only person who wasn't surprised by his stage transformation was Ann. 'That's where I first saw him, on stage. I was at Kettering High School, and he was at Kettering Grammar. The boys were in one half of the building, and the girls in the other, but we had a communal hall, and every year combined to put on a Shakespeare play. It was *Romeo and Juliet* that particular year. I was only a mere third former, and John was a fifth former. John and this other fellow played the two comedy parts, and this girl that I went with, Angela, we sat and – well, we just laughed and laughed.' He was playing Sampson, who opens the play with a volley of *doubles entendres*, a suitable début for an embryonic dame.

SIX

The Chancel

On August 29, Emma telephoned us in London to say that Rene Kirk had died. She'd been in hospital, but had seemed to be getting better – had sat up and waved cheerily as Bert left the ward after his last visit. Emma sounded very shocked. Rene was one of those dependable, modest people whom everyone relies on, and she was a year younger than Emma.

When we were in Barnwell just over a week later, I called on Bert. He gave me a warm handshake, said he had someone with him, and asked if he could come round to us when they'd gone. He arrived bearing a glistening home-grown cucumber. He said he would have brought runner beans, but the gales had ruined many of them, and there were slugs in the potatoes – which *would* happen just when Pauline was having to get used to preparing the vegetables the evening before for their dinner the next day after they both came home from work. Helen and Pat, who are both married and live nearby, were supportive in every way, but he knew it was important for Pauline to get things planned in her own steady routine. They'd only got one domestic detail left to sort out – the coalman, who called tomorrow. His most unexpected difficulty had been not knowing where Rene kept things, although their places were perfectly logical once they were found.

He told us about her illness, how unexpected her death was, and, with unconcealed but controlled emotion, what a good wife and mother she had been, and how it was up to them for her sake to re-order their lives and sort out how best to run things. He'd already started helping the Gunns again, had been coffin-bearer at a funeral the day before: it seemed better to get started again.

He presented all the information to us thoughtfully; an ordered description for neighbours who had not been there of what had happened. Keeping the record straight, for Rene's sake.

Dulan and I visited her grave in the All Saints churchyard. It was still smothered with flowers, the posy of sweetpeas from her grandsons, Nathan and Harvey, now limp. The Chancel had been especially loved by her, and she had helped look after it and raise money towards its upkeep.

While we were strolling round, our feet sinking into the old, old turf, we met some visitors. One of them, a man originally from Norfolk, said it was the most 'bootiful' churchyard he'd ever seen, and that he'd like to be laid to rest up in that corner where no one would walk on him. We talked about some of the graves – the carved stone cross commemorating Corisande, wife of E. Basil Ludlow that is placed squarely in front of the Chancel echoing the similar cross on its roof; the golden-lichened headstone to Virtue, wife of Borrett Bletsoe; and the ancient monk's grave, with his horizontal image carved upon it. Ever since Kath Batley and Norah Blunt were children, Norah told me, 'We've always gone and scrubbed the monk and scraped the moss off him every year. I've always said I'm having my ashes buried at the bottom of his feet, because I thought he'd keep an eye on me.'

Many of the headstones are in family groupings – the Stricksons, the Chapmans, the Russells, the Toughs, the Kirks – and just reciting the familiar Barnwell names sounds like a kind of benediction. Not all of them have survived to this generation, but they still crop up frequently in conversations with older inhabitants. Jim Waite went to work for the Stricksons at Bright Pitts Farm when he left school. 'Six shillings a week I used to get. And then I asked for a rise one Saturday, and he gave me a shilling extra. And then he hung himself on the Monday morning. When we went to work Monday morning, we found him hanging in the stable. It frit me very near to death, I run a mile. John Strickson, that was. He's buried up at this churchyard. 2nd of June that were, I remember that quite well. I think it were money worries.' It used to be said that Barnwell's suicide rate was very high, but it may just be that no incidents of it are ever forgotten. I knew the details of several within a year or two of coming to the village; people I would otherwise probably never have heard of, but who will inhabit my memory for ever.

All Saints Church was built in the early 13th century, and the lost manor house about two hundred years later in the fields beyond. During the 16th century the Montagu family, who owned Barnwell Castle and its adjoining Manor, took over the All Saints estate too. By the 19th century the manor had disappeared, and the same rector was responsible for both churches. In 1821 he petitioned for the demolition of All Saints because of its bad state of repair.

Legend has it that he needed the support of the villagers for his petition, so he promised a free pint of beer to all men who voted for the demolition. All but three voted in favour, and one man said he'd vote for St Andrew's to be pulled down too if he got another free pint.

An Act of Parliament authorized the demolition, 'the whole to be pulled down saving that of the Chancel', which was to be preserved because of the vaults of the Montagus, Earls of Sandwich, beneath. Tom Litchfield describes what happened:

> ... some of the materials were used to create 'a good and sufficient wall' around the neighbouring Church and Rectory of St Andrew, whilst in a more secular direction, other stone was used to build the Market Hall in Oundle. After the demolition much of the remaining material lay around the churchyard and the Chancel itself stood with its arch gaping until 1893 when the then Rector of Barnwell, the Rev. G. W. Huntingford, launched a public appeal for its restoration and repair. The response was moderate except for the generosity of the seventh Duke of Buccleuch who contributed three-quarters of the total cost.

The heavy key to the Chancel door is kept by Peter and Joyce Watson at The Limes, next to the churchyard, and walking round to them straight from All Saints is like a brief trip in a time capsule. Outside their back door Peter is creating an elaborate patio, full of novel decorations and diversions, where that summer they held a Barn Dance. 'Did you hear the music last night?' Emma Babb had asked me the following day. 'It was up at the Watsons. It sounded nice, didn't it? They were clapping away. Sounded as if they were really enjoying it.' According to an old plan, the long tree-lined court leading to the lost manor house was sited through their land.

Dulan and I fetched the key that day so that we and the visitors could see inside the Chancel. It is crammed with

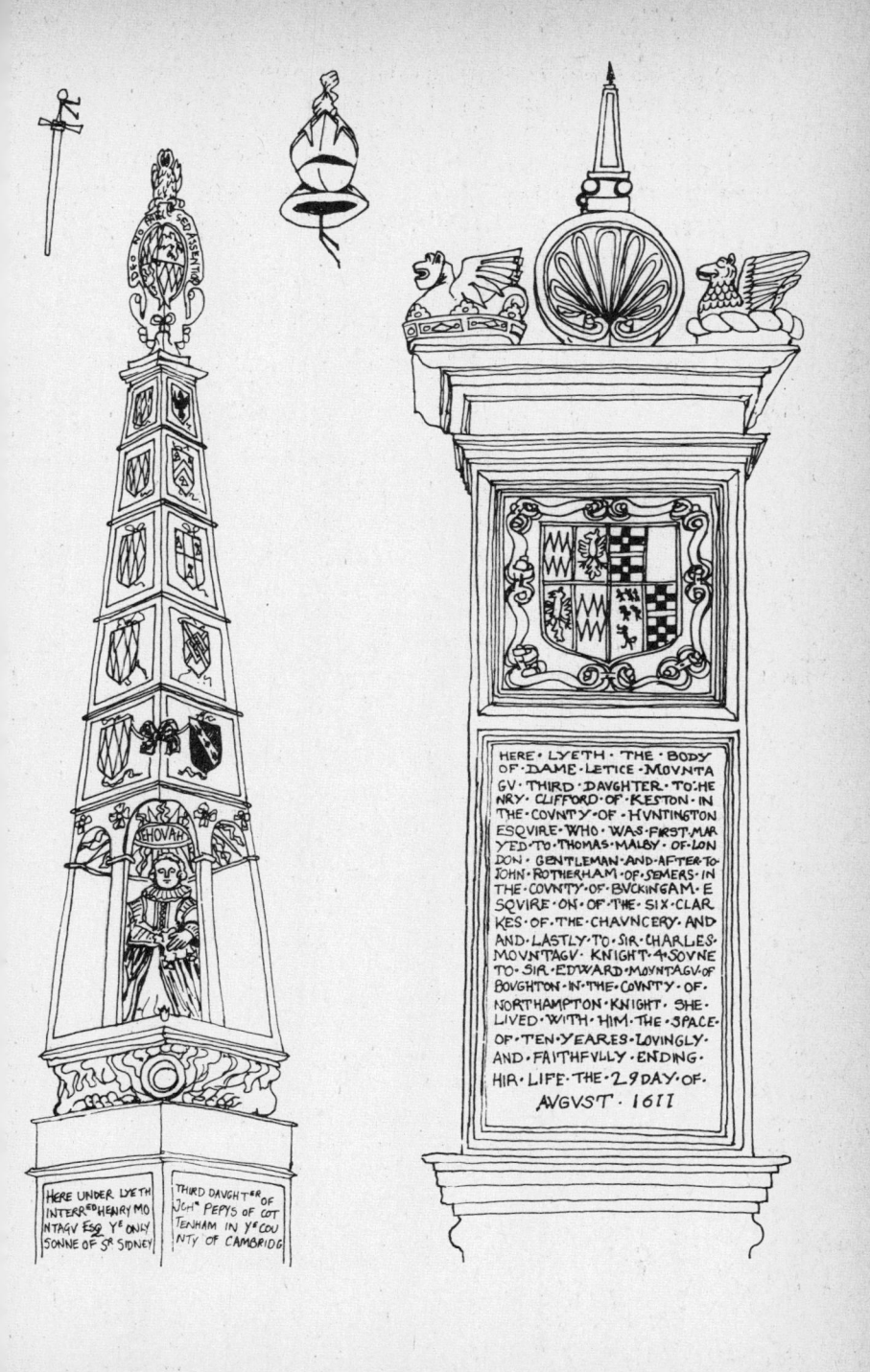

HERE·LYETH·THE·BODY
OF·DAME·LETICE·MOVNTA
GV·THIRD·DAVGHTER·TO·HE
NRY·CLIFFORD·OF·KESTON·IN
THE·COVNTY·OF·HVNTINGTON
ESQVIRE·WHO·WAS·FIRST·MAR
YED·TO·THOMAS·MALBY·OF·LON
DON·GENTLEMAN·AND·AFTER·TO
JOHN·ROTHERHAM·OF·SOMERS·IN
THE·COVNTY·OF·BVCKINGAM·E
SQVIRE·ON·OF·THE·SIX·CLAR
KES·OF·THE·CHAVNCERY·AND
AND·LASTLY·TO·SIR·CHARLES·
MOVNTAGV·KNIGHT·4·SOVNE
TO·SIR·EDWARD·MOVNTAGV·OF
BOVGHTON·IN·THE·COVNTY·OF·
NORTHAMPTON·KNIGHT·SHE
LIVED·WITH·HIM·THE·SPACE·
OF·TEN·YEARES·LOVINGLY·
AND·FAITHFVLLY·ENDING
HIR·LIFE·THE·29·DAY·OF·
AVGVST·1611

HERE·UNDER·LYETH
INTERRED·HENRY·MO
NTAGV·ESQ·Yᵉ·ONLY
SONNE·OF·Sʳ·SIDNEY

THIRD·DAVGHTᵉʳ·OF
Jᵒʰⁿ·PEPYS·OF·COT
TENHAM·IN·Yᵉ·COV
NTY·OF·CAMBRIDG

monuments saved from the main body of the church, including a famous one to Henry, the infant son of Sir Sidney Montagu, who was drowned in a pond by the lost manor. As well as the little boy's statue, set in a tall obelisk decorated with texts and symbols of water, there is panelling on the right-hand side of the altar which opens to show a description of the tragedy, painted on vellum. Part of it reads:

> Thursday 16th May 1622 Borne
> Much rain falling Aprill 1625 filled a pond wch
> wth a scoopet lieing by was supposed ye occasion of his end
> Thursday Ascension Day Christened
> Thursday 28th April 1625 dyed

On the inside of one of the opening panels there is a representation of the mantle which covered his hearse, which the vellum explains was 'the same which covered him at his christening, and was set with true love knotts of black ribbins, made by divers of his friends.'

A morning service is held in the Chancel on All Saints Day, and, every so often, evensong. The presence of fresh mouse droppings demonstrated the need for the protective plastic over the altar frontal. We craned our necks to look at the rusty rapier and visor, displayed high on the wall, which were part of the funeral panoply of the Montagus. Someone tried a few mellow notes on the little harmonium. Looming large by the door is an old wooden coffin cart, with iron wheels.

We went outside into the bright day, and I was aware how shrill the wind sounded as it cut round the northern wall of the church.

*

Those early September storms that had battered Bert Kirk's runner beans seemed to sweep away summer. Green leaves which had been prematurely torn off the trees became shrivelled and crisp underfoot.

Walking along the Armston Road past the Manor, I noticed that the middlemost bough of an old ash tree in the grounds was gashed down, the splintered wood pale as a chicken breast, but with a dark centre where it had begun to rot. I walked past Empty Spinney as far as the row of estate houses built by the late Duke of Gloucester for his model farm. Empty

Spinney used to be the place where they penned the sheep years ago for washing in the brook at the point where it crosses Gypsy Lane. 'There used to be some slides,' Jim Waite recalls, 'to hold the brook up. There'd be a wall all round. And there'd be hundreds, thousands of sheep come there of a summer time to be washed. They'd put 'em in, roll 'em round, and let them swim out the other side. Just to get the wool clean. You got more for the wool if it was washed.'

On the way back, I felt a soft thud in my armpit, and stopped to see a dragonfly which had collided with me. It flew briefly near the hedgerow, its metallic colouring matched by its staccato machine-like movements – backwards and forwards, side to side. Combined with its big goggle eyes, it made me see why dragonflies used to be regarded fearfully and called the devil's darning needle – though in fact they do not have a sting. A few yards along the verge is a clump of blue sow-thistles, the only slightly scarce wild plant I've ever identified. It was still in flower, looking very like the common dandelion-type sow-thistles, except that its flowers are a powdery blue.

By the Manor gates, one road leads straight back to the village green, and the other, Well Lane, goes over a bridge and up a small hill past Stone Cottage to the old station house and the main road. That particular bridge, and the horse chestnuts on the bank beyond, are sometimes a particular haunt for young boys. Out of view of the main village, and with space to shelter under the bridge on the water's edge from wind and rain, there is a pocket of privacy.

Like boys, wind brings down conkers before they are ripe, and I picked up one of the prickly, sappy cases and tried to prise it apart. But it was reluctant to yield its premature harvest, whose shells were still as white and smooth as wedding satin.

The Parish Council met early in September, and I wondered whether Dolly would come without Rene as her companion. They had been close friends. She did, but said it had meant a particular effort.

The main item on the agenda was the Wigsthorpe bridleway, and not only was Mrs Sandra Williams – the horse-owner who it seemed had raised the matter recently – there, but also two officers from the District Council. The latter were both suitably solemn, though the rosy-faced fair one just slightly less so than his thin, bearded colleague. They explained that the bridleway designation was official, that it had been claimed as a bridleway in both 1934 and 1953 by the Parish Council, but that it could be downgraded to a footpath at the next review if an application were made.

'Well,' said Norah Blunt, 'it's called a bridleway, but you can't get up it with a horse. We want the matter clarified.'

'As far as clarification goes,' said an officer, 'it is a bridleway.'

'I've tried to get through,' said Sandra Williams, 'but a stile was in the way.'

'No one's been able to ride through for fifty years,' said Norah.

'In a village,' said Sandra, 'there should be bridleways. My horse is frightened of all the heavy vehicles on the road.'

'The 1927 map,' said Walter Woolman, 'shows the bridleway. And I know where the gates are.'

'What happened,' asked Graham Wise hopefully, 'in 1953 when it was designated? Whose responsibility was it?'

'I can remember field gates higher up,' said Norah, 'but before you got to them there were the kissing gates.'

'And after that,' said Ian Fox, 'the track as marked takes you straight through the Chancel graveyard.'

'Couldn't it be diverted round the Chancel?' suggested Sandra.

'Diversion orders have to go through the usual channels,' said an officer.

'Before you get as far as the Chancel, the path as marked goes right through Mr Watson's greenhouse,' announced Norah cheerfully.

The council officers explained that designated rights-of-way were the responsibility of the owners whose land they crossed, though a quarter of the cost of any reclamation might be met by the council. However, if a path hadn't been used for fifty years, a landowner might have a case for not keeping it open.

'What happens if I jump someone's gate and break a fence?' asked Sandra.

'It would be a matter between you and the landowner,' replied an officer judiciously.

Graham enquired how much expense would be likely to be incurred in reclaiming the bridleway, and exactly whose responsibility it would be. Dolly reminded us that the kissing gates had been there when she and Tom Wells were courting nearly fifty years ago.

'I've only been in Barnwell three years,' said Sandra, 'and I was unable to get my horse down there.'

'*All* young people want to ride across country away from juggernauts,' remarked Walter Woolman expansively.

'But if it's never *been* used as a bridleway,' said Ian, trying to cling on to the terra firma of reason, 'what *is* the position?'

'If it's never used,' said an officer, 'the landowner has a case for it to be downgraded.'

'There doesn't seem to be any tangible evidence that a horse was ever ridden there,' said Ian. 'And the whole route from here to Wigsthorpe crosses five or six landowners' property.'

'But there's a notice up saying it's a bridleway,' said Joan Crump nervously but firmly. 'What happens if the notice is followed, and a horse or rider gets hurt?'

'I don't want to be in my grave before that bridleway is used,' said Sandra.

Graham proposed that the landlords be approached by letter. The officers undertook to do an inspection of the pathway right through to Wigsthorpe and to make it a joint affair between the District Council and the Parish Council when approaching farmers.

The meeting passed to other matters. Mention of Mr Watson's greenhouse had reminded me that another of his projects had been to organize a horticultural project for handicapped boys on his land for several years. And he'd also made an adventure playground for the village, though that had to be stopped when someone broke a leg. But most of all, as far as Dan was concerned, he'd provided 'The Hut'. It was a simple, wooden structure that became endowed with legendary qualities because the younger teenagers were allowed to treat it as their own private territory. 'We used to play records and smoke cigarettes. And we could do it all day long. It's hard to think now why it was such great fun – but it was.'

Walking back from the Reading Room, I wondered how other horseriders in the village managed without access to Wigsthorpe, and whether my approach to public footpath signs is wrong. Virtually all those around Barnwell point directly into unpathed fields and I make no attempt to follow them. But there are several broad, unsignposted tracks leading through lovely farmland which I've used without restriction for years.

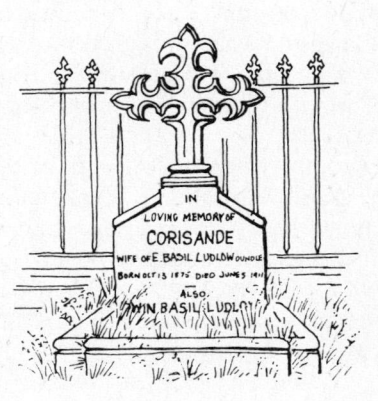

SEVEN

Parish News

The September storms, with their accompanying heavy rains, postponed the colour effects of autumn. By the third week in October, most of the trees in the open landscape were still green, but looked as if they had been lightly washed with a transparent tint of dun. The fields that had been planted with winter wheat were already the sort of pure emerald one associates with spring and soft rain, and the sun shone from open blue skies.

In the village, the limes along the brook were turning coppery, but the grass everywhere was lush, and our gardens, which had been so parched and scorched in August, were sprouting with densely self-seeded weeds and grasses and summer flowers. Those teeming patches of poppy and marigold and cornflower – the seedlings packed far, far too tightly to grow their proper size – posed a problem. If we thinned them carefully – the fiddliest job in the garden – we might be rewarded next year with strong plants, flowering early. But deep frosts and lingering snows could wipe them out. If we left them as they were, and then, if they survived, thinned in the spring, they would be irredeemably straggly of habit. We could, of course, purge: hoe them all away and forget about them.

Recently the *Parish News* had informed us that in 1985 parish documents over 100 years old would have to be deposited at the County Records office, and I went up to the Rectory to look at them while they were all still kept in the heavy metal chests in Peter's study. He gave me an inventory of the documents held, and brought the ones I selected into the dining-room. Centralization of records is a sensible precaution for future historians, but I was glad to be able to leaf through Barnwell's most ancient and interesting document, known as 'The Bridge Book', at a table facing the floor-to-ceiling sash windows overlooking the Rectory lawn and the west doorway of the Church.

It is a thick, battered manuscript book, bound in dilapidated parchment, which records how the parish's money was spent over a period of nearly 250 years. It begins in 1549, nine years before Elizabeth I became Queen of England, and at first the old script is indecipherable to a non-scholar, but a note by Tom Litchfield explains that it records 'the names of the two Bridgewardens appointed annually whose duty was to report to the parish the condition and monies required to maintain the four principal bridges within its area.' The accounts of annual payments each Ploughmonday up to 1684 are duly noted, together with orders of the Parish, and then the book contains the Constables' accounts from 1698–1797.

In May 1755 a 'Whiping Post' was set down at a cost of four shillings, and later painted for a cost of two shillings. The Mole Catcher's annual payment rose in 1741 from five shillings to seven-and-sixpence. Many of the payments recorded in the 18th century were for lodgings given to people with passes, such as 'April 9 give to five lame sailors with a pass and for lodging 6d'. In 1758 Thomas Kisbee was paid for use of his cart and horse 'to carry a deserter to Oundle' – perhaps he had tried to flee the Seven Years' War with France.

I noticed in the green marriage register (begun in 1837 and still in use) that Annie Pask, daughter of a later generation Kisbee, was married in 1915 when France was no longer the enemy. A recent entry, recording Heather Cook's marriage to Per Norum, reminded me of the hot, blowy Saturday in July, when a large Norwegian flag had rippled from the pole outside the school and the whole village had seemed *en fête*. Many guests had travelled from Norway, and all day knots of people – some in Norwegian national costume – strolled around the village. Then in the afternoon a smart gig pulled by a dappled grey pony arrived to take the principals to the Church. Back and forth, back and forth, went the top-hatted driver, and I walked up to join the onlookers gathering at the gate.

Inside the churchyard, photographers were desperately trying to organize page boys and bridesmaids into well-composed groups, while Peter Bustin waited with a patient smile in the porch. Then the gig drove up for the last time, and

Heather, smiling and sunburnt in creamy lace, arrived with her father. They both looked very happy.

Flipping back through the register, one signature stood out boldly: Elizabeth R., witness to the wedding of Prince Richard of Gloucester in 1972.

In the white baptism register, I discovered that Michael Black, one of Dan's childhood friends who now lives in Nassington, had a son in March and brought him to Barnwell to be baptized – Jason Michael. I felt almost absurdly pleased. Dan had said of him recently, talking of their friendship, 'He had that Marlon Brando in *On the Waterfront* sort of charm. He seemed to have his feet on the ground a lot less than everybody else, and that's what made him really great to be with. He could always make an interesting situation out of the most boring. And he didn't try, that was the thing. It just came completely naturally. Everybody wanted to be where he was. He was so scatty, he was just really charming.'

The burial register is black, and I looked sadly at the most recent entries: Irene Bessie Kirk, and old Joe Owen from two doors further down. He'd been on his own since Emma, his wife, died, and the last time I saw him leaning on his gate, and we exchanged a few words, his eyes had a dulled glaze. He died in September before the lonely long nights of winter set in. 'I miss Joe a lot,' Sid Batley told me. 'We used to go down to the pub, Joe, Jim Waite, and a friend from Oundle, and have a game of cribbage. But we're one short now. We still play with three, but we miss him.'

Among the documents I skimmed was the Terrier and Inventory listing all the items belonging to the parish. Everything from the Montagu helmet and sword in the Chancel to the Flymo (1969, unserviceable) in the garden store of the Rectory. And from a loose sheet updating the stock of catering equipment at July that year, I learned that numbers had remained undepleted since the previous official count: 68 plastic saucers, 70 plastic cups, 72 plastic teaspoons.

To be placed alongside that sort of minutiae is the fact that since 1978 Peter Bustin has been the Rector of three parishes – Thurning and Luddington as well as Barnwell – in addition to being Rural Dean of Oundle. 'Of course there have been rectors before who've had more than one parish,' Peter said, 'but for us it was a major change, and it really meant rethinking.

One good thing that has occurred is that people have taken on various work for the Church so that things could continue, which perhaps previously were done by a rector. So there's been a change from an individual ministry to a shared ministry, and the parish is almost more active than ever because people are doing more themselves.'

'I do think Barnwell is a caring community,' said Anne.

'Oh, on the whole, I think it is,' Peter agreed. 'But perhaps we should talk a bit about the position of the Church in the community. The Church is there, in the centre of the village, and I think the building is an outward sign of the Church's faith. You can get a beautiful building as a museum – which is a perfectly good function – but our hope is that the Barnwell Church is a place of worship, and not just an outward sign of history, so the building represents the Christian faith and the life of the Church. We are trying to maintain what we believe to be a true faith and to work for its expression in Barnwell, and that leads to such things as the baptizing of people, teaching the children, the sharing in preparation of marriage, and trying to help in the daily life of the community. And then sharing in sickness, illness, death, bereavement. I think it would be true to say that there is a living Church in Barnwell.'

The actual building feels alive when you step inside. Perhaps knowing a little of some of the people who care for it helps. There is the pile of guides by Tom Litchfield documenting with careful detail the 600-year history of the Church; it has a sketch on its cover signed 'A.' – Princess Alice. Maggie Head does much of the cleaning. 'I start at the altar. I scrub the top half of the Church where the choir is, and then I have a long mop, and do down the sides, the big stones. Then I hoover all the carpet straight the way down. I like to do me cleaning and that Saturdays so it's clean for the weekend. Then for weddings I'm there to clear up afterwards, and the same for funerals. When I go up to do my chores, I sit there for a little while.' The rosters of flower-arrangers and brass-cleaners in the *Parish News* give an indication of the many hands responsible for the burnished ornaments and filled vases. Signs of movement behind a screen in the north-west corner on a quiet afternoon might indicate that Dora is freshening some of the flowers.

Charlie Head cuts the grass and helps tidy the churchyard, which in 1982 and 1983 was judged the best-kept in Northamptonshire. It has a magnificent cedar and other fine conifers, but also borders and beds of flowers – massed scarlet tulips in the spring, geraniums in late summer. The most familiar figure to be seen among the gravestones mowing the grass a decade ago used to be that of Colonel Fred Berridge from Castle Farm. (Simon, who runs the farm now, is his grandson.) He was awarded the DSO and MC for outstanding bravery in the First World War, and in the Second was Zone Commander of the local Home Guard. I used to glimpse him over the churchyard wall, absorbed in his task, his capped head bowed against wind and drizzle.

Ron Rutterford is one of the churchwardens. 'From the top to the bottom, from the tower to the graveyard, it's in our charge. But, being Barnwell, jobs have been organized in the past and you've just got to keep things moving, keep the wheel turning. We've got a nice routine working at the moment in the churchyard. Mr Head cuts the grass, Mr Warner, who used to be butler of the Manor, meself, and Mr Kirk, we do the churchyard. Mr Elcock's been helping. Mr Elcock had an operation you see, and so he couldn't do any lifting, but he come in and helps me do the trees and so forth. Last year we got the highest score in the competition, but I don't think we've done anything this time, because we had trouble with the mowers. Both mowers broke down, and I've been going backwards and forwards to Gidding to get them mended.' It was a few weeks later that the 1983 award was announced.

Arthur Malster, who used to own Crowsons, is the second churchwarden. He and his wife moved to Oundle when they retired, but remain closely linked to Barnwell. He looks rather serious, with neat silver hair and a self-effacing expression, like an old-fashioned schoolmaster who has never needed to raise his voice to keep the class in order. He'd been churchwarden for about eight years when Ron received a telephone call from Pat. 'I was at Cash & Carry. And she rung me up and said, "Mr Malster's been on the phone. Would you like to be churchwarden? Nothing to it, he says. There's nothing to it. You just have to go to church. You just be there." Little did I know! By taking on the churchwarden's job, by being voted in, I've never stopped.'

Before that, Ron had been unconcerned with the possible variations in ritual and decoration within the Church of England. 'Until I became churchwarden and I saw the differences, I didn't know there was any class distinction in churches. Well, it's not class distinction, differences. It's surprising, when you start to talk to people, a lot of people won't talk about religion. Although there are religious people in the village, they won't talk about it. There are some people who will bow to the cross when you're saying the creed. I didn't realize this, until I stood at the back of the Church and watched it. Didn't know you could bow, if you wanted to. I don't like it high, but I do like to see a little bit of colour.'

Real candles, lit for services; altar frontals, carefully looked after; any ceremony thoughtfully planned and performed; these are some of Ron's practical concerns. The theological implications he properly leaves to the clergy. If a stranger comes to St Andrew's, he would like them to enter a welcoming church and join in a well-ordered service that has a touch of exhilaration and spectacle. Like when the Bishop comes to take a service. 'The churchwardens – how do you put it? – you take him to the vestry. And then you bring him out from the vestry, and you have the rods you see, and he doesn't like it really, not very much. You have to be quick with the Bishop. When he comes down to meet the choir, you stand at the side, and then the choir leads off, and he comes at the rear. You procession him, and you go down to the altar, and when he's finished, his sermon and the service, the churchwardens go up and take him back to the vestry. Well, if you're not quick enough, he's off his chair, straight through the door. Gone. So what we did this time, we stood at the altar rail, so he couldn't come out, then we directed him into the vestry, the proper way.'

Opposite the Church, next to the School, is Rectory Cottages, where Peter and Peggy Scopes live. He is the Church's Treasurer. 'Mr Scopes is the most excellent bloke with figures,' Ron said. 'He's very good with the Church accounts. He's put us back on the road. In other words, although we're struggling, we're not struggling too deep.'

Mr and Mrs Scopes had lived with their three children in another Northamptonshire village, Isham, after Peter came out of the army, and there Peggy was chairman of the parish council and deeply involved in village activities. When they moved to Barnwell, needing a much smaller house for their retirement, Peter applied for the post of Parish Clerk when it became vacant. 'I was the only applicant, that's why I got the job. It was interesting and I quite enjoyed getting to grips with it.' 'I think they all got quite a shock when they got you,' remarked his wife. I remembered what Mick Burns had said when we'd been discussing the PC. 'Mr Scopes picked it up quite a bit, didn't he? When he started, it was a bit dying off. Not too much enthusiasm. And he did work very hard, no doubt about it. Got all the minute books straight, all indexed. You know, a lot of extra jobs.' 'I decided that the minute book was really the history of the village, and so wrote it accordingly. And I indexed them all, with cross references,' said Peter.

Both he and Peggy are very straightforward and decisive. If the PC could not come to a decision over an issue and was about to leave the matter on the table to be referred to the next meeting, Peter would try to prevent such evasion. 'I'm a benevolent dictator,' he said smiling. 'He kept tidying the parish noticeboards,' Mick had said – also smiling. 'He kept putting the whist drive notices at the top so you couldn't see them. So every morning when I took Santa round for his walk I'd move them back to the bottom!' Peter held the post of Parish Clerk for five years and then stood down. 'I thought five years was about right.'

In the entry for Isham in the Shell Guide to Northamptonshire, there is the following remark about its church: 'There are gay hand-worked hassocks and altar-rail kneelers, made in Isham.' Now any description of Barnwell's Church would probably include a reference to its hassocks, with their bright emblems and flowers. 'I've always done embroidery,' said Peggy Scopes, 'I've done hassocks all over England.' 'Including Westminster Abbey,' said Peter. For the past three years she has run embroidery classes in the Reading Room of which the hassocks are a product. Although advertised only in the *Parish News*, people come from quite a wide area. 'I've got a waiting list. I wanted about fifteen, but I'm up to twenty-eight. And I'm beginning to get the younger ones. To me it's marvellous. To think that people are so keen and want to do it. It's all creative. People have no idea what they can do. They say, Oh, I don't think I could possibly do that, or could I? And away we go. Like Rosemary Pratt, who's absolutely super. She had no idea how good she was.'

The day I spoke to the Scopeses came at the end of what had been a very special week for them. Their daughter, Victoria, who had been born with a bad heart, died fifteen years ago at the age of twenty-five. When she was seventeen, she was paralysed down one side after a stroke. She battled throughout to lead as normal a life as possible. 'She wanted to live like everybody else,' Peggy said. 'But of course everything she did was doubly difficult. She was a very tiny little person. But we had so much help from so many people who were devoted to her.'

Vicky left her body to medical research, and the hospital released it for burial unexpectedly quickly. Her parents were abroad and did now know what had happened, and she was buried in a depressing cemetery not of their choosing.

'So,' Peter said, 'we thought we'd like to get Vicky here.' They approached Derek Gunn to see if this could be arranged. 'And we went up on Thursday of this week, and she came down on Wednesday. And yesterday we had a little service and buried her ashes just inside the gate of the churchyard.'

'So she's home now,' said Peggy.

I looked through the window across to the Church. From certain angles, sky can be glimpsed through the spire's open lights. I'd never heard of Victoria Scopes before that morning, but I felt glad she'd come to Barnwell.

Inside the Church, high on the wall of the chancel, is a painted effigy of Nicholas Latham who was Rector from 1569 to 1620. He built and endowed the almshouses, above whose entrance is the carved inscription, 'Cast thy bread upon the waters'. Originally known as 'Parson Latham's Hospital', it housed in Thomas Bell's time a warden and eleven 'poor persons'. Each inmate was allowed £2 yearly for fuel and washing, and every other year a black cloak was given to the men and a black gown to the women. The small community hall and chapel is no longer in frequent use, though it comes in handy as a base for a travelling chiropodist's surgery.

Stepping into the quiet courtyard, one might think that the buildings had changed little over almost four hundred years, but in fact behind each of the eight closed doors is a one-person flat, fully modernized. As in the rest of Barnwell, comparative newcomers live alongside members of old Barnwell families. Jack Sharman, whose mother once lived here, always used to be one of the first people who greeted me with a smile when I walked down into the village after an absence. He'd sit on his bicycle by the shop or the main bridge, and if Dan wasn't with me he'd always say first, 'How's Danny?' and then ask a question about some recent happening in London he'd heard about on the news. Because of his lame foot, bicycle was the easiest way to get around, and his tall frame in working clothes topped with a knitted hat seemed almost welded to the iron frame of his machine. He was a gardener, and 'If he'd had really good feet,' Bert Kirk remarked, 'he'd have been the best batsman that we could have turned out. In those days we used to practise on the village green, and you couldn't bowl him out.' He's outside seldom now. On Sundays I've often noticed Charlie Head carrying a covered dish up the street around lunchtime, and learned that it was Jack's Sunday dinner.

One problem people sometimes face when they move into Latham Cottages is that their furniture doesn't fit the small, high-ceilinged rooms, and they don't want to get rid of it. 'But if you want a small place really badly, particularly when you're getting on, who wants a lot of furniture?' said Miss Constance Greenwood sensibly. She herself is short and plumpish, like a benevolent character in a traditional nursery story, and looks completely at home in her bright little sitting-room. 'Of course I worked in London for thirty years. The last job I had there was with an accountant's. I used to go out auditing. All over the place. I was in an office in the City when the Queen visited the City after her coronation.'

Miss Greenwood came to Barnwell with her friend Miss Winifred Thomson after they had both retired. Miss Thomson lives in a house up Horseradish Lane, and Miss Greenwood has lived in Latham Cottages for the past ten years. I asked if they had taken to Barnwell quickly. 'I suppose we did really. We joined the WI of course. I was Treasurer for seven or eight years, and now I'm Treasurer of the over-60s.' In 1982 they had a nasty car accident. 'We caused quite a commotion. Because we were just going out shopping. And there was a dog at home. But it's surprising how quickly things get round. I don't quite know how Mr Bustin came to see us, who telephoned first. Mrs Allen, Win Allen, she went and got the dog. That was Kim. He was lovely. He died in November. He had kidney trouble, and we had to have him put down. They said, "What do you want done with this dog?" So we said, "Well, you'd better keep him." But I said to Miss Thomson, "Oh, when you've had a dog for fourteen years, since he was a puppy, you can't just abandon him. I mean, I think they take them to the lime pit. So I said, I want him home. So we buried him in the garden. It seems a bit silly, but ...' A framed photograph of Kim, a handsome sheltie who used to bark an alert at all passing strangers in the street, proclaims his specialty.

Miss Ethel Groome lives next door; like Miss Greenwood not a native Barnwellian, but someone who has been here long enough – twenty-five years – to sigh over the gradual passing of those of her own generation and feel that things have changed inexorably. But that suggests someone who has retired from action. Not at all. Every year the *Parish News* announces that there will be a 'Coffee and Sherry Morning and Sale, 10 a.m. in Latham's Hall (organized by Miss Groome and Mrs Steer in aid of the All Saints' Fund).' Then in a subsequent edition thanks are expressed to all who supported the morning and helped to raise something between £160 and £200. How, I used to wonder, does an event of this kind, on a weekday, in a parish this size, run by two ladies in their eighties, raise so much money? Is it the sherry at 10 a.m?

'It's such a friendly little do,' said Miss Groome. 'We have sherry or coffee or both. I think, oh well, if we give them a glass of sherry they'll spend more. It gets them going!' Mrs Annie Steer and her husband Jack, a retired keeper, live in a bungalow opposite the almshouses. She and Miss Groome are 'collecting bits and bobs all the year round' for their knickknacks and good-as-new stalls. And of course there is a cake stall. 'You can always make money on cakes. And we have a very good raffle, with super prizes. We do ever so well. The number of people who respond to an appeal for the Chancel is really amazing.' Miss Groome used to live down the village near the Chancel in the 'Duke's row' looking after her brother who was valet to Prince Henry. Before that – 'many moons ago' as she puts it – she was a hospital sister, and she still has the calming, enquiring air of someone who will understand uncomfortable symptoms and try to suggest a remedy.

One frosty evening when the stars were shining, I walked up by the almshouses on my way to eavesdrop on a choir practice for the carol service. Smoke the colour of the fur of blue Persian cats floated from their chimneys into the violet sky. A barrow loaded with blue plastic bags of coal stood on the pavement outside: David making deliveries. The Church was floodlit, and inside it was unusually cold. Children were scampering around, and one boy tossed off a few soprano alleluiahs. Shirley Burchell, Arthur Malster's daughter, was briskly calling them to order when she remembered she'd left her music at home in Oundle. One of her sons was sick, and her day had been frantic. She rushed out to her car, and Mrs Sheila Akroyd, who is an Associate of the Royal College of Music and plays the accompaniments, led the children into 'O little town of Bethlehem'. 'Longer *the* on "the hopes and fears",' she said at the end, her still-Yorkshire voice reminding me that choirs were practising from Halifax to Brixton, honing their Christmas praises.

James Rutterford, mittened and duffle-coated, smiled sociably across the aisle. 'It's *cold*, isn't it?' he said. 'Cor, it's cold.' He towered above the other boys. His excellent treble had deserted him some time ago.

During 'Hark! the herald-angels sing' Shirley returned and took over with studied calm. 'A little bit more noise with your voices. Mark, please get rid of what you're eating. You can't possibly eat *and* sing. My apologies for leaving my music at home.'

The adult members of the choir began to arrive and a new carol was tried. 'We belong to the Royal School of Church Music.' Peter Bustin had told me, 'we buy some music from them and try as best we can to put fresh life into the services. But it's not a question of trying to copy a cathedral. It's just being a village church choir.' The carol sounded difficult to my inexpert ear. 'Don't try the tenor line yet, James,' Shirley said. 'Now, trebles. Sing out as though you really meant it.'

The children left the pews and went with the adults to sit in their correct places in the choirstalls. James next to Walter Woolman, Marion Leesons next to Juliet Wise. Juliet sings alto, and Marion later told me she wished she could too. 'I often can't reach the top notes of the treble. But Shirley says of *course* I can.' Still, she added, when Shirley and Mr Spelman were in full voice, she couldn't actually hear herself singing anyway. Ray Spelman, who like Shirley sings with the Peterborough Operatic Society, has a bass voice which he occasionally unleashes in church with thrilling effect.

The next carol was a lullaby. 'Remember, you're singing to a baby – who's *sleeping*,' Shirley urged the trebles. Doing as bid, they forgot to observe the instruction printed by the last verse. 'Mr Woolman made a notable fortissimo as marked, which the trebles didn't. Really blast it out before the final, very quiet, "Sing lullaby".'

My nose and feet were perishing. Mr Woolman was wearing a very sensible heavyweight bodywarmer over his jacket.

The practice concluded with a try-out for Oliver Berridge, the soloist chosen to lead 'Once in Royal David's city'. I could see him in profile, his mouth opened into a wide oval, singing with that sense of urgency that gifted choirboys emit. When told he would be singing out in front while the rest of the choir processed up to him, he protested. Everyone would stare, he said. 'It'll be candlelit,' said Shirley, 'and no one will be able to see you properly.' Juliet, who'd been standing at the back of the Church testing for audibility, said it had sounded very good.

The door opened behind her, and Peter Bustin came in. He was horrified by the temperature. Why hadn't anyone turned the heaters on? It seemed no one had liked to, for economy's sake. He looked perplexed, then smiled. 'Perhaps the essential purpose of a vicar is to switch the heater on.'

The Archdeacon had dropped a bombshell at Sunday morning service ten days before. He had announced that Peter Bustin was leaving Barnwell.

Dora Robinson told me about it. 'Oh, it was a shock. I don't think anybody had any idea. I couldn't believe it. I knew the Archdeacon was coming. But, well, I mean we took it all in the ordinary way – well, they do come sometimes. And then, you see, he announced it. So, *well*, when the service was finished, he came down as Mr Bustin always does, shaking hands and talking to people, and he said, "Hello, how are you?" "Absolutely shattered," I said. And I was. I couldn't have said anything else. I was so taken aback. I just couldn't think what to say. I think everyone was the same. I mean we rather looked upon Mr Bustin that we'd got him for ever.'

December's *Parish News* concluded with the statement:

I have been appointed Vicar of Southwold, Suffolk, in the Diocese of St Edmundsbury & Ipswich. The date of my

Institution has not yet been arranged but is not likely to be before Easter 1984, so I continue with my present work until then. The coming months should give us an opportunity to work out what will need to be done when I leave. Meanwhile, let us prepare to celebrate *Christmas*!

'You knew Mr Bustin was leaving, did you?' Maggie Head asked me. 'It's such a shame. He's going down near the part I came from in Suffolk. I think Mrs Batley's going to get a bus on so we'll go down and see him inaugurated.'

That morning I'd seen Charlie walking towards their house carrying a Christmas tree and holly garland. Maggie had almost finished decorating the tree when I went in. 'We're having grandchildren's day on Boxing Day, so there'll be a bit of a rumpus. I love everyone together. But you see it was eighteen last year, and with Tracy pregnant her head gets bad quickly, so we've had to work it so we halve them. But of course a lot of them that's coming Christmas Day have said they'll come back Boxing Day.'

Before we parted, she remarked: 'There's going to be a frost tonight. I hope the kids all get home safe before the roads get bad. John and Trace come from Cooks to Thrapston. Maurice comes from Wellingborough to Thrapston. Ken's on the estate. And the other one, he comes from Stamford to Oundle. I'm at the window at quarter past seven in the morning to see John and Trace go past. He blows his hooter. He's got a queer hooter. He always pips it when he goes down just to let me know they're all right. Because he knows I whittle, you see, if the roads are bad.'

I heard the hooter next morning just after I'd been out to fetch some coal. The horizon was pearly purple, and the frozen washing creaked on the line. There were William Morris patterns on the insides of some of the windows, and patches of ice on the brook.

In the middle of the day, I went for a walk round by the Manor. The winter jasmine spilling over the wall was in flower, a cascade of yellow stars. There were sheep in the field which slopes up to the Church, and the winter sun shone low behind them, making the outline of their fleece iridescent. Birds scrabbled among the decaying leaves by the hedgerow as the sun softened the frost, and my footsteps made the blackbirds cry loud warnings. Some boys were playing in the secret place under the road bridge; they stared at me, alert and slightly hostile, like rabbits disturbed in an unfrequented meadow.

EIGHT

The End of the Year

At half-past eight the following Sunday morning the sun was lolling on the horizon beyond Emma's orchard, slanting soft light across the powdery frost.

I decided to go for a walk, and John Lillyman greeted me over the fence: 'They say there'll be snow tonight.' I glanced up at the harmless blue sky; it seemed unlikely.

Out in the street, the only people abroad were dogwalkers. Young Bill Metcalfe was going slowly along the brook bank with his stately white pyrenean mountain bitch. Turning down the Thurning road, I passed a boy in a black leather jacket with a beautiful alsatian; I didn't recognize either, and thought that it was unusual to see a teenager out so early on a Sunday. In the fields behind the Manor just by Fox Covert was the distant figure of a man with two dogs. I recalled, as I invariably do when I look at that spinney, that Major Colin Cooper's ashes were scattered there after he'd died in Kenya. He'd requested that they should be because he'd so enjoyed hunting over the estate, and had kept his own pack of harriers.

The pond in front of Castle Farm was clustered with ducks, and the open lawn pale with frost. It is this generous, comfortable lawn fronting the classic stone house – three windows upstairs, one either side of the front door down – that makes most visitors pause and say, 'Oh! I'd love to live there.' Along the verge the frozen moisture on the molehills glistened, and the shallow puddles looked like iced milk. I pressed one with my toe and it squeaked and splintered just as a gunshot cracked loudly from the spinney. For a split second I thought of broken glass and bullets.

The field beyond the cart track that leads up to the ridge has a hill in it. Some Mays it is alight with flowering rape, cadmium dayglo surging into the sky. At other times, under plough, it looks dark and dramatic, especially against stormy skies. Now it was covered with the frosted green shoots of winter wheat, and the low sun dodged behind its shoulder as I came near and walked onto the track. When the sun re-emerged on the other side it dazzled my eyes, and I turned my back to it and faced the village, where the cockerel on the weathervane of the Church shone like a Christmas star.

There was wheat too in the big field that leads up to the top of the ridge, and tough little rape seedlings in the one that slopes down the other side. I was conscious of nearby repeated gunshots, much quieter than the ones from the spinney, and thought they must come from a mechanical birdscarer. I'm ignorant about these, and wondered whether it would be foolish to get in the way of one. Reason suggested that they must be safe, and I much prefer this walk when I can carry on down to the track that leads back to Lower Farm, rather than return the way I came. Sometimes the planting forbids this, but there was a clear path now. Another shot made me hesitate again; but I was perfectly visible and wouldn't go near the edge of Foot Hill spinney, where I might be camouflaged.

I walked alongside the heavily-docked hedgerow, looking across the intervening fields to the roofs of Wigsthorpe, and picked out the one that belongs to friends who'd given me such a good supper the previous night. Suddenly there was a movement about twenty feet in front of me. The hedge seemed to thrust up a tree-figure, greeny-brown like itself. I stopped. Then I saw a khaki head, hooded like the SAS. For a split second my nerves froze, and I realized I could turn and run. Clutching at the absurdity of that thought, I walked on. I saw the figure had straightened up from a hide and was holding a rifle.

'Hello.' I tried to sound both confident and apologetic.

'Hello.' An unsure, friendly young voice.

'I'm sorry. Have I disturbed anything?'

'That's quite all right.' I could see his grey eyes through the balaclava slits. I might have recognized him without his helmet.

'I'm never sure whether I ought to go through these fields. But it's such a nice walk.'

'It's not very safe at the moment.'

'No. I'm sorry. What are you shooting?'

'Pigeons. There's one up there somewhere.' He pointed to the top of the field.

'I hope I haven't frightened him off.'

'It's okay.'

I walked quickly down to the track. At the point where it bends towards Lower Farm, there is a midden, big as a row of pigsties, which was beginning to steam warmly in the sun, its rich smell in the frosty air giving promise of produce to come.

During the rest of the day, while I was doing some clearing out indoors, I had the wireless on a good deal, and listened to many reactions to the film *The Day After* which had been shown on television the previous night. It seemed I could not avoid thoughts of war. Indeed, with the jet nuclear fighters that shave the peace from the tops of Barnwell's trees and spire almost daily, it's not possible to forget that aspect of reality for long. One went over once when I was talking to Peter Bustin in the street, and he bowed his head for several seconds. It's the first time I remember hoping that someone was praying. Marilyn and Nigel Burrows, when I spoke to them, were surprised that I hadn't watched the film – 'everyone else did'. They talked very honestly and sensibly about it, and about the impossibility of England's strategic position. I was comforted that villagers, contrary to some opinions, aren't ostriches, and also felt very helpless as phrases such as 'complete wipe-out' were spoken in front of Andrew and Trina. They didn't seem to mind, but had those sealed-up expressions that mask children's feelings completely from grown-ups.

That evening I'd been invited to join the Youth Fellowship for their Christmas party up at the Rectory. The Fellowship is run by Pat Rutterford and Juliet Wise, and creates an opportunity for children from Barnwell and nearby to play together on Sunday evenings. 'And we try to tell them what goes on in the Church year, and why we do certain things. And what it means to us. And what we hope it could mean to them,' said Pat. Usually they meet in the backroom at the Rectory, but for the party the Bustins had lent their dining-room and kitchen. Pat explained that everyone had been asked to bring an edible contribution, in a big enough portion for two. 'Does that mean we'll all have twice as much as we need?' one of the children had asked hopefully.

When I arrived, it looked as though that hope would be fulfilled. Pat was in the kitchen cutting meal-size sandwiches into quarters, and plates were being loaded with crisps and cakes and sausage rolls. As the children arrived, the boys went fairly silently to one side of the room, while the girls gathered on the other, giggling. Juliet was whirling around with her usual wholeheartedness – making us welcome, sending herself up, setting out soft drinks and paraphernalia for games, and complaining that she was tired. She'd arrived home yesterday towards the end of *The Day After* just wanting to relax briefly before going to bed, but the ensuing discussion of the film on the screen and the one with Graham afterwards just could not be avoided.

The Bustins came to join us, and the first game got underway. Two boys from Thurning were wearing heavy metal T-shirts and studded jackets. The incongruity of Iron Maiden, Thin Lizzie, AC DC and Judas Priest logos in that setting was somehow reassuring.

The next game involved everyone sitting cross-legged in a tight circle, throwing a dice in turn, and the first to achieve a six hastily putting on a scarf, cardigan, red woolly hat and gloves, and trying to open a parcel with a knife and fork. Meanwhile the others continued to throw the dice, and as soon as another six turned up, the clothes and the parcel were snatched away. Learning that the parcel had chocolate inside, Marilyn Allen looked perturbed and said, 'I hope it's chocolate I like.' Peter Bustin threw the first six, and got as far as donning the hat, which made him look like Doc in *Snow White*, before Marilyn snatched it away. She scrabbled frantically to put on the clothes and managed to break open the parcel and cut one piece of the chocolate. 'Is it all right?' someone asked. 'Yes,' she said thoughtfully, as a boy grabbed the clothes off her, 'yes, it's nice chocolate.' She had the concentrated expression of a wine connoisseur who has been unexpectedly pleased by the contents of an unpromisingly-labelled bottle.

Just before tea they played passing an orange held under the chin from one person to another, no hands, two teams competing. There were urgent attempts to cheat and impossible feats attempted – such as conveying an orange from mighty James Rutterford to elfin Kirsty McIntosh. The winning team yelled in triumph, an orange hurtled up the room like a cricket ball, Anne concealed her alarm for the safety of a picture, and everyone rushed to the table.

Afterwards, when the clearing up was finished, Juliet, Pat, Anne, James and I sat around the kitchen table talking. James told me about his school's computer and the one he has at home, and I tried to understand the fascination of programmed 'quests'. Because he knew I was finding it extremely difficult to learn to drive a car, he assured me how easy it would be when all cars were completely computer-controlled. Then he looked a little bewildered. 'I don't know where it will all end.' Nor did I, on the day after *The Day After*.

Peter came into the kitchen quietly in his Damart slippers and prepared a dish of food for their cat, a thin-tailed, plump-bellied tabby that came with them from London thirteen years ago. When she'd eaten, she allowed me to stroke her before she crossed the terracotta tiles in the hall and went upstairs to bed. I wondered what she'd make of the move to Southwold.

Anne, who had gone outside, announced that it was snowing. We went to watch the flakes falling through the dark air, caught by the light from the house. John Lillyman had been right after all.

The snow hadn't settled by morning. When I drew the living-room curtain back, a large white drake stomped imperiously across from the brookbank and stood quacking in the road below. I broke up a thick slice of stale bread and threw it to him, but when he'd gulped it he looked most aggrieved that there was no more.

*

An hour later there seemed to be machines everywhere. A canary dredger tractor, followed by a big lorry, was crawling along the brookside. It lowered its scoop into the water, and dragged up sloshing clumps of dripping weed and mud which it deposited into the lorry. The grass was churned and tyre-marked, and the water murky. Cars puffed exhaust fumes into the cold air. Scarlet and blue, mud-splashed and shiny, they had an air of urgency and self-importance as they backed out of gateways and revved off to work and school.

They reminded me that Dolly Cole had been knocked down by a lorry on a crossing in Peterborough last week. Her face was badly cut and at first they'd thought her jaw was broken. She always looks so fragile that the idea of her being hit by a lorry was rather like thinking of an eggshell being cracked by a hammer. It meant that she and Fred had missed the Friendly Club's Christmas outing to The Falcon in Fotheringhay, an event much relished, judging by the accounts I'd heard.

'It was super,' said Maggie Head. 'We had a choice of soup, grapefruit or orange for starters. And then we had turkey, pork, brussels sprouts, peas and baked taters, and gravy. And then we could have Christmas pudding and brandy sauce, peach melba, or sherry trifle. And then we had mince pies. And we had a glass of wine with our dinner. And, you know, it was beautiful, it was really lovely. We went in with white faces and we come out with red!'

The Barnwell Entertainers' pantomime would not be performed until February, but rehearsals were in full swing in December. I asked Margaret Smith, the producer, if I could sit in on one. 'If you're mad enough to want to, of course you can.' She has a cheery, Birmingham voice. Two people had told me earlier that day how her cat had gone to church on Sunday. It had followed her up the road and there'd been no time to take it back home. It was the service when the children each took a toy up to the altar to give for families in need, and Margaret's daughter became shy and wouldn't leave her. Margaret couldn't face walking solemnly up the aisle clutching the cat, so she plonked it into the arms of a man in the pew behind.

Putting on a pantomime in the Reading Room is like having a party in a bed-sit — you can't imagine afterwards how everyone fitted in. When I arrived, Juliet Wise was trying to get Ali Baba and three others to do a quadrille. They circled cautiously while Juliet played the piano with attack. 'I am a lonely camel driver,' sang Ali Baba, alias John Lillyman, to the *Gondoliers* tune 'I am a courtier grave and serious'. 'Do-si-do,' cried Juliet, 'or rather, half a one.' 'Do-si, perhaps,' said Mrs Elizabeth Berridge, infant teacher at Barnwell School for many years. Grey-haired, elegant and tall, her impeccable vowels seemed splendidly out-of-place in the vulgar world of pantomime.

Juliet soon had to rush home to her children so that Graham, who was playing one of the comedy duo, could come and rehearse. The other comic was Alan Richardson, once the village's policeman and now in charge of security at the Manor. He's big, blond and boyish, while Graham is slight and bearded, with the high forehead and melancholy dark eyes of a Renaissance portrait. As Mustapha Dubbuhl and Mustapha Nutha respectively, they competed with puns.

It was supposed to be the first run through without scripts. 'Sorry, I'm completely off key tonight,' claimed Alan, picking up his script after stumbling over some early lines. On the sixth take of a scene with Elizabeth Berridge he cried, 'O lady of infinite circumcision', instead of 'O lady of infinite circumspection'. 'Perhaps I'll keep that in. On the Saturday night, anyway.'

Margaret's husband, Andy, was playing the Robber Chief, and when he and the two comics kept faltering in a scene, she said, 'Go on.' They stared, and she said it again, louder: 'Go *on*.' 'We can't. We've forgotten the next line.' 'Go on!' she yelled. 'That *is* the next line.'

At one point John Lillyman had to be prompted on almost every other word. 'John,' wailed Margaret, 'Your *lines*.' 'I knew them perfectly yesterday,' he said, 'but I've had two hours' sleep and I've been driving all night. I'm tired out. I learned some of them in a lay-by on the A1.'

Julie Grant, the principal girl, forgot her lines while being wooed by Thelma Allen, the principal boy. 'I can't remember,' she cried histrionically, collapsing at Thelma's feet, while Thelma gazed down at her trying not to laugh.

At the end, everyone swore they'd be word perfect by the next week.

John invited me to go with them to the pub, and I was talking to Judith and David Brown when I noticed a very fair young man smiling rather shyly across at me. His face was so familiar, but just for a second my memory fumbled. Its stored images of the same face were younger, those of a child and a teenager. But, of course, it was Richard. Richard Black.

'When the Blacks left the village,' said Graham Wise, 'we lost half the Youth Club football team.' There were five of them. Richard was the eldest, followed by Michael, Geoffrey, David and Andrew. They were all blond, and our cottage directly faced their house in Montagu Terrace with its sloping path and scuffed lawn. For years the customary picture in the window frame was fair boys playing, running, fighting, talking, motorbiking and courting. When their parents decided to move, it was a shock.

I went to join Richard, who introduced me to his wife and asked after Dan. I told him that he was married too, and that Barb loved Barnwell and they were going to spend Christmas at the cottage. Then I told him I was trying to write this book. 'What was it like for you, growing up in Barnwell?' I asked. There was a slight pause. Then, like a testimony, he said quietly, 'It was wonderful. Quite wonderful.'

'The Blacks' house was always the centre of things,' Dan had said. 'That was where everything happened. Because there were so many brothers, there was always someone calling for one of them.'

'We've still got a photo somewhere,' said Richard, 'of Dan, with us in cowboy suits.' 'I've got it too,' I said. In it, Richard is grinning over his shoulder into the camera while he points a toy gun at Geoffrey and Michael. They're all dressed in resplendent new cowboy outfits and are aged about four, six and eight. Dan, aged two, is clutching a gun, rolling his eyes, and, from the look of it, talking.

The photo must have been taken immediately after Christmas. Three days before Christmas, a twenty-year-old diary tells me, I'd gone to Oundle to buy a turkey and a tricycle. Dan had found it difficult to ride the trike and had howled, and the 18-pound turkey fell through its paper carrier onto the pavement. At that point, Carry Akroyd, who was ten, appeared at my elbow. She rescued the turkey, calmed Dan, and came back on the bus with us. And in the afternoon 'Carry + 6 others, came round to balloons, crackers and chocolate.'

Two years later, Dan had outgrown his London nursery school before he was old enough to be given a place in a primary school, so my mother suggested we ask Mrs Edith Beswick, the headmistress at Barnwell, if she would take him. She did, and my mother stayed at No. 22 to look after him during term-time. Then one day she noticed a hand-written 'For Sale' sign in the window of No. 58, the last of the old numbered cottages up by the Post Office. She'd not had her own home since my father died, and wondered whether the cottage, which had been modernized, would be within her means. It turned out that No. 57, which had a tenant, had to be bought as well, but the price of the two was reasonable and she went ahead.

Big, jolly Mrs Coppard lived in No. 57, and thin, nervous Mrs Folker in No. 56. There was a right-of-way through my mother's back garden to their kitchen doors, and they used to sit out on her garden seat for a chat when the mornings were fine. She writes of them, 'All the four years we lived so close together we never used christian names. Mrs Coppard, despite all the years she had lived in England, was very Irish. She would drink a morning cup of tea with me in my kitchen and relate fascinating stories of Irish/English discord. It was as though she was there as a girl playing a vital part, but one knew the stories were before she was born, but very real to her. She and Mrs Folker had an off-hand, but genuine, liking for each other. Mrs Coppard would like to find out in advance if Mrs Folker was going into Oundle or Peterborough on a certain day, but Mrs Folker would like to keep her movements to herself. Sometimes I was informed but "not to tell *her*, remember". Very bewildering to me as I could not see that it mattered at all. When Mrs Folker made a fruit cake (and no one could make a nicer one) Mrs Coppard, just to tease her, would call "I can smell you are making a cake, shall I put my plate out?" Mrs Folker always gave her a generous slice, but she hated it to be taken for granted.

'Mrs Folker was very self-effacing and yet she longed for people to take notice of her. She would leave her cottage, which was just opposite the Church, on a Sunday morning too late for people to greet her, and she would hurry across the road after the service. Sometimes, later in the day, she would say to me, "No one spoke to me, not the Rector, not anyone." In vain I would try to point out that she should linger in the churchyard like the others did and talk to them, and the Rector, but she would shake her head. I remember her as a dear neighbour and friend. She would bring a packet of sweets, or some fruit in for Dan and sometimes try to engage this young boy whom she didn't really understand in conversation.'

Both are dead now, but they remain vividly at the centre of

my mother's experience of Barnwell. When Dan was eight and came back to London to go to school, she sold her cottages and came too.

About five years later, main drainage was brought to the village, causing much upheaval because a layer of rock had to be blasted through in a long section of the road by the brook. We turned the old washhouse and coalhouse at No. 22 into a kitchen and bathroom, and built a cloakroom onto No. 21 for Eric. The trips up the garden to the bucket privies had come to an end. 'Somehow I found going up the path and sitting peaceably with the door open, looking through the leaves of the apple tree, hearing the birds, smelling the flower scents or the mown grass, a distinct improvement on modern hygienic life,' said my sister, who used to bring her boys to stay. 'I must have just always been a bit prissy about loos,' said Dan, 'but I always found it highly unpleasant. *And* there were spiders there.'

'It always felt,' he said, 'as though I'd spent about seven years living in Barnwell, not just four. Because we went back for all the school holidays from London, it stayed my main social life until I was about fourteen. All that sort of growing up that one does amongst friends was done in Barnwell.'

As they became old enough, his friends, including Richard and Michael, began to acquire motorbikes. They'd meet in a gang up at the green, and if someone would let him, Dan, aged thirteen or fourteen, would ride on their pillion. He wasn't supposed to, we'd strictly forbidden it. 'It was great fun, riding on the back seat. Oh yeah, I remember you used to get cross. Especially that one time, you went absolutely bananas. I mean you didn't go sort of YAYAYA or anything like that, but I could see it in your eyes. But when I remember some of the things we used to get up to, and the amount of alcohol that had been consumed, not that much by an adult's standard, but a lot by a sixteen-year-old's, it's like so many times in your childhood, you look back and think, well, I'm lucky to be here.'

His other special friend apart from the Blacks was Stewart Burrows, Nigel's younger brother. 'Of course, one of the major things for everyone was sport. Both Stewart and Richard wanted to be professional footballers. I remember I asked Richard once for a stick of chewing gum, and he said, "It's my last one," and I said, "O well, sod you then," and he said, "In a couple of years, when I'm playing for Leeds United, I'll buy you five thousand packets of chewing gum."'

The Blacks left at about the time Dan fell in love with London and formed a band. 'Michael and I were the ones who always used to keep time to records, rapping on the table. We used to play along to Gary Glitter records because the drum sounds were really prominent. He had the same sort of dreams as I had at that time, of just getting involved in music. All we really knew about it was Top of the Pops, and the idea you could go on Top of the Pops and play drums was really great. I don't remember anyone being particularly enthusiastic about going into the sort of jobs that older people were doing.

'It's the ideal way to be brought up, country and town. Because then it's sort of in your blood. I don't actually remember missing the countryside. I don't remember thinking, Oh, I wish this were a field instead of a street, or anything like that. But certainly cities are that much colder because there's so many more people. It's impossible to walk down the street and say hello to everybody. I've never consciously felt, Oh, it's horrible that there's so many strangers, but you know even in my street I couldn't possibly know even half of the people. What I do miss is that you can throw yourself around in the country somehow, it's just softer. You can fall over and you don't hurt yourself. Even now, if I'm in a park, I don't walk along the road bit, I always walk on the grass, because it's that much more springy and my feet feel at home on it.'

After I'd said goodnight to Richard and left the pub, the air outside felt much warmer. There was no hint of frost. Nevertheless, when I got back to the cottage and unlatched the door, I revelled in the unaccustomed enveloping warmth that greeted me. During that month, a great change had been taking place.

Ever since Eric died, his cottage had remained empty. Dulan and I had talked about joining the two and converting them properly, but had never had enough money or, really, the will, to alter them that much. So at last we decided just to annexe Eric's as simply as possible, and make a couple of alterations to ours. These Mick Burns was in the process of completing, but the main one, installing a new stove, he'd already done. It stood in the opened-up old fireplace, with a wedge under one of its elegant cast-iron legs because the old brick floor is so uneven, glowing.

Before Mick started, I'd said a private goodbye to the old, collapsing range, setting a match to the paper rubbish gathered in its grate and reading the little plate 'Amies & Son, Peterborough' screwed to the door of the broken oven that had once cooked the 18-pound turkey. The flames were orange with black edges. As they died down, I noticed there was the stub of an old candle among the ashes and it went on burning for several minutes, like an offering.

I kept the ring hob on which one could boil a kettle over the open fire, and it now hangs, the only ornament, on the newly-revealed brick mantel.

The first night I slept in the cottage with the new stove and bigger living-room space downstairs, I was so excited I got up at half-past four and went down to look at it all and riddle the ashes. On one side of the stove stood an old wicker basket which had belonged to Eric, full of kindling. On the other stood a very wide bucket, half full of coal. Emma and Bob had said, 'Would you like this for your coal? It's never been used. Someone gave it to us years ago, and then there was no need for it.'

So I gave it a coat of black paint, and the lavatory bucket looks rather convincing in its new role. It'll be something for Dan and Barb to explain to a subsequent generation.

NINE

The Dinosaur's Lair

Pat Rutterford had photographs of the Fellowship party to show me when Dulan and I came back to the village in January. Also ones of the skyline behind the Post Office before the dead elms were cut down. It is on that kind of winter late afternoon, when the horizon is a blinding gold, that one perhaps misses the elms most, with their dark, knobbly silhouettes.

'So what's happened in the last month?' I asked.

'Not a lot,' said Ron. 'Oh – one thing. The publican's wife's pregnant.'

'Oh.'

There was a gale roaring up from the south-west during the night. It tore round the corners of the cottage and over the thatch, and every now and then there was a loud rip, like the crack of a sail. In the morning, the surface of the brook was heavily corrugated, and the shrubs in the garden were lurching and waving. A hooded, blown figure out in the road waved up at me as I stood by the window – Basje on his way to school.

We met Jeanne while we were out for a walk, and she spoke of efforts that were being made in the Oundle area to start a peace studies class and said she'd visited Greenham Common recently. She was wearing a snowy white anorak, and a full skirt with black suede boots, and I thought of all the ridiculous slurs that have been made against women concerned with peace; anyone less unwomanly or slovenly would be hard to find.

One person's reason for thinking Britain should have nuclear weapons as a deterrent I could understand. 'I think it's better to have the bomb,' Agnes Broome had said, 'because I've lived through two wars when we weren't prepared. Our airmen were brought down in the Second World War because we weren't prepared, and the boys all rushed to join up in the First and they weren't properly trained. Old Kaiser Bill knew we weren't prepared, and so did Hitler; they knew very well we weren't. But I mean, just have it as a deterrent. Not to use it at all. Because I remember them being dropped in Hiroshima and Nagasaki. It was awful. It's terrible to think of it.'

Below the Chancel, Norah Blunt and Liz Fox were in deep consultation. 'We're planning where to plant trees for the future,' Norah called out across the brook. Liz caught us up outside her house and explained that the Parish Council had decided to take up the District Council's offer of some free trees. People had been rather apathetic when it was first mentioned, but bearing in mind how many have been lost in recent years, she and Norah felt they should do something.

The gale had blown down a lot of dead wood, and we were carrying paper sacks for sticks. I'm always tempted to pick up more than I can comfortably carry, and a walk turns into something of a struggle. The weather was still stormy, the light so dramatic that the whole village looked like a stage set. The sky in the east was electric blue and overhead there were thick black clouds, while in the west the sun blazed, spotlighting the houses and making any white paint on windows and doors dazzle.

It was a day to make one feel protective towards creatures outside, and Dulan had taken some carrots to feed to Chunky and Freckles and a bag of stale bread to the ducks huddled under the bridge by the ford.

A day, too, when a pub like the Montagu Arms comes into its own. The low, beamed ceilings trap the warmth, and a whisky mac or glass of red wine or pint of strong ale banishes the shivers.

Ralph and Sylvia Harrison, who bought the Montagu two years ago, bear out a theory of mine that the landlords of agreeable pubs seldom conform to the 'mine genial host' image. Also, they frequently have a special chief barperson who complements their own disposition – in this case, Shirley Sharman.

The Harrisons lived in America for four years, where Ralph worked in the aerospace industry in order to save enough to come back to England and buy a pub. He has a quiet, private manner, listening seriously to one's order and then checking on preferred finer details before dispensing it. Whenever possible in the evening he goes to the electric organ at the far end of the bar and, with his back to the room, plays through arrangements of light music such as Gilbert & Sullivan operas and standard American musicals. He keeps the volume down, and seems quite engrossed in the soft web of familiar tunes which he weaves for the inattentive clientele.

'He took some terrible ribbing to start with,' said Gerry Allen. 'But he took it all in good part. One night Nigel Davies brought in some of those earmuffs that tractor drivers wear. He took all the mugs down from the hooks and hung these earmuffs, and put up a notice saying, "For Hire, Earmuffs, while the Landlord is playing". So Ralph was there, happily playing away, and he suddenly looked up and saw them. He stopped, got up, walked slowly over and took one of them down and put it over his ears and went and started playing again. He'll sit there all night playing away; he's in a different world.

'But,' he added, 'I think the transformation he and Sylvia have made at the pub is marvellous.'

They've turned it into a family pub with one long bar where people can have all kinds of snacks or meals, and drink cordials or cocktails or coffee as well as a good range of beers. There's a terrace to sit out on when it's fine, and children can play Krazy Golf and run up into the field where a few caravans park in summer.

Until the early 1970s, there was one snug bar for regulars, and a larger – often empty – one for visitors. The only foods were crisps, nuts and chocolate, and children were allowed into the stone entrance passage between the two bars to buy these and drink bottles of Vimto and Thackeray's ginger beer. 'I think it had a more friendlier atmosphere then,' said Nigel Burrows. 'You knew everybody when you went in there. And now you don't.' Then it was a place almost solely for the village – and mainly for the village men who'd have their dinners at home. Now, like many pubs, it caters for a wider public's expectation of variety combined with friendliness and efficiency. But it's still a stronghold for darts and cribbage, or a gathering of the Cricket Club. 'One thing you can say about the Barnwell cricketers,' said Gerry, 'they beat everyone at the pub. There's no question about that.'

The Harrisons have three children, and the news that Sylvia was expecting a fourth had spread pretty early even by village standards, since the baby Ron had told me about turned out not to be due until mid-August. 'They go away on holiday, and look what happens,' said Shirley Sharman, smiling.

Shirley must have been born friendly. She grew up in a children's home in Wales because her mother died, and gets angry when people assume it must have been horrible. According to her, it was companionable and caring. When she was fifteen she had to leave the home, and she went to Corby to live with her brother who worked in the steel industry. Her first marriage, which happened when she was seventeen, broke up, and she met Brian Sharman when she was potato picking one summer. He's a member of an old Barnwell family, his father, Joe (who used to carry around a bag of peppermint lumps which he shared with children he happened to pass) being Jack Sharman's brother.

Brian and Shirley make a notable contrast. He is broad, fair and quiet, and she's very slight, dark and talkative. One gets a sense, when he's in the pub while she's working, of their instinctive mutual support. Support which has been essential as her three children, who to start with were not all enthusiastic at being transplanted from Corby to Barnwell, grew up. Now her daughter is married and Shirley is, amazingly, a

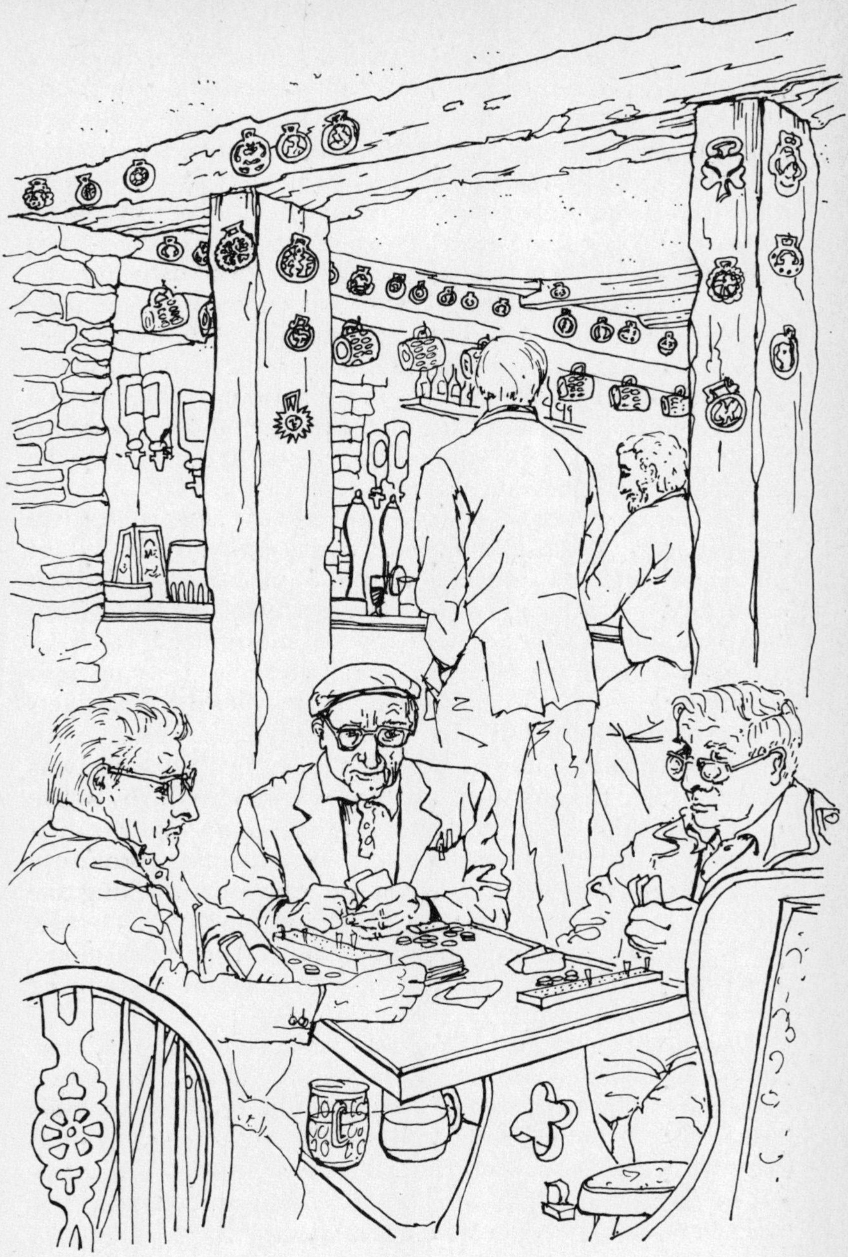

grandmother. Two tall, striking-looking boys, who might be socialising in the pub or helping out on the terrace if it's a busy Sunday lunchtime, are her sons. The younger, Andy, acquired a motorbike as soon as he could, but after two spills Shirley said either it was sold or she smashed it up. Since she looks as though a gust of wind could blow her away, this seemed an idle threat. But, judging from the expression in her amber eyes when she's determined, it wouldn't be one to put to the test.

Dulan and I aren't regular pub-goers (which isn't to say we're not regular drinkers), but through my needing to be out and about more we enjoyed dropping in at the Montagu. Once, just as we were sidling out through a near closing-time crush, someone said, 'Hello, aren't you speaking to me?' It was Pat Shacklock, sitting with her husband, Alan, who invited us to join them.

The meeting, one of those impromptu ones that pubs make possible, lightly forged a natural link, since the Shacklocks live next door to Emma and Bob, and although we've always passed the time of day, the four of us had never had a conversation together before. I'd not imagined them other than in their Barnwell context, but we discovered that Pat originally came from the East End of London and Alan from Yorkshire, and could see how the different veins of energy and independence from those backgrounds had contributed to their personalities. When they came to the village, Alan had a job with rented accommodation; now they have built a bungalow and he runs his own engineering business. Their three grown-up sons remain very close. Graham, the youngest, chose to work with his father; Gerald, like Geoff, is married and lives nearby, and this sense of continuity, of having established sound family roots in a place they care for, gives Alan and Pat great pleasure.

It is when something distressful occurs in a close-knit, successful family that one sees clearly how fragile the structure of happiness is. On January 17, Pat's birthday, an event took place which pleased her more than anything – her first grandchild was born. She was Gerald and Ann's baby, Jemma Elizabeth, and, after having three boys herself, a granddaughter seemed just perfect. But Jemma had something badly wrong with her digestive system. She had to be operated on, and Ann was not able to take her home when she left hospital. When Pat walked by our window – as she does at least twice a day with their dog, Tess, her shoes clopping briskly on the road so I know it's her without looking up – her normally positive expression had been wiped away and she seemed to walk without seeing.

In the middle of February, I asked after Jemma. It was clear from Pat's reply that, during the one month of her life, she had become a unique personality who, whatever happened, would always be part of her world. 'If love and prayers can bring her home,' she concluded, 'she'll come through.'

The February frosts were spectacularly lovely. At first, in the morning, the garden would be subdued and pale under a swansdown mist. Then, very gradually, the sun penetrated the vapour until the rime on every twig and bud, and on the spiders' webs that hung from every bush and plant, were like silver silk threaded with glass. After the freezing nights, the snowdrops were limp and translucent, but by midday they had thawed and stood upright, restored to opaque white and green.

One day the weather shifted. The air felt mild, and the winter trees looked air-brushed rather than etched along the blurred horizon.

The deep sound of an engine chugged over from Emma and Bob's, and when I opened the door, I recognized the heady, damp smell of cut grass. Bob was mowing – in February! It seemed inexpressibly exciting to have that foretaste of summer. Soon the noise moved out of his garden, along the brookside – which he cuts from the Shacklocks' down to us – through our squeaking gate and up the narrow path to first Eric's side then ours. Whenever I see Bob walking slowly behind his heavy mower, deaf to the rest of the world, I'm always reminded of Joyce Grenfell's phrase, 'Stately as a galleon'.

It was still warm on the evening of the final performance of *Ali Baba and the Forty Thieves*. Owls were hooting from both sides of the village, and there was a line of parked cars stretching from the Pub way past the Reading Room. All five performances had sold out, people coming from Polebrook, Thurning, Hemington and Luddington-in-the-Brook, and some Barnwellians seeing it twice.

There's a fascination in watching people one knows in everyday life semi-transformed on stage. 'He *is* a tall boy, isn't he?' murmured the lady in front, as the curtain went up to reveal James Rutterford greasepainted into an Arab cobbler. Judith Brown and Marilyn Burrows, with sprigged net veils across their faces, appeared – most uncharacteristically – as slave girls. 'Into your tent I'll creep – with me boots on carrying me truncheon,' sang Alan Richardson in an approximate version of *The Sheik of Araby*.

John Lillyman, loosely robed in beige, and in a perpetual state of Victorian vapours, wafted round the stage singing, 'I'll be your sweetheart' in a deep baritone. A hint of make-up indicating five o'clock shadow could not begin to transform Thelma Allen from a sweet willow of a girl into a boy. Elizabeth Berridge, aristocratic in kaftan and turban, ordered her unfortunate stage husband to 'Sittt!' à la Barbara Woodhouse.

The scenery changes on a stage about the size of three double beds were impressive. The cave did 'Open Sesame' on command, and when the dozen or so children playing the Forty Thieves suddenly erupted through a door at the back of the hall, they made most of the audience jump. Their menacing Robber Chief provoked vigorous boos and hisses, and when he pinched my cheek as they exited I remembered being seven years old and not quite sure where the audience ended and the pantomime began.

Everybody joined in the knock knock jokes and the singing. Instructions to drone on cue for an Arab chant led unexpectedly into a hummed bag pipe opening to *The Mull of Kintyre*. The lyric sheet unrolled, and the sentimental song was given a wholehearted, lump-in-throat rendering. Someone announced that it was Mark Lillyman's thirteenth birthday, so we all sang 'Happy Birthday to You' to a surprised, suddenly shy, young robber, and then, after a brief pause and a few Why-are-we-waiting's, the curtain went up on the transformation scene.

A pillared palace, smothered in reflecting silver foil, dazzled our eyes. Ali Baba implored 'May the sand snakes never, Wriggle up your knicker', and Elizabeth came down to the footlights swinging a rope of pearls to a cascade of catcalls and cheers for her turquoise miniskirt and black lace stockings.

Marilyn and Judith threw off all traces of servitude and exhorted the audience to stand up and join in the inexorable *Birdie Song* – 'With a little bit of this, And a little bit of that, And shake it all about' – complete with actions. It had been Marilyn's first experience of performing on stage and she looked very pleased and happy. The most vigorous, gleeful shakes I could see among the backs in front of me came from Norah Blunt.

Then the company made a presentation to David Brown for 'Scenery surpassing anything we've ever done' – unanimous applause – and we put on our jackets, neighbour exclaiming to neighbour, 'Weren't they *good*?'

Apart from the pantomime, the main topic of conversation that month was the announcement in the *Parish News* about the appointment of a new rector – except there wasn't going to be a rector but a Priest-in-charge. 'I'd always understood priests were Roman Catholics,' said someone dubiously in the Post Office.

> The Bishop proposes to suspend presentation to the Benefice of Barnwell with Thurning & Luddington for the time being and to appoint a Priest-in-charge for the Parishes, resident at Barnwell Rectory. The Archdeacon of Oakham consulted the Parochial Church Council about this proposal at a Meeting on 17th January and explained the reasons for it, chiefly that it would be a more flexible arrangement than the appointment of a Rector, in view of the need to work out the best pastoral care of Oundle deanery as a whole, in future years.

'Consulted' was not a word some members of the Barnwell Parochial Church Council felt was apposite. The Bishop, they gathered, already knew whom he was going to appoint, which was fine, but why go through the motions of a consultation? It rather underestimated their intelligence. Others thought these feelings should not be mentioned, it wasn't fair on the incoming man, and after all the Bishop was the Bishop.

There was likely to be a four-month gap after the Bustins departed, and Peter was anxious that all practical church matters should be ship-shape and up-to-date. At his last PCC meeting – held in the School – everyone agreed that the interregnum might prove difficult, but that it would provide a challenge to the community. Peter's good wishes to his successor were greeted with applause.

'By and large the church accounts are healthy if prudently watched,' Peter Scopes summed up after their presentation, though the All Saints Fund would have been in the red were it not for donations in memory of Rene Kirk. Collections as a whole were slightly down, but attendances were up, and Ron reported an increase in volunteer help for the churchyards. Arthur Malster could not be present so Ron read his report, and held up a hymn-number display board which he had just made for St Andrew's.

Shirley Burchell asked for reactions to the introduction of music to the communion services, and Kath Batley said she thought it was very nice. Ron raised the point that there was a change of atmosphere when the choir suddenly stopped singing in the middle of people walking up to the altar, and Shirley said it was difficult to judge the length of a piece in relation to the size of the congregation. She'd try in future to have an extra item up her sleeve. She felt rather dubious about conducting while people were going up, but it was necessary if the trebles were going to sing an anthem successfully.

Mr Rowland Parker would be turning in his grave, I thought. He was both the village schoolmaster and, from 1873–1926, the church organist. 'He didn't agree with women in the choir,' Agnes Broome had told me. 'He wouldn't have them while he was organist. Rector Baillie wanted them, but he wouldn't have them. But they had to have women in the end because there wasn't enough boys.' And not all boys were reliable. 'I used to blow the organ for him when I'd just left school,' remembered Jim Waite. 'I'd sit there during the sermon and drop off, and when he wanted to play he couldn't start because he needed some wind. He was a cripple – they used to take him in a bath chair – and he couldn't get out to tell you. Poor old Parker!'

During the Rectory change-over period, things were extremely busy for Ron; but, when I walked down from the Oundle bus one Thursday and realized just as I reached the Post Office that I'd left a new curtain track propped up against the Market Hall, he immediately offered to drive and fetch it. I had an awkward, bulky bundle under my arm – a rag rug I'd just bought – and he wouldn't listen to my protests but said he'd go and look for the track and then come and see the rug.

He arrived – bearing the track – just as Emma and Bob were inspecting the rug. Made mainly of grey, umber and vermilion scraps, it lay on the bumpy brick floor looking singularly at home. Ron and Emma immediately began to reminisce about how they had made rag rugs as children. Both families used to cut up old clothes, and Ron's used to sort them into different colours which they put into sugar bags. The sorting was important for making patterns; Emma and Bob's family didn't bother with patterns. Old hessian bags were cut up to make the backings, and a new rug was always put in front of the fire, while the others were moved to less and less conspicuous places around the home as they got older. All three of them were tickled by the idea of my buying such a rug, made out of brand-new scraps, in a craft shop.

It was from Emma, some days later, that I first heard the news that Jemma Elizabeth was home.

When Pat walked past our window, she had her customary optimistic air again. And when Tess frisked and pleaded for stones to be thrown – her favourite game – she threw them with zest.

*

Like most dogs in the village, Tess is indulged but disciplined. It used to be said that country people don't get soft-hearted about their domestic pets, but that's certainly not true in Barnwell.

Santa, the Burns's golden labrador, is one of the older dogs, and every morning he tries to persuade Mick to amble very, very slowly round the brookside rather than take a brisk, pre-work walk. His coat is very pale, and with particular joy he will take a rather stiff roll on the dewy verge, streaking his back with mud.

The main street ducks that have already been mentioned belong to the Pywells, but most of the village seems to feel protective towards them. The ducks themselves soon sussed out the softest touch: the Gunns. Just a day after one of them hatched a brood of ducklings, she route-swam them to the point of exhaustion along the brook from Chancel Terrace and then led them up into Crowsons yard. Eileen reported that at one period they were receiving three visits a day from two families of ducks. 'I don't mind,' she said, frantically buying up all David's yesterday's bread one afternoon, 'but we do get a *bit* fed up with hosing down the yard afterwards.'

She and Derek are even softer towards their cats than we are to ours. 'They've only got to look at him and he reaches for a tin opener,' said Eileen. Since Christmas, a wild kitten called Holly had been their main preoccupation. She had hidden in the hearse, which is garaged up the Armston Road, and had been unwittingly driven down to Crowsons where she emerged and took refuge in the woodpile. Finally she was enticed indoors, but by mid-February was still spitting at strangers from behind the chintz valance of a chair.

As well as the hearse, the Gunns have two limousines which they hire out. Derek gave me a lift into Oundle in one of them, and it felt very posh gliding along, cushioned by the thick upholstery. My shopping went reasonably well, and I came back with my usual muddle of bags and bundles, managing this time not to leave anything behind. Then, just as I was walking by the almshouses, my blood ran cold. I stopped, and for about three seconds I thought the cumulative effect of David Brown's wineboxes had affected my mind at last.

Down beyond the green on a trailer, with its head outlined against the sky above the roof of the pub and its green body tapering along the pub's length, was a dinosaur. Its jaw was slightly open, and it had red lips and a long, leering line of triangular teeth.

When two children came into view on the other side of the bridge and stood staring at it, I felt mightily relieved. At least they could apparently see it too.

By the evening, it was ensconced at the back of the pub near the Krazy Golf. Its head reared above the wall, gawping in the direction of Dolly and Fred Cole's garden.

'It belongs to a chap in Finedon,' explained Gerry Allen. 'He hires it out for fêtes and things. But some of the local lads took it out of his yard and parked it in the middle of the night on a roundabout. Which rather upset the local constabulary. Then it was moved to a pub, but the kids started getting air rifles and shooting its teeth out. And then they tipped it right over. So someone from here said, "There's a field at the back of our pub, why don't you graze it there?"'

So he did.

TEN

The Wren and the Butterfly

During the first week in April, the crocuses started to collapse like swooning soldiers, and the clumps of hyacinths and daffodils were waiting for a warm day in which to unfurl. Beneath the old apple tree there was a sparkling blue and white patch of scillas, which by next year will have spread forward to touch the edge of the lawn.

One morning, in the dense labyrinth of clematis that smothers half the tree, a wren was singing like some Dionysian reveller celebrating the rite of spring. I had to walk up the garden to look for him, to make quite sure that the noise really was coming from a creature only three inches long.

He eyed me from the swirls of the bare stems – the same brown as his feathers – then scuttled upwards, trilling coarsely. It was as though he had a microchip amplifier in his tiny throat. I hoped he was going to nest in the clematis; it's a place the cats can't penetrate, and at the end of the month we were going to bring them down to Barnwell for the whole summer.

I felt less happy about the sparrows under the tiles of the bathroom roof. Midler, our youngest cat, would certainly discover their whereabouts. And for a different reason I was dubious about three more families of sparrows and one of the starlings that were busy building under the lip of the thatch; they had squeezed under the wire which we should have had tightened last autumn. It's only two years since the new thatch was completed, and it was daft to let the birds begin making inroads already. Still, as our genial thatcher from Cotterstock always takes months to materialize, and would feel as bad as I about turfing birds out of their new homes, it was easy to decide to do nothing.

The District Council's trees arrived last month when I was in

London, and I was having difficulty identifying the new sapling on the brookside near our gate. 'Someone said it's a beech,' said Emma. 'Funny sort of beech,' I replied.

I met Norah Blunt, who told me that when the trees were delivered at Orchard End, Liz and Ian Fox were away in Hong Kong, and she and John Lillyman fetched them, only to find they had Latin labels. 'I could recognize the horse chestnuts and some others by their buds, but several stumped me, so we called in Mr de Bock.' 'What's the one outside our cottage?' I asked. 'A cherry, I believe.' Funny sort of cherry, I thought. 'We were well organized,' she said. 'Fetched the trees at ten, and they were all planted by eleven-thirty. We'd dug the holes first, and the Telecom man had to inspect the sites – the sewage and electric people took our plan on trust. One hole we dug was filled in. Someone didn't want a horse chestnut near them.' Certainly there are unenthusiasts, people who like to look out of their front windows and see what's going on the other side of the brook, rather than gaze at a lot of trees.

Werner de Bock confirmed that our tree was a cherry, but not the sort I had in mind. It was a bird cherry, with white almond-scented flowers in May followed by small, shiny black berries. It should look well near the little rowan we planted a few years ago – provided the latter picks up a bit; it's grown very, very slowly, and I'd like it to be one of those sturdy, round-headed rowans, smothered in flat red bunches of berries.

Up and down the village, filling in gaps or standing in the wings near ageing trees, were sapling birches, limes, willows and whitebeams, planted, as Norah and Liz had said, 'For the future'.

By midday on April 10, the sun had enough heat to penetrate one's clothing between the shoulder blades. The clumps of different kinds of daffodils began to open, and a faint, sweet scent drifted from the hyacinths.

On one of the spreads of aubretia – lavender, mauve and purple-red – a pale, acid green butterfly appeared. It was a female brimstone, the first butterfly I'd seen outdoors that year. Probably she'd been hibernating in the ivy at the top end of the Lillymans' fence.

I pruned the rose of Sharon and lad's love bushes hard back; spring's the right time to do this, but it always feels strange to decimate them just as everything is beginning to grow. The lad's love has a pungent, herby smell that makes one try to nudge out sealed memories of forgotten gardens and old medicines.

Whilst I was working on the perforated strip of asphalt by the gate – once the slope up to Eric's demolished car shed – which sprouts expanding mats of thyme and veronica and acaena, Mick called across the brook: 'Are you all right? Is everything I did working all right?' 'Oh, yes. Thanks. Everything's absolutely fine.'

John Lillyman, who had recently bought a handsome blue lorry for his growing business, appeared in his garden. I asked what the Barnwell Entertainers' next production was going to be. 'It's a comedy about a repertory company. But we're all sworn to secrecy about the parts we're playing.' 'I always knew you wanted to play the ingénu.' 'No. I've always wanted to play a randy vicar. But they won't let me.'

Part of my preparation for our summer-long stay was to visit the library van and get an advance stock of biographies for my mother. The van stops outside the almshouses and the shop every other Friday afternoon, and has two staff anxious and able to provide a personal service to each reader.

Mrs Mary Thomson, who lives just by the green, had enquired the previous fortnight about a particular book on Venice; it had proved unavailable, but the girl librarian had brought along three others. Shirley Sharman was housebound with torn ligaments in her leg – she'd fallen (sober) down the Montagu's cellar steps – and twenty-two of her favourite addiction, romances, were ready to be taken down to her. Kath Batley also likes romances, and the library man was helping her find 'The rape and pillage books I know you Barnwell ladies enjoy!' Norah Blunt prefers real life – preferably Catherine Cookson's – and I was quickly discovering that the stock of biographies was extremely good and up-to-date. 'I'm afraid temporary borrowers are asked to deposit ten pounds,' said the girl librarian shyly. 'Oh – we'll vouch for her,' chorused several ladies, and the request was immediately withdrawn.

Mention of Venice, my favourite city, had made me nostalgic, and Mrs Thomson invited me in for a cup of tea to talk about it. A friend had persuaded her to go on a short visit, and she liked to be prepared. Several of her husband's watercolours hang on the walls of her sitting-room – he was a retired surgeon who died a few years ago – and she talked about his painting and how he had suffered from migraine and sought solitude in the landscape. Suddenly my excitement about Venice waned. I wasn't sure that I would be much good at going to new places, the fabulous ones that is, without Dulan.

There was a knock on the back door. Hanneke had come for a chat with Mrs Thomson. The sun streamed in, brightening the covers of the books: the canals and the palaces. Outside it shone on the bridges and the brook. Just now, when we'd all clambered into the library van, it had shaken slightly with our weight, and been filled with our teasing and laughing. It was silly to cast shadows when everyone else worked hard to keep them at bay.

Palm Sunday, two days later, was Peter Bustin's penultimate Sunday in Barnwell. It was cold and wet, and with some trepidation I decided to go to morning service; I hadn't been to church apart from three funerals, two weddings and one christening since I left school. I walked up with Juliet Wise, who soon dispelled my self-consciousness.

She was wearing an anorak which over the months I had come to regard as special. Mainly it is an ordinary navy blue, but in each of the interstices of the diamond-shaped top-stitching it has a metal stud, and these studs, which catch the light like sequins, combined with the serviceable navy nylon, have somehow become a private metaphor for Juliet's personality: thoroughly down-to-earth, but with a quicksilver energy and enthusiasm that opens almost more doors than she has time to enter. That day her three daughters, Amy, Hannah and Esther, had mumps; she wasn't at all sure of some of the music the choir were supposed to be singing; and she'd promised to compile the *Parish News* – which Liz Fox would type and duplicate – after the Bustins had gone. She'd be bound, she said, to muddle or forget the saints' days and so get into trouble with one of the more fervent parishioners.

There were about fifty people in Church. Norah and Phil Cook were the sidesmen, greeting everybody and handing out prayerbooks. I saw Shirley Sharman in a pew near the back, and asked if I could sit next to her. 'No need to ask,' she said. It was the first time she'd been able to get to church since she hurt her leg. She told me that she'd been brought up as a Roman Catholic, and had recently been confirmed into the Church of England. I explained I hadn't been to church for over thirty years, and she helped me find the right places in the prayerbook.

Embarking on the first hymn, 'All glory, laud and honour/ To Thee, Redeemer, King', my head recognized the melody though my voice could no longer reach all the notes. Peter brought the different elements of the service deftly together in the traditional mix of praise and prayer, admonition and celebration. I was struck by the switchback of impact between strong and soft language: between the Litany entreating delivery from the crafts and assaults of the devil, from everlasting damnation, pride, vainglory and hypocrisy, and a submissive hymn that sought protection for 'Us thy frail and trembling sheep'. The setting for the Benedicite was lovely, Ray Spelman's voice underpinning the invocation to the Works of the Lord – Stars, Showers, Lightnings and Clouds, Seas, Whales, all Beasts and Cattle – to praise their Creator.

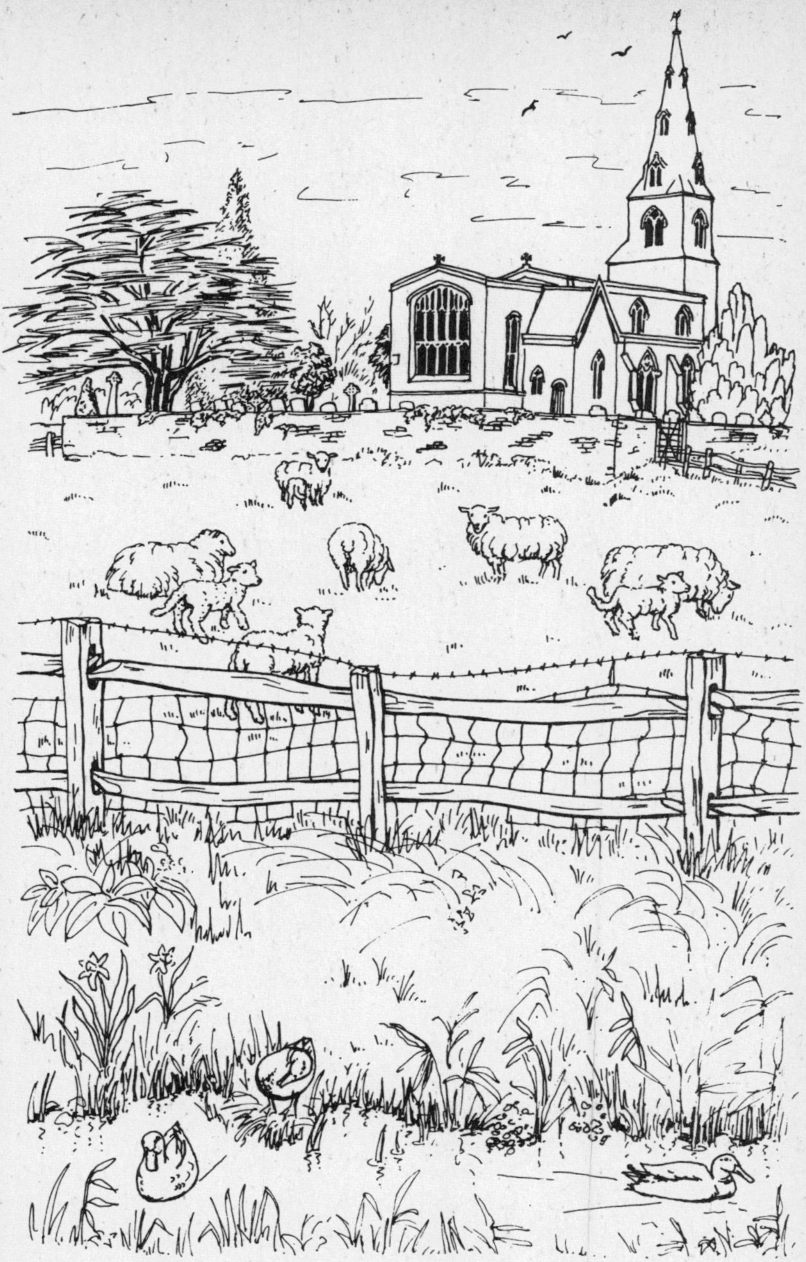

In the silences of the service, the birds were singing loudly outside.

During the announcements, Victor Crump and Audra Graley's marriage banns were read for the third time, and notification was made of Peter Gliszczynski and Susan Knight's marriage at Luddington Church the following Sunday.

At this point, Anne Bustin leapt to her feet and rushed from the Church. A few heads turned, and signals were made. Three minutes later she was back, flushed, carrying the little palm crosses she had forgotten to bring over that were about to be handed out to the children before they left the service for Sunday School in the Rectory.

Finally, after the last words of the blessing had died away, the last private prayer made, and we had stood quietly while Princess Alice and her secretary, Miss Betty Chalmers, left the Church, everyone suddenly seemed to start talking. Mrs Malster turned round from the pew in front, saying, 'You're from the village, aren't you?', and we caught up briefly with the years since we'd last spoken. Shirley Sharman gave me news of Neil, her elder son, who after three medicals had joined the army for a week, but had then been sent home disappointed after a fourth. Mr Elcock came to have a word, and, as I passed Peter Bustin in the Church porch, he remarked that the recent PCC meeting had been rather fun.

I walked down the path beside Reg Larkins, taking the opportunity to thank him for agreeing to put a shaft on a hammerhead for me. I'd found the head, a nice heavy one, in the garden, and Bob had said he'd ask Mr Larkins if he could fit it up when he came to collect some eggs. I hadn't known he did jobs like that. It was just a hobby, he explained, no charge; and would about fifteen inches long be right? – he'd got a suitable piece of hickory. He and his wife, Jessie, live in Chancel Terrace, and he drives around in a pale blue three-wheeler because of chronic hip trouble. He's nearly always smiling as he passes.

The hammerhead is one of several things rescued from our garden and Emma's. Mostly they stand on a shelf in the kitchen: old bottles, heads of clay pipes – one with 19th-century prize-fighters embossed on it, fossilized oyster-shells, a tiny pottery jar, a glass sardine container, a green marble, glass bottle stoppers – one shaped like a crown. As I passed by No.

20, Emma and Bob were working in the drizzle and cold in their garden, and by chance had just unearthed a slender little turquoise bottle, about three inches high, and a pre-plastic, moulded model carthorse, probably from a farmyard set. 'Thought you'd like them,' said Emma, watching my pleased expression as she gave them to me.

*

Our friend Maureen Duffy drove our whole household down from London two weeks later: Dulan and me, my mother, three cats, and bags and cases and boxes galore. As the luggage and cat baskets were set out on the London pavement, it didn't seem that they could all possibly fit in.

It was the gentlest of April days. When we turned off the A1 and drew near to the Northamptonshire boundary, the sunlit landscape with its distinctive spires and well-kempt fields seemed like a measureless welcome mat. Even Perkie-Liza, our middle cat, didn't cry all the way down as she usually does.

After we arrived, Pudding, our eldest cat, who has always adjusted immediately to Barnwell before, seemed to concur with my mother in finding the expanded spaces inside the cottage very strange. Midler was full of confidence and curiosity; he quickly located the nest in the tiles, viewing the parent sparrows' exits and entrances obsessively, both from the path below and the deep windowsill of the small back window in our bedroom. It wouldn't be long before he jumped down onto the kitchen roof.

*

Maureen was staying the night, our inaugural guest in the room which had once been Eric and Aggie's. The two small landing rooms, with their new connecting door, were Dulan's and my workrooms. I unpacked my files and arranged things on my new trestle table: settled for the summer.

After supper, and a visit to the pub, we opened the doors of the stove, put on some of the logs Bob had left for us, and talked until the small hours.

Outside, there was a light frost bruising the pale magnolia petals under a skyful of stars.

At the Parish Council meeting the following week, I learned that a start had been made on the Wigsthorpe bridleway. Ken Preston had changed the stiles into his field to gates so that a horse and rider could pass through. Two evenings later, Dulan and I went to try them out on foot. We walked across the meadow at the back of Montagu Terrace and came to the first sturdy gate. Inside, we could see a cow and a bullock, some geese and hens, and several lambs, one of which – a dark one, with sticking-out ears – came flying towards us bleating hopefully. It had obviously been raised by hand, and it seemed a shame to raise its expectations further, so we left the gate untried and went round to the five-barred one that leads to the road at the side of Tom Litchfield's house.

As we passed the Post Office, Pat and Ron, who were unloading stock, came down the path to talk to us. James was just cycling off to the Youth Club; he'd been on a school skiing holiday, where he'd lost a stone and dressed up as a flasher in a donkey jacket and bathing trunks at the last night party. The Friday fish and chip van came, and we wished, on sampling one of Ron's packet of chips, that we hadn't just eaten. In the morning he was going in a coach with other parishioners to attend Peter Bustin's induction at his new church in Southwold.

The *Parish News* had already informed us that our Priest-in-charge was called the Reverend Professor William Frend, and that he was a Doctor of both Philosophy and Divinity, and a Fellow of the British Academy, the Society of Antiquaries and the Royal Society of Edinburgh. At present he and his wife were in America for a few months, where he had been made a Fellow of Harvard University and was seeing a book to press. Ron told us that he understood he was sixty-eight and that this would be his first parish. Most of the village was slightly bemused by this combination of facts.

We said good night, and as Dulan and I walked past the front of The Croft, where the Prestons live, I remarked that I'd had no idea they kept so many animals. When I talked to Barbara Preston some weeks later, she said she wasn't surprised.

'People see the house from the road, and they don't realize we have three acres at the back. It was always Ken's ambition to have a place with a little bit of land, in case we wanted to do anything. Then of course when we got here, he said to me, "What do we do with all this land?" And I said, "Look, it was your idea, you think of something." "Well, we could have a few geese," he said. So that first year we had geese and goslings, and the grass was so high you couldn't see the goslings. So I said, "Ken, there must be some better way than this."'

Ken Preston was a major in the army then, and their two sons were still at school. Now he works in a business which takes him abroad, and Stuart and John have grown up and are away from home. Barbara, who was in the WRNS when she met Ken in Germany, had never looked after any animal other than a cat before she came to Barnwell.

'Ken got to know a few farmers, particularly Norman Beesley who's been very helpful to us. And he said, "Why don't you keep a few sheep?" So we started off with one cade lamb, and then Norman said to Ken, "Well, why don't you borrow the ram and have lambs from your ewe?" So we borrowed his ram, and that's a story in itself.

'We fetched the ram, and the ewe had never seen another sheep. She thought he was human and she was absolutely petrified of him. He approached in a friendly manner, but she just ran. For two days, she ran round bleating helplessly, hiding behind Ken's legs. It was ridiculous. Finally he decided to lock them both in the stable so they could have an enforced honeymoon. Poor girl!

'But, before that happened, he'd looked out of the french window one morning to see the ram put his head down and go straight through the fence to join Trevor Marriott's flock on the other side. He was obviously fed up with our one who wouldn't play at all. But of course they were a different breed of sheep. So it was all hands to the pump. "Barbara! John! Stuart! Boots on, you've got to go and round this ram up."

'So there we were, trying to catch the ram, in the middle of about seventy sheep. Oh! it's the most difficult thing, trying to catch a ram in the middle of a herd of sheep. Ken said to me, "When they break, throw yourself on the ram." "You must be joking," I said. "I've never had anything to do with sheep before in my life."

'Anyway, in the end we eventually isolated it and hog-tied it. And then of course we had the problem of how to get it back again. There it was, on its back, and I said, "You can't lift it over the fence, you'll break its back." So we borrowed Ron's van with the sliding door, drove it round, and when we got to the paddock it was so muddy it stuck. So we got the wheelbarrow out, and there was this ram, upside down in the wheelbarrow. And we had to wheel it round the outside of the house just as everybody was going to Church. I was most embarrassed.

'Anyway, they had the enforced honeymoon in the stable for about three days, and she was all right after that. She had a lamb. And now we keep usually about six sheep and they produce six or eight lambs for the freezer a year.'

Three years ago, Ken decided he'd like to keep a cow. 'I wasn't a bit keen. But then I was taken to see this herd of Dexters, which are a small, black Irish house cow, very, very docile. What I didn't know was, they have horns, and that threw me. But she's just a soppy thing. Of course she's had two bull calves these last two years, and I'm rather careful because the elder, Bertie, is a bit handy with his horns. They're lovely animals, I must say, though I was dead agin it at the beginning.

'It's lovely at this time of year because the animals feed themselves pretty well. But in the winter, when the water's frozen and you have to go through the ice and snow, it's not funny at all. Sometimes, when Ken comes home from work and says, "I don't know what you do with your time all day," I could scream. Because we produce all our own vegetables and fruit. I think he thinks they jump out of the ground and off the bushes, wash and shell and peel and blanch and chop themselves, jump into bags, and then get into the freezer all on their own!'

And what about the Wigsthorpe bridleway? 'Well, when we came, and as far back as Trevor Marriott can remember, there were the stiles. And then Mr Elcock approached me one morning and said, "Do you know, it's all wrong, that should be a bridlepath, and it should be wide enough to allow an ass with two panniers to pass." So I said, "Well, I don't know anything about that, Mr Elcock. My husband's in the army and in York, and I really can't cope." I hoped everybody would forget about it. And then of course I became a parish councillor and it was raised during the time I was on the council. So I asked, "Well, who is interested?" And they said, "Oh well, someone *might* want to ride a horse through there." And I said, "Oh, really?" And it all dropped again. Then it was raised again this year, and because they persisted Ken had a letter from the Council saying that he had to put in proper gates, and of course it took him three weekends. Trevor Marriott's refused to do the same on his land. But we felt, being sort of newish in Barnwell, we couldn't really stick our necks out.'

At what point does one stop feeling newish? When can one confidently say, 'I don't care if asses with two panniers can no longer pass through my land?' I'm not sure. Because there have been occasional, more crucial, cases concerning rights-of-way in Barnwell; incidents when newcomers have tried to ride roughshod over very necessary, and reasonable, access needs, putting their own personal privacy above co-operative custom and practice. At those times, it is perhaps quite salutary to keep the principle of the itinerant legal ass alive.

ELEVEN

'Queen of Months'

John Clare called May the 'queen of months'. In *The Shepherd's Calendar*, his long poem about Northamptonshire village life at the beginning of the last century, he describes a schoolboy blissfully truanting through the May countryside, lured by the lambs and birds and blossom. It has always been my 'queen of months' too; my birth month, when the new leaves and lush waysides are almost heartbreakingly green.

But, this year, it only just retained its title. We were gathering firewood right through, it was so cold and drear, and to begin with it was also dry, the ground hard and chill so we couldn't plant out Emma's seedlings. One sight, however, couldn't be dimmed by the weather: the rape fields. They flowed, fluorescent yellow, beneath layers of dense grey cloud that seemed to suffocate the sky.

Nowadays rape oil is used for margarine; once it burned in miners' lamps and sanctuary lamps. When a meeting of the Girls' Brigade, held in a back room at the Rectory, sang a lusty rendering of the hymn, 'Give me oil in my lamp, keep me burning/Give me oil in my lamp I pray', I couldn't help being literal and thinking of the embryo lampfuls of oil flowering up the Thurning road.

The Brigade is run by Norah Blunt, assisted by Marion Leesons. The company was started about a decade ago by a newcomer, Betty Neave, who, Norah said, 'Had been practically born into it. I think they were Baptists. Because the Girls' Brigade is basically Non-conformist. I can remember her coming to a PCC meeting in her uniform. Then, when it had been going about two years, she came into the Oundle Bookshop one day, and said they were making baskets, and did I know anything about it. I said, Well, not a lot, but I'd done a bit at the WI where you're dabbling with all sorts of things. So she said, Right, come and help. So I started helping her with the baskets, and then I started helping generally. She kept going on about having to pass an exam to be an officer, and I said I thought I was too old at fifty-eight to be an officer. She said, Well, the thing is, if you pass the exam you'll have a say at the meetings and it makes one more opinion. So I went to Northampton, I don't think I'd written so much for years. I spent all morning writing and answering questions, and all afternoon learning drill. And, about six weeks later, I had a certificate come to say I had passed, and I was then commissioned as a lieutenant.'

Not long after that, Betty and her husband moved to another area. 'So I had to take over as captain, having never really been a lieutenant. All Betty said was, here's the bit of red braid to put on your uniform. So really, I have to find out as I go along. Because I've done Girl Guides before, but I've never done Girls' Brigade, and it's totally different. Some of the girls won't come because their families aren't very churchified and so they don't get awarded marks for attending church. But to me that doesn't make any difference. The main thing is to get them together out of school, and they seem to enjoy it.'

Recently she had been finding out about alcoholism, drugs, gambling, euthanasia and abortion – aided by the staff of the library van. 'The older ones are doing this project. Mind you, they don't always turn up, so we don't get very far. I think the project's called Christian Living – something like that. Angela Shanahan, she's eighteen, and she's a Roman Catholic, she likes nothing better than a good discussion. And Thelma still comes occasionally, she's nineteen now. Trina stays on with the older ones, she and Kirsty are two odd ones – not quite old enough really, so I went and asked Marilyn Burrows if she had any objection to the abortion or the euthanasia or any of it. "Well," she said, "I'd sooner she discussed it up there with you, than discussed it down the bottom by the lamppost."'

Angela lives in Armston, which is a hamlet. 'I feel really isolated. I lived in a town until I was twelve, and I've had to spend my teens in a very small, *very* small place. I missed on going out a lot, being just able to get on a bus and go to a cinema, or go to people's houses just for coffee or something, because if I want to go anywhere I've got to ask my Dad to take me, and I've got no freedom as such.' She wanted to be a nurse. 'But I think I've decided against it because there's so many unemployed. I can't face studying until I'm twenty-one and then not getting a job. I couldn't cope with that. I'm taking my 'A' levels at the moment, in history and archaeology, and I've got a job in the Peterborough Museum when I leave.'

Angela had helped Norah and Marion to entertain the younger ones on the Rectory lawn at the earlier part of the meeting, and then she hitched up her elegant pencil skirt and joined in a jumping game. In between their turns over the rope, the girls did headstands and handstands and cartwheels and somersaults on the soft turf. The empty house looked rather forlorn, with its long white shutters closed and the white lilac in full bloom.

After some games and hymns indoors, Norah said to the younger ones, 'Hats on!', and they assembled in a straight line – with a short wait for Hannah Wise, four years old and donnishly bespectacled, whose legs had become entangled in the bars of her chair and was briefly in a heap on the floor. Norah, magisterial but with a broad twinkle, blew her whistle. 'Ready? Company dismiss. Good girls – after a fashion.' They clattered off down the back stairs to waiting parents, leaving the older girls to make some coffee and draw closer together for their discussion.

Gambling was the first subject. Norah came in for a good deal of stick because she confessed to putting 30p on the football pools each week. 'That thirty pence could be going somewhere worthwhile,' said Angela. 'To a charity. If you put that thirty pence a week in a bottle, at the end of the month you'd have one pound twenty, right? And if you think, over a whole year, that money – which you're paying out for no reason – that money could feed a child in Cambodia or something.' 'Yes, Angela,' said Norah meekly.

'The men who go down to the pub on a Saturday lunch time,' said Marion, 'and take their bag of twopence pieces and play crib, probably not for more than ten pence throughout the whole game, they really enjoy that. And they're not doing any harm, they're doing it amongst themselves. That's not hard gambling.'

'I suppose it's all right for some people,' conceded Angela. 'Because they can control themselves. But other people can't. And you don't know yourself whether you're strong-willed enough not to let something get out of hand.'

'It says here,' said Norah, consulting the Girls' Brigade's

handbook, 'that gambling's a social evil. It's a sin against the family. Like a father who visits the greyhound track or betting shop immediately after pay day. The trouble is, we haven't got any of those fathers around here. I mean Jack wouldn't even put five pence on the football pools, let alone my thirty pence.'

The discussion passed to drugs. Angela made out a very good case for not testing drugs on animals because they have a different make-up to humans. Marion pointed out that because of her heart she couldn't keep going without the drugs she has to take. 'But they're always testing things that are proven,' said Angela. 'They're good, and they're still testing them. You can test things much better on a computer. Because you can feed in human characteristics, and feed in characteristics of the medicine, and it comes out with the correct answer.' Both agreed that they would rather like to be vegetarians, but it was difficult: Angela because of her parents, Marion because she sometimes ate with her grandfather.

Norah read from the handbook again. 'It says here, "How can we help people cope with the difficulties of today without resorting to taking tablets of one sort or another? What can the Christian Church do in the face of the growing problem of drugtaking to help an addict or would-be addict to combat the false philosophy of life that leads to drugtaking?" Well, I don't think we've got a drugtaker in Barnwell, have we? Any ideas? Do you know anybody?'

'No,' chorused everyone.

Somebody suggested there might be some in Thrapston. 'Well, Thrapston, yes,' agreed Norah. 'And there's some in Oundle, I think.' Someone suggested there were in fact a lot in Oundle; particularly glue-sniffers. But no one knew anybody in Barnwell who sniffed glue. It reminded me of a conversation I'd had with Pat Rutterford. 'We don't know we're born in Barnwell,' she'd said; 'We don't really see the hardships and horrors that go on.'

I asked the girls how Barnwell compared to other villages they knew. 'It's prettier,' said Marilyn Allen. 'More of a community,' suggested others; 'There's more to do.' 'The people in Barnwell are really nice,' said Angela, 'that's why I come out here. They wanted me to go to a Youth Centre in another village, but I didn't because the people aren't very nice. They don't mix; they're all back-stabbing at each other. It was very friendly to me, Barnwell. It doesn't matter where you come from.'

'That's the trouble with our discussions,' concluded Norah. 'We all agree – except for my thirty pence on the football, of course.'

When I happened to see Angela some weeks later, she told me she'd become a vegetarian after all, had managed to persuade her parents. I was not at all surprised.

Ever since I first came to Barnwell, there have been murmurings from older inhabitants about the decline of the May Queen ceremony. Judy Beswick, the headmistress's daughter, was the first May Queen I can remember. She grew up to be a teacher too, and is married to Reg and Jessie Larkins's son, Geoffrey. Shortly after her reign, the then rector called a halt to the ritual altogether – partly, so I was told, because the children used to be invited into the Pub for a drink of lemonade after they had processed around the village.

In John Clare's village, Helpston, the May Day ceremony died out during his own lifetime. The cowslip balls he mentions were still made in Barnwell ninety years later when Agnes and Dora were young:

> No flowers are pluckt to hail thee now
> Nor cotter seeks a single bough
> The maids no more on thy sweet morn
> Awake their thresholds to adorn
>
> Wi dewey flowers – May locks new come
> And princifeathers cluttering bloom
> And blue bells from the woodland moss
> And cowslip cucking balls to toss

Princifeathers are lilacs.

During the last few years, Barnwell School has revived the

ceremony, though its pagan origins have become somewhat blurred, and it takes place at a time to suit various sections of the community rather than on the first of the month.

This year, Sarah Lillyman was due to be crowned on the Rectory lawn on Sunday, May 20, after church. There were some complaints that this was a ploy to get people to the service who otherwise wouldn't go, and a few people thought the children should still sing and dance right around the village, but by the time Sarah walked up the churchyard path on her father's arm, transformed from a long-legged tomboy in shorts to an impish queen wearing a long, pale apricot dress, past years were forgotten, and people turned to one another and whispered, 'Doesn't she look pretty?'

The service was rather long, particularly for the younger ones, but at last we made our way from the churchyard, through the gate into the Rectory garden, thankful to see that the promised rain hadn't yet begun.

One question which had caused some concern was, Who should crown the May Queen? Princess Alice had crowned Amanda Davies last year, and no one wanted this year to be an anti-climax. Then the perfect solution was found. Somebody pointed out that it was seventy years since Dora had been May Queen, so, wearing a tailored coat and a dashing, wide-brimmed hat, it was she who crowned Sarah with a circlet of flowers, and made a short speech. Her words carried clearly across the lawn to all the spectators – who included Princess Alice – and a tradition, though changed, endured.

The children performed some prepared dances, and then their parents were asked to join in. Fathers were mercilessly seized by small daughters and whirled around the grass with bemused or slightly embarrassed expressions on their faces, while their sons, happy to be stretching their legs at last, forgot the niceties of the steps and galloped away like young ponies.

A boy's face, carved six hundred years ago on a capital of the Church's north door, gaped out of a surround of leaves. The boy is a Jack-in-the-Green, a youth who, on May Days then, would camouflage his head with a wicker canopy covered in leaves and dance among the girls, making passes. So the pagan was part of the Church right from the start.

For the rest of the day it rained, and for most of the next two as well. But it was warm rain, and we were able to plant out seedlings during the dry intervals. Then the sun came out, and Kirsty, Hanneke and Amanda called to play in the garden. They sat on the grass making daisy chains, with apple blossom branching over their heads and bluebells in the border behind. From a distance they looked Arcadian, but near-to they sounded real enough, gossiping away about their close and not-so-close schoolfriends, and arguing about new clothes.

Kirsty was among the first to arrive outside the Reading Room for the start of the Family Walk organized by the WI on Bank Holiday Monday. The weekend had been so wet – it was on course for the wettest bank holiday ever recorded – that doubts had been cast on the likelihood of the walk taking place. But by half-past ten the rain had virtually stopped, there was a bit more light breaking through, and people tentatively began to assemble.

The walk is not a strenuous affair. It was started a few years ago simply as an opportunity for people to walk together in the countryside at a beautiful time of the year. David Brown does the map reading, and this time he had worked out alternative routes; one across fields which would be very wet and muddy, and the other by road and track. The routes converged at Polebrook, and from there we could all take the same path on to the pub in Ashton.

There were about thirty of us at the outset, and it took time to decide who would and who wouldn't take the muddy way. In the end a dozen did, and we set off after David up the Thurning road. When he turned into a field with tall, wet rape growing right up to the edge of the ditch and hedge, and promised us we were on course because the map showed a footpath here, I was not particularly surprised. His daughter, Rachel, being only four began to complain, but Judith said firmly, 'The whole idea is to *enjoy* the walk' – which she did once David had hoisted her up on his shoulders.

Kirsty's Scottish mother, Bobbie, is not one to fuss, and even when the sopping rape closed completely over the head of her seven-year-old John, she was unperturbed. 'Come on!' John yelled at his elder brother James and Jonathan Fox if they showed signs of falling a yard behind, 'Come on!' With his face wet, and his fair curls plastered with yellow petals, he looked ecstatic.

We reached a slope, clear of the rape, where we could wipe the pounds of mud off our boots and look out over the tops of spinneys to the slender spire of Oundle church. Most of the leaves on the deciduous trees weren't yet fully unfurled, and their shades of green varied widely, the tints of gold and pink making them look almost like trees in flower. 'Och, this is better than being shut up indoors with the television all morning,' said Bobbie. Thelma and Roy Reed, who had just recently come to live in Barnwell, agreed. Settling in, they said, was proving remarkably easy. All the children on the walk had been given a list of objects to find, and their daughter Nicola was on the look out for such things as a 'leaf like a hand', a pine cone, a bluebell and a fossil.

Skirting round the back of Polebrook, those of us who did not know that a circus has its permanent quarters there were astonished to go into a perfectly ordinary field and find ourselves stared at by two dromedaries and several llamas. 'They'll never believe this when I get back to Canada,' said Mary Thomson's daughter, Elizabeth, raising her camera.

However, the English rural image was completely restored by a glimpse through a gateway of a perfect spring meadow along the Ashton road. It had high hawthorn hedges on all sides which were just beginning to flower, and the tall grass was thickly scattered with rusty sorrel and golden buttercups.

The pub at Ashton has benches and tables on the village green, and ideally we would have refreshed ourselves and walked back to the Reading Room where the WI was putting on a tea. But one or two people with small children had already arranged to be met, others had sneaked back swiftly to get cars, and as the wind got colder and the clouds lower, the rest of us were grateful to accept one of the numerous lifts offered. I went with the McIntoshes, who live in Montagu Terrace, and as we drew away from Ashton, rain mizzled against the windscreen and Donald turned the wipers on. John was shivering in the back, and when James said, 'Can we put our pyjamas on when we get back?' it sounded like rather a good idea.

*

Earlier this year, Bill Groom went to stay with a member of his family and then decided not to come back. One day, council men arrived with two vans to clear his house out, and a few weeks later Mrs Nene Pywell – of duck repute – and her teenagers, Teresa and Paul, moved up there from Chancel Terrace. Paul does some of the more daredevil wheelies in Barnwell, and soon the McIntosh boys were streaking after him, hell-bent it seemed on turning their small bicycles into flying machines. I was reminded of the days when the Blacks were still there and Victor and Martin Crump and Stewart Burrows were still teenagers, when I saw Paul leaning against the wall by the road talking with Andrew Burrows, and the Sharman and Melton boys.

It was David and Jean Melton who came to live in the Blacks' house when they moved, and immediately one saw their children rushing up and down the garden path and steps, the change no longer seemed sad. On Sundays the whole Melton family delivers the papers around the village, supplying one of the weekend's musts.

In the May *Parish News*, a notice asked everyone to be particularly conscientious about litter, because the judging of the Northamptonshire Rural Community Council's Tidiest Village/Churchyard Competition would take place between June and September. Probably those who are conscientious anyway went on being so, and those who aren't continued to scatter the packets and wrappers and cans which I suppose they must see simply as part of the natural landscape, but on the first Saturday in June a special purge was to be made, and people were asked to come and help.

Not very many were turning up at the stone bridge at ten o'clock to receive instructions from Graham Wise and Liz Fox as to where to trawl with a blue plastic bag. However Hanneke and Basje, Amanda and her brother Miles, and the policeman's son, Matthew Smith, said they would accompany me and do the brook and verges from the Pub up to the Manor. Matthew, aged eight, stood in the middle of the stream and solemnly declared: 'Say your prayers, rubbish, because here we come!'

Basje's first catch, a motor tyre, would probably be missed, since Hanneke said the children used it as a target for throwing stones at while they waited for the Oundle school bus. Various bottles, bits of metal and plastic sheet were dredged up, and then the inevitable happened – Amanda got stuck in the mud. Until then, since I wasn't wearing wellingtons, I'd kept out of the brook, but I slid down the bank and squelched up to my calves in water and smelly mud to try to give her a hand. Just as it seemed I was more likely to get stuck myself than unstick Amanda, Matthew said brightly, 'Do you know what this makes me think of?' 'What?' 'A nice cup of tea!' Hanneke decided she'd better save the situation, and instructed me to get back up the bank while she waded out and somehow got Amanda up on the other side. 'My best friend rescued me. Well done, H!' cried Amanda, in a good imitation of a school-story heroine.

It was sunny enough for the wet and mud not to matter, and we finished that section of the brook and turned up the hill to Stone Cottage. The banks of the road were foamy with keck – the local name for cow parsley – and the chestnut trees towered above us, mountainous with white candles.

We called in at the Post Office for icecreams, which Ron allowed us at a discount since we were being useful, and when we got back to the stone bridge we learned there was still an untouched stretch of brook along by the Chancel. The Harrisons' children were on the green, and Brett, who is ten, wanted to come and clear the brook with us. However he was supposed to be looking after Kirk and Tiffany – aged two and three respectively. I said they could walk with me if they'd hold my hands, so two extremely suspicious small people took my fingers as though they were handgrenades and watched Brett as he waded happily into the water. His mother, I knew, had not been well and was having injections for embolisms. For a while, his eyes seemed to lose their slightly troubled look. Sylvia had told us that, if the new baby was a girl, she wanted to call it Melody, and if it was a boy, Clint. She liked boys' names that couldn't be shortened. The trouble was, said Brett, a short name didn't stop people inventing nicknames. It was obvious, as we walked home together, that Tiffany and Kirk would have trusted him to the ends of the earth.

As we passed the house that had once been Joe and Emma Owen's, there were signs of activity both inside and out. Jean Hastings (once Gliszczinski) and her husband Bert had bought it, and improvements were underway. A few days later, Jean cycled by when we were working in the garden. She offered to bring us some 'bits' from plants she was transferring from her old garden at Chancel Terrace, and we said we hoped there were some things in ours she'd like for the new one. She'd come and have a look round soon, she said, just now she was off to buy oranges and lemons and sugar to make wine. What kind of wine? we asked. May blossom, she replied. She and Mary

Marriott had been out in the fields and gathered simply masses of it.

May blossom wine! It sounded like nectar.

TWELVE

One Red Rose

When the Duke and Duchess of Gloucester bought Barnwell Manor in 1938, they were looking for a country house where they could enjoy family life and each pursue a particular interest: farming for the Duke, and gardening for the Duchess. Since the Manor is built beside a ruined Castle which makes it look as though someone of historical note should live there, the Royal connection, though fairly recent, seems to fit the village naturally.

The Le Moine family who built the Castle were granted the land by the Abbot of Ramsey in 1170. But they omitted to get a licence for the building, and had to forfeit it back to the Abbey a century later. A legend about the Le Moines concerns one Berengarius who fell in love with his cousin. She, however, was already in love with his brother and, when Berengarius found this out, he ordered the brother to be walled up inside the Castle and left to die. As soon as his cousin heard what had happened, she seized a horse and rode down to the River Nene to drown herself.

This story, which has variations, has helped to substantiate the idea of the existence of a Castle ghost. Besides Tom Litchfield's story, several reports of mysterious lights seen at night inside the castle, and ghostly figures seen moving on its walls, have been passed down. Susan Burns, who with her sister once worked as cook at the Manor, had an experience in the road outside which still makes her shudder when she tells of it:

'It was Josie's night off, and I had to walk home on my own. I didn't like it at the best of times. Regularly I used to meet Mr Goodson, he used to go out for a walk, and I saw this shape coming, and I thought it was Mr Goodson. I didn't think more of it until I got abreast of it, and when I got abreast of it there were nothing there but white. I don't think it clicked for a start, I just saw this white thing, and everything went cold. I went ever so cold. And I just started running. It wasn't till I got past that I realised it wasn't Mr Goodson – do you know what I mean? I just ran. I didn't stop running till I got home. I didn't tell Mum for ages and ages. I just daredn't. I just didn't want to talk about it. Every night after that when Josie wasn't there to walk home with me, I just used to come out the gate and run without looking.'

The Castle started to fall into ruin while it still belonged to the Abbey of Ramsey. Occasionally stewards of the Abbey lived there when overseeing the surrounding estates, but by the time Henry VIII was preparing the dissolution of the monasteries, his Surveyor-General, John Leland, who visited Barnwell in 1539, reported that 'At Barnwell remain yet four strong towers of Berengarius le Moine's castle. Within the ruins is a meane house for a farmer.'

Henry VIII granted the Castle and its lands to his Chief Justice, Edward Montagu, who had recently built Boughton House near Kettering, about twelve miles away. Montagu did not take much interest in Barnwell, but his son Edward, who was knighted by Queen Elizabeth, built the manor house which forms the central part of the present building. Its entrance faces the entrance to the Castle, separated by a forecourt and lawn. Sir Edward's son was then created 1st Lord Montagu of Boughton, and during the Civil War, when he was an old man, he allowed the Royalists to store small arms inside the Castle. As a result, he was imprisoned by the Parliamentarians in London until he died.

The 3rd Lord Montagu (who became the 1st Duke of Montagu) was far too busy turning Boughton House into a smaller version of Versailles to bother with Barnwell. He even instructed his agent who lived there to strip stone from the Castle to implement his building projects. The 2nd Duke stopped the demolition, and also made additions to the manor house. When he died in 1749, his lands were left jointly to his two daughters, and through the marriage of his granddaughter they passed to the Dukes of Buccleuch, who continued to use Barnwell as an outpost to the main seat at Boughton.

During the 19th century, Barnwell Manor was inhabited by a succession of agents, apart from a brief period when the second son of the 4th Duke of Buccleuch lived there. Then, in

1890, the Earl of Dalkeith, who became the 7th Duke, leased the property, before finally selling it in 1910.

When his daughter and son-in-law bought the Manor, together with the by-then much smaller estate, in 1938, it wasn't a very propitious time for establishing home roots. The Duke of Gloucester was away a lot during the war, but his thoughts were often of Barnwell: 'How I long to be home to see it when all the spring flowers are out,' he wrote in a letter to his wife.

Their two sons, Prince William and Prince Richard, were born, and people in the village were pleased when, as small boys, they came up to the shop or to the station. 'They always had their chocolate from me mother-in-law when she had the shop, they used to come for their rations,' said Dolly. 'Ivan, who used to work at the Manor, he had this big horse, Prince,' explained Mr Elcock, 'and he used to come up here to the station, with the cart, to fetch the laundry. Well, the lads worked it with Ivan to come up just when the goods train come in. They used to get on the engine, and go up the line, and do the shunting on the engine. They used to love it.'

In July 1972, Prince Richard and Miss Birgitte Van Deurs were married in Barnwell Church. Many members of the Royal Family, including the Queen, attended, and Barnwell was awash with journalists and camera men. Eric Garratt had a lovely time buttonholing reporters – who wanted authentic anecdotes about the Gloucesters from the locals – and telling them his war stories.

Photographs of the occasion, kept in many Barnwell albums, largely feature umbrellas. 'Poor old Richard,' said Dora, 'it poured and poured. Oh but, dear, the people I had, different friends that had come over, and I had to find frocks and goodness knows what for them, because they got absolutely soaked. I rigged them up in all sorts. Oh, we had quite a day.'

Just seven weeks later, Prince William was killed. He was thirty years old, and crashed while taking part in an air race. Agnes Broome remembers how her neighbour, Flo Grimes, came in with tears streaming down her face, saying, 'Have you heard the news? Prince William is dead.'

The Duke, who had been ill for several years, died two years later. As his elder son, Prince William had been expected to succeed to the title, but in the event it was Prince Richard who became the present Duke of Gloucester, and in that same year the young Duchess gave birth to their first child.

Princess Alice, in her mid-eighties, still carries out a full schedule of royal duties. But, whenever she can be, she is in Barnwell, and the Duke and Duchess, together with their three children, come down for weekends and holidays.

Betty Chalmers arranged for me to meet Princess Alice briefly in the garden to inform her about this book, first taking me indoors into the sitting room in case I wanted to ask any questions. It is a large room, but its grandness is so overlaid with evidence of family life that one expects dogs and children to come running in at any moment. Tall windows overlook a terrace with balustrades covered in roses and clematis, and beyond is a lawn with shady trees and an open view of the fields which rise towards Fox Covert.

When we went out, the policeman on security duty told us that Princess Alice was working in the Silver Garden. This circular area, bounded by a yew hedge, was laid out and planted in 1960 as a gift to the Duke and Duchess from the staff at Barnwell for their silver wedding. All the foliage of the bushes and plants in the beds was in shades of silvery grey, and at the centre there is a stone well-head decorated with wrought-iron.

Princess Alice, in brown corduroys and a quilted jacket, was pulling the weeds from between the rough-cut paving stones. She peeled off her gardening gloves to shake hands. Some of the silver plants had died, she said, and the green alchemilla had seeded everywhere. She supposed it ought to come up, but it was rather pretty and she thought she would leave it for the moment.

Talking of Barnwell people during the times when the estate had a large staff, Princess Alice particularly remembered that there were two woodmen who never spoke to one another. She recalled this battle of wills with amusement. She asked if I knew Miss Robinson, since she would remember a lot of things and be a good person to talk to.

Three or four times a year, on Sunday afternoons, the Manor gardens are opened to the public. There are guided tours of the Castle, and teas are served in the stable block. Dora is usually among the people who are helping. Over the years I've noticed that the younger teenage boys from the village seem particularly to enjoy going around the gardens in a group, peering through the Castle's slits, dodging round the tall hedges, and swaggering up the gravel forecourt.

I like to look into the row of teak-framed greenhouses in the kitchen garden to see the seedlings and vines and hot-house flowers that are under the care of Nicholas Warliker. Nick, who keeps bees and writes about gardening for a local newspaper, is also the village's honorary wasp destroyer. Report a nest, and he'll come and deal with it as soon as he can.

One Saturday in June, the gardens were made available for a Family Day for disabled people organized by the district Rotary Clubs. It was perfect weather, and cars and coaches flocked up the access road through the farm which the late Duke built. There is a rather deserted air about its buildings now, for with changes in farming policy, and the demise of the pedigree Guernsey herd which was Prince Henry's particular pride, the estate no longer needs them all, and some are being let off as private workshops. In the fields beyond, the thick green corn was growing tall, and the first creamy saucers of elderberry flower were just beginning to appear in the hedgerows.

In the meadow separated from the Manor lawn by a ha-ha, there was the smell of sausages singeing on barbecues, and all kinds of entertainers were making preparations for performances later. The Peterborough Medieval Society were going to put on a joust, and so matronly ladies in gold and crimson gowns and men in cod-pieces were rushing around in the very hot sunshine creating an arena. A teenage page, dressed in black and carrying a dagger, was anxiously trying to cheer a drooping damsel wearing a long white dress and a silver crown. Later I saw them walking hand in hand up to the entrance of the Castle, looking rather as if they were going into their own home.

Betty Chalmers said that one of the people in wheelchairs whom she spoke to told her that she had danced for Princess Alice at Boughton House on her wedding day nearly fifty years ago. And, when the Oakleaf Country & Western Band struck up, a little mongol boy leapt and danced on the grass and looked so happy, she had found herself crying.

There was more dancing outside the Manor towards the end

of the month. This time it was in the forecourt where the children of Barnwell School came to pay their annual rent of one red rose to Princess Alice.

This is an old custom, dating back to when Nicholas Latham built Barnwell's first school on land given by Sir Edward Montagu for an annual payment of one red rose on St John the Baptist's day. The custom had long died out, but the School decided to revive it in 1980, and each year a little ceremony takes place at its presentation.

Princess Alice comes to the front doorway to greet the children, and as well as the rose they give her something they have made to symbolize the occasion. One year it was a fabric collage picture of the village with emphasis on the various school houses.

The first is Latham's school for boys, now Tudor House. The second is a building which has a curious history. Another village benefactor, William Bigley, who had himself attended Latham's school, bequeathed money for its erection in 1838, stating that it should help 'fifteen poor girls' of Barnwell and Oundle. Its site was what is now the south-east corner of St Andrew's churchyard. Then in 1875 the 5th Duke of Buccleuch built the present, larger, school for both girls and boys, in exchange for the other two school houses. In 1915 the owner of Barnwell Estate, Horace Czarnikow, had the girls' school dismantled and re-erected near the roadside in the Manor grounds as a house for his butler. The Gloucesters' retired butler, Mr Dennis Warner, lives there now, and it is referred to as 'Bigley's Bungalow'. There is a fourth school house, No. 8, next door to the Reading Room, where Ray and Judith Spelman live. It was built in the last century by the poet and schoolmaster Thomas Bell as a small private boarding school for 'the sons of gentlemen'.

Little knots of people, some with toddlers and push chairs, gathered by the side entrance to the Manor just before the schoolchildren arrived over the crook-backed bridge. Teresa Pywell, in very trendy casual clothes, looked up at the grey sky and tossing trees, and remarked she was glad she'd decided to put on her thermal vest. The sheep in the meadow below the Church had just been shorn, and were bleating continuously.

The gate was opened, and we went to stand in a semi-circle around the forecourt. Princess Alice, in bright coral pink, came out, and one of the boys read out a short introductory speech. Then, accompanied by the distant sheep, the children sang 'Summer is icumen in' and six-year-old Nicola Ferguson presented the red rose. Three dances followed; one, a famer's jig, got the dancers into a slight tangle with inevitable giggles, and I wondered exactly what it was that John McIntosh whispered to Jane Fox as they skipped hand in hand across the gravel looking misleadingly angelic.

Ann Lillyman, who had come to see Sarah take part, murmured to me that perhaps gravel wasn't the best surface for dancing on, and when Princess Alice walked round to have a word with parents afterwards, she came up to Ann and said exactly the same thing.

One day when I'd gone up to the School it had been break time, and some of the girls, including Sarah, had been playing a game which I suppose they had invented after watching newsreels. They all pretended to see a bomb, and ran off just a second before it exploded. But one girl was injured and fell to the ground, lying there until someone – Sarah – dared to come back to rescue her.

The main outdoor game that is played there is the headmaster John Parkes's favourite – nationball. It is a game that fits on to a small playground, and it can, with a little restraint from the older ones, accommodate a mixed age group of players. It appears to consist mainly of one side hurling the ball at the other to hit them below the knee, and it was played by both parents and children at a fundraising evening in June.

Graham Wise, who can organize things without apparently ever raising his voice, refereed a match between the mothers and fathers. One or two of the players gave the impression they were in the world final of the Battle Between the Sexes; others just got hit as quickly as possible so they could escape to the safety of the schoolroom, where Margaret and Andy Smith were dispensing food and wine.

The evening was to raise money to buy books. With thirty children on the School roll, and a village that feels the School is an integral part of the community whether they have children there or not, adequate fundraising is not difficult. £120 was collected that evening, and as the sun faded and it became past some children's bed times, hardly anyone seemed anxious to go home. Yet another game of nationball would be demanded – by both children and parents, and Bobbie decided the remaining orange squash could be given free to thirsty kids.

John Parkes is a tall, bearded, gentle man, committed to the natural, open quest for knowledge and information that characterizes the modern primary school. Until recently, the head teacher at Barnwell always lived in the schoolhouse, but the Parkeses wanted a larger place of their own for their growing family, and as property has become expensive in Barnwell they had to find somewhere out of the village. It was a change which loosened the close all-the-year-round geographical link between the head teacher and the community.

Spending time with the children in the School – and John welcomes visitors – is more like being among an extended family with plenty of resources than in a classroom. The infants are in one room with Mrs Berridge, and it is possible to appreciate each of the juniors as an individual, rather than be forced, as happens with large classes, to pretend to support the theory that schoolchildren should strive to be identical parts of an assessable whole.

A carved stone lintel, brought from Nicholas Latham's school, stands over the doorway of the School office where Wendy Davies – Amanda and Miles's mother – works as secretary. It reads:

INSTRVCT ME O LORD
THAT I MAY KEPE
THY LAWES

Around the walls of the junior classroom this summer, there were brightly illustrated re-tellings of the story of the Resurrection. The fruits of a previous year's fundraising stood below: a computer with its software.

One amenity the School and village has lacked is a proper playing field. Goal posts have been temporarily erected in various places on occasion, and for years the Cricket Club had its pitch in a field behind the Manor. But by the early 1970s the pitch was gone and the Club had collapsed. Shortly after it re-formed in 1977, a drive began to establish a permanent field for the School and the Club. 'If I'd known it was going to take over five years,' said Gerry Allen who chaired the working party, 'I'd probably never have started.' However, at the May Parish Council meeting he could report that the Education Committee had finally signed a document guaranteeing their contribution, and by the summer of 1985 Barnwell will have a home ground again for its cricket matches, ninety-three years after the Club was founded by Trevor Marriott's grandfather.

The Marriotts have remained a cricketing family. David plays for the Northamptonshire Boys' team, and Trevor is an umpire – always using an old penny for the toss. According to Bert Kirk, when Norah used to come out and put on pads during the team's practice when she was a girl, her father would say, 'Bowl as hard at her as at a boy.' Bert himself holds the village bowling record. 'I got ten wickets once against Thorpe, and I got ten wickets against Glapthorne. No – I didn't, I got eight. But no one else got any because we had two run out.'

Recent years have been rather trying, with fixtures always having to be played away. Stewart Burrows, the captain, resigned this year, and Mo (Maurice) Head took over. 'Stewart battled on for three years,' said Gerry, 'with the hassle of every week having to get eleven people to turn out to play cricket away from home. Though mind you,' he added, 'I'm fixtures secretary, and people always ring me up and say, "We must have a fixture with you, we enjoyed it so much playing Barnwell last year, we had such a good evening," – because there are always at least ten of us in the pub at closing time. They never mention the standard of the cricket, and I think for two seasons we didn't win a game!'

The site chosen for the playing field is in the glebe meadow next to the Litchfields' house; it was used for grazing by Trevor, and tends to flood badly. 'We picked that particular field,' said Gerry, 'not because it was the flattest or whatever, but because everybody going in and out could see the team playing and we hope people will stop and watch – or make fun of us.'

It was known that there had once been a drain which ran across the meadow, then under the road, through the spinney and down the adjacent field to a ditch in Well Lane, but the rumours concerning its exact whereabouts and demise varied.

'It was all put in my hands,' said Gerry. 'The Council said to me that the culvert under the road should go about twenty yards from Tommy Litchfield's fence. So Mo Head and I spent one Saturday morning digging through the spinney. Then Bob Chapman from South Lodge came to fill the pond in in the meadow, and while he was doing it he discovered the old drain. So young Bob Chapman came along with his two wires, and followed this drain right across to the roadside hedge. Someone came with a digger, and dug down, and there was the other end of the drain. So they rodded it all through and cleared it out, and then tried to rod under the road, and that's when they discovered where it was blocked. So we abandoned the original digging in the spinney, and moved up opposite what we'd found, and Ted Booker and I found the old drain under the field. But it was broken and blocked under the spinney where the tree roots had grown into it. Also when they laid the mains water supply into the village, they'd broken the drain under the road. So we put in some plastic pipe and connected it up to the old drain. Then Ted Booker came and flushed it out, and Ian Hamilton came and helped as well.' Ted Booker and Ian Hamilton both work for the Manor estate farm.

'I've just arranged for some top soil to be delivered,' Gerry continued, 'and Robert Marriott's coming to level it out. And the man's coming to fence it within the next week or two. We hope this year we shall put up – well, it may be a ramshackle pavilion, it may be a decent pavilion, but at least we'll have a base to put all the kit in, and put the roller in and mowers and everything. And then we can develop it from there.

'I hope eventually we'll get the old fixture with Sandringham back, because that used to be a traditional one, when the old Duke was alive.

'Anyway, as I said to Trevor Marriott, "If the Cricket Club folds up, and the School packs up, at least you'll have a much improved field back."'

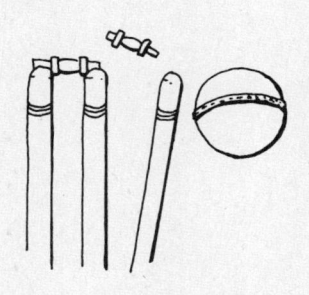

THIRTEEN

Songs of Praise

The flowers in our garden were shimmering in the heat.
   Myriads of shirley poppies leant over the path, shedding their pale petals on the grass. The huge oriental poppies – vermilion, black-and-white, and that shade of pink which was once called shocking – shone like Thai silk. Ordinary field poppies grew straight and tall, and yellow Welsh poppies flourished under the apple trees. There were spires everywhere – spires of lupins, delphiniums and monkshood; and there were sheaves of delicate sky-blue linum, their coin-like flowers nodding in the hot air.
   It was the day before the Barnwell Church Festival. Would the weather hold?
   We had taken flowers to add to the bunches being collected to decorate the Church. My mother had dressed a doll for a 'Guess the Name' competition. Ann Lillyman had been deputed to ask us if we would make a cake for the cakestall, and had looked most disbelieving when we said we didn't know how; she'd give us a recipe, she said. So we explained we ate cake too seldom for it to be worth learning to bake now, but we promised we'd buy one. She was also collecting for the second-hand bookstall which she and John organized, and didn't at all mind relieving us of boxes of unlikely titles such as *The Psychology of Aviation*.
   Then Dulan broke the sacrosanct rule of cakestalls by asking Jeanne, who was helping to run it, to save him a chocolate one in case we were late. My sister was arriving the next day around lunch time, and we weren't sure we would get to the Rectory for the start of the Festival at two-thirty.
   As it turned out, my sister was early, and we just about breasted the metaphorical tape for the opening of the cakestall equal first with Sandra Wilkins. The day was as lovely as the one before, a silver band was playing, and the Rectory lawn

was packed with people going round the various stalls and being served tea at garden tables and chairs.

The west door of the Church was open, and just inside James Rutterford was offering tours up the spire to see the bell-chamber. All around the sides of the nave an exhibition of arts and crafts made by Barnwell people had been set up. Its size and range were remarkable. There were patchwork quilts, designed clothes, tapestries, embroideries, carvings, models, carpentry, paintings, poems.

Among the embroideries was an intricate work-in-progress by Peggy Scopes: a lovely communion kneeler decorated with the flowers of the Bible. Princess Alice, who earlier in the day had been on the balcony at Buckingham Palace for the Queen's birthday, was looking at it when my sister and I returned to the Festival at the end of the afternoon for the 'Songs of Praise'.

Families came into the pews in their shorts and summer dresses, glad of somewhere cool to sit. The younger children looked as though they had come from a carnival; a face-painter had been transforming them into devils and mythical beasts. 'Songs of Praise' was a new idea to round off the Festival; each village organization had been asked to choose a favourite hymn, which was then introduced by a spokesman who gave the reason for their choice. 'Jerusalem' received by far the lustiest rendering from the choir and congregation.

After supper, we walked up to the end of the No Through Road. The sun was setting behind the Chancel and, when we had passed Friars Close and drew near to Lower Farm, we could hear voices and laughter.

At a table in the front garden of the farmhouse, shaded from the dazzling golden light, a celebration was taking place.

'Did you enjoy the cake?' Mary Marriott called to us.

As Dulan and I had left the Rectory garden that afternoon, the chocolate cake being carried flat on his palm like a votive offering, we'd met Mary with a big dish of squares of yeasty cake which she'd held out to us. 'Take some,' she'd said. 'It's called friendship cake.'

'Yes,' I shouted across the brook.

Jean Hastings raised a tall glass to us. She and Bert, and Trevor and Pat Shacklock, were helping Mary and Alan Shacklock to celebrate their shared birthday.

Nothing could appear more parochial than the group outside the farm at the end of the No Through Road. Yet there were among them three people, Pat from London, Alan from Yorkshire, and Jean who was born in Germany, who had gravitated to the village years ago from far afield and had become what to most people would now be considered part of 'old' Barnwell. So foundations become renewed and strengthened.

When we walked up Well Lane two evenings later, the air was heavy with the scent and particles of seed from haymaking. We stood in the gateway of a field which had large rectangular bales scattered across it and our shadows reached right into its centre.

Pat came out of the Post Office when she saw us, saying she felt shattered after all the work for the Church Festival. Ron was still at Cash & Carry, and he was finding life without the Bustins rather difficult. A rota of visiting clergy took the services on Sundays, and there was everything from mowing the Rectory lawn upwards to organize. On top of this, Sharon Booker – Ted Booker's daughter – who helped with the Post Office shop, had been very ill and had been taken to hospital. But then James poked his head out of the window and said he'd made – guess what? – a chocolate cake at school, and would we like some? Slices were brought out, and when Ron returned, looking fagged out, he found us all eating and laughing.

We reached the Pub just before time was called, and after we'd had a drink, and commiserated with Shirley because Ralph was away and two barrels had finished and one was malfunctioning, a very tall young man in a red and blue rugby shirt turned round and insisted on buying us another drink. It was Stewart Burrows, whom we'd not really talked to since he was a child. Only a few days before, his mother, Dot, had been telling us she worried that he was not really taking care of his life now he lived on his own in Oundle, so it was good to see him looking as relaxed and well as anyone might wish for.

'I remember going up to Number 58 when Dan's granny lived there,' he said when he'd asked after Dan and my mother. 'We used to watch *Superman* and she always gave us a drink.'

'Remember when you came to stay with us in London?'

'Yes. I was homesick. And Frank, Dan's dad, how's he? I remember meeting him. You two haven't changed a bit. You're still in jeans, and Dulan looks exactly the same.'

Which, given we'd both put on well over a stone since those days and I'd gone grey, made us feel rather good.

We wandered back to the cottage and sat talking about people, both in the past and the present, until we heard the ragged, sharp beginnings of the dawn chorus. It was a quarter to four. We went out into the luminous garden and listened as a cuckoo called softly.

July 1 was a Sunday, grey and rather dismal. It had been so chilly the night before we'd lit the stove.

Ron had told us to rouse him in the afternoon and he'd show us right round the empty Rectory. I'd wanted to see it because I thought it was such a lovely house, fantasizing how exciting it would be to have so many rooms. I felt very different, however, by the time we'd seen every bedroom, boxroom, pantry and passage.

I hadn't realized how sprawling the older, back part is, and seeing it empty, with all the surface imperfections in even the main rooms, made it suddenly seem depressing. There were the lingering aspirations – smells even – of past generations: the disused tiny chapel, which was now virtually a store cupboard, with its broken stained-glass window; the lady's and gentleman's dressing rooms attached to the main bedroom. I felt that Professor and Mrs Frend would need all the enthusiasm and energy they could muster when they moved in.

The following day, Sharon, who had returned to the Post Office but was still very pale and uncharacteristically subdued, turned up for work wearing a stud through her nose. Knowing the alarm with which Pat regarded her boyfriend's sensational Mohican haircut, we didn't, as we probably normally would have done, make some jokey comment – Sharon always giving as good as she gets. And, indeed, by about the third sighting the stud seemed as normal as an earring, while just lightly emphasizing Sharon's natural air of independence as she attends efficiently to the everyday business of looking for butter beans or weighing cheese.

A cultural challenge on a very much larger scale was beginning to tax village opinion. Over the August bank holiday weekend there was to be a rather hastily-planned pop festival at Lilford Hall, a mile and a half away, and thirty thousand people were expected to attend. Oundle shopkeepers were up in arms, and a police sergeant had been on the local radio advising them to board up their shops when the time came – though this advice had been countermanded at a higher level.

Barnwell Parish Council debated the matter during the course of its July meeting, and a proposal was made by Walter Woolman to uphold the District Council if they tried to suppress the festival. Several of those present had probably assumed that everyone would agree to this, until Graham quietly said, 'I think a lot of people are getting neurotic about it. I accept it's going to cause problems, not least the fire hazard for farmers, but I'm in favour of living and let living until there's a reason to stop it.'

'If that nearby wood, which is all pine trees, gets alight, with a wind behind it,' said Walter, 'it will be down into this village. The fire will jump the road if the wind's in the south west and these so-called firemen can't contain it. We should uphold the District Council if they suppress the festival.'

'You're assuming the Council will suppress it,' said Graham.

'Well, they will. It's been on television.'

'We can't anticipate how the committee will vote,' said Ian Fox. 'And, if there *were* adequate safeguards for farmers, traders, etc., then one should approach the festival with an open mind. But two months is not long enough for it to be adequately planned and thought through.'

Graham proposed an amendment to ask the Council to ensure that the problems of sanitation, fire-risk, traffic control, etc., were minimized. Ian felt there was merit in this, provided it included compensation for any damage caused.

'They won't be responsible for anything outside the Lilford

perimeter,' said Norman Beesley, whose land abuts it, and who had seconded the original proposal.

'Can you assume they'll be thirty thousand layabouts?' Norah asked Walter, who was looking askance at the amendment.

'They're *not* all layabouts,' said Joan Crump, whose younger son, a joiner, would probably want to go.

'There's the other that goes with it,' said Walter. 'Junkies.'

'There were a couple died at Glastonbury, in a car, of an overdose,' added Norman.

'Well, at least they did it peaceably,' remarked Norah.

Ian proposed an addition to Graham's amendment, 'That the East Northamptonshire District Council fully consider the environmental consequences before granting a licence,' which Graham seconded, and the amendment was carried.

Outside afterwards, Dolly said, 'Of course there wasn't pop music and drugs in my young day. And the trouble is, the drugs make people do silly things.'

*

Three evenings later, the Foxes, John Lillyman, Godfrey Pratt, and several others, were busy putting up stalls on the village green and along the side of the road to the Reading Room. Notices had appeared signposting the way to toilets, car park, tours round the Manor gardens, veteran car rally, and a clay pigeon shoot.

The next day, Saturday, was Country Day, an event which used to be linked to a gymkhana, but 'This year,' announced the *Parish News*, 'stalls will be in the centre of the village, and there will be a number of craftsmen demonstrating spinning, thatching, stick dressing, glass engraving, woodcarving, knitting, patchwork, jigsaw making, etc.'

I was sleepily aware, very early in the morning, from a glimpse of sheeny light through a white mist, that the weather forecast was going to be true: a fine hot day, with temperatures into the eighties.

By midday, there was the first traffic jam I think I've seen in Barnwell. Veteran cars were arriving, together with stall-holders, and displays by the police and the fire service, and a huge transmitter van from Hereward Radio who were going to do a live broadcast throughout the afternoon. Judith Spelman, who was the chief organizer, hurried from one point to another, looking fraught but firm. All proceeds were going to the upkeep of the Reading Room, of whose management committee she is the secretary.

Mrs Ivy Vinson was preparing refreshments in the Reading Room, slightly hampered by the fact that no one was able to give her a remotely confident estimate as to how many people might turn up. Victor Vinson is the Manor's estate manager, and their cottage, on the far side of the Reading Room, was about to have its own craft display, when some very handsome new thatchwork was done along the ridge of the roof.

The veteran cars were meeting in the field opposite. Their burnished paintwork – Cherry Blossom boot polish red, stove black and holly green – shone against the pale gold stubble from the hay. A steam tractor was beginning to snort out plumes of black smoke as it prepared to take children for rides. The smell reminded me of the old steam trains, and Norman Elcock's stories of the dramas that had taken place at what had looked like just a quiet country station.

During the War, he'd told me, army stores had been kept in some big sheds on the Duke's land. 'We had 3.7 guns coming here, 3.7 barrels coming, ammunition coming, all different equipment for radar. Then we had rocket guns. We used to have to put them on the lorry, take them up to the sheds, and they'd probably be up there a day or two, and back they used to come.

'And we had American hospital trains coming in here. The platform was lengthened for them. I'd be in bed, fast asleep. Front door would be hammered on, and the policeman'd say, "Hospital train in an hour's time!"'

The biggest excitement was when the Queen came down in the Royal Train for Prince William's twenty-first birthday.

'The station was all done up. Eastern Operating Superintendent from Cambridge, and another Superintendent came from Watford, and they was talking in the office, about where they were going to put the train, you see, and they couldn't make up their mind where they were going to put it. So I said to me boss, I says, "May I have a word, sir?" He says, "Yes, Norman, if you can help us out." "Well," I says, "Look. If I was going to do anything about this. Over the other side, where we had the ambulance trains come in, you've got hard road there. I'd get the engineer people to come up," I says, "and take up three of those fence posts, and take the wire down, because they can always put it back again, and allow the cars to come in there." And he says, "Why didn't we think of that?" So we had the Royal Train on the down line. It stood in there from eight o'clock in the evening, until four-twenty in the morning when she moved out, went back to London. But she didn't go down to the Manor till – about twenty-past two, I think it was.'

'Well,' corrected Mrs Elcock, 'she came in at eight o'clock in the evening, but it was between nine and ten that she went down there. Because they came back early hours of the morning, didn't they?'

'That's right. Twenty-past two when she come back. And then she had a couple of hours sleep, before they moved off out again.'

A ride on a steam tractor, which the Duke and Duchess of Gloucester's children had on Country Day, couldn't really compare with the regular engine rides their father used to have as a boy. 'Still,' said Mr Elcock, 'if they're like their dad, they'll have a go, and enjoy it.'

There was, of course, among the stalls, a WI cake one, and

we again competed in the unseemly rush at its opening, coming away with two cakes as we were expecting visitors. (This time Sandra Wilkins had out-manoeuvred us in advance by becoming one of the stall organizers.) When Mrs Barbara Hamilton told me later that the stall had been completely sold out by the time Princess Alice reached it, I felt slightly guilty.

    The Lillyman bookstall, which at last found a buyer for *The Psychology of Aviation*, was next to a plant stall from a nursery that specializes particularly in hebes. We kept going back for one more look and purchase, the temptation of plants which we like and don't have being irresistible. Once we met Win Allen carrying some herbs away from the stall. They might help her to cook something tasty, she said. We had heard that Gordon was very poorly and could eat very little.

Stretched out in the sun on a lounger outside the Pub, Sylvia Harrison was directing cars that were just visiting Country Day away from their car park and up to the one where they had to pay. With one month to go before her baby was due, she was looking much better, but had been told to rest.

We took our new alpines and hebes home, and lined the pots up on the yard under the kitchen window. The ground was too hard and dry to plant them out.

Two days later, Norah stopped me by the footbridge opposite Horseradish Lane. 'I saw from my five-year diary that it's just a year since you came over to tell me about the book.'

'Yes. You're right. I've been thinking I can stop my Barnwell journal now. It was only supposed to cover a year.'

I ended it in the garden on the next day:

At four-thirty it is a grey morning in which the colours of the flowers look enamel bright. The madonna lilies and the roses are quite formal after the rush of poppies.

A dove coos loudly on the Kirks' television aerial, and two cockerels crow. The rooks that fly home in a noisy, sky-filling mass every evening at about a quarter to ten, are setting out quietly in twos and threes and fours to their feeding grounds. A few bees, their wings humming loudly, clamber in and out of the larkspur and the canterbury bells.

Bob's ducks wake up, and a swift arcs across the garden. Perkie-Liza pads over the damp grass, her black feet brushing the still-closed daisies. Indoors, Pudding and Midler stay in their sleeping-places, unimpressed by this early rising.

POSTSCRIPTS

Early on Monday, July 30, John called me over to the fence and said quietly, 'You probably don't know, but I'm afraid Gordon Allen died yesterday evening.'

We both stood for a moment. Over John's shoulder, across the intervening summer gardens, I could just see part of the grey roof of Gordon's shed.

In the autumn, before he was ill, I'd rather tentatively stopped him outside his yard and asked if he would talk to me one day. He always struck me as a very private man, and I wasn't sure he would approve the idea of this book.

He said he would like to, one evening in the winter, and that since the Allens are one of the village's oldest families he could probably tell me quite a lot of things.

It was a conversation I had particularly looked forward to.

*

On the afternoon of Friday, August 3, which was very hot and oppressive, many people in the village were at the Church for Gordon's funeral.

The library van was practically deserted, but Brett was there helping Tiffany and Kirk to choose their books. I asked after his mother. He smiled and said the baby had arrived at five minutes past one that afternoon. She was a girl.

*

During early August, the news filtered through that the organizers had cancelled the pop festival.

*

Very late in the evening on August 21, the combine was still thrumming in the distance on Berridge's farm.

For days, the tractors pulling trailers of corn had been passing our window once more, and it had been good to see that Neil Sharman, like Brian, had been in charge of one of them.

There was a loud knock at the open door, and Ron appeared with an armful of ripe corn.

'I thought you'd like to have this. I was getting some before it was threshed, for the Harvest Festival in October.'

The *Times* headline next day read: 'EEC fears record harvest.' Fears.

The corn, with its drooping heads, stands in a pottery jug on a shelf under the beams.

*

A week later, Barbara Preston reported that someone had appeared on their section of the Wigsthorpe bridleway for the first time. 'Leading a horse. A lady, I don't know who she was, leading a rather magnificent horse, I must say. Coming up from the village, and she could see me picking peas in the garden, and she shouted, "Is this the bridleway?" And I said, "Yes, it is." And I watched very carefully to see that she closed the gates, and she did.'

*

Miles said to Dulan that the long tendril, with its flat leaves, which a nasturtium had put out over a bushy heather at the top of the garden, looked like 'a flight of steps to the end of the world'.

*

On September 1, Maureen drove us back to London. In our luggage was a present from Ann and John: a watercolour which Ann had secretly painted of our garden at poppy time.

Dulan and I didn't admit to one another until the next day how sad it had been when people came to say goodbye.

'When I walk round with Santa in the morning, if your cottage is empty,' Mick had said, 'it don't feel right.'

*

Professor William Frend was licensed as Priest-in-charge on September 3, and the October *Parish News* began with his first message to his parishioners:

> Dear Friends,
>
> It was an honour and a wholly unexpected surprise to be invited to follow Peter Bustin at Barnwell with Thurning & Luddington. It is a wonderful parish, and we have been overwhelmed by the kindness and help we have received from all sides. After 35 years in academic life I don't expect to find work in the very many activities of parish life at all easy. We all, however, have some contribution to make, and we will do our best to make ours.
>
> With every good wish to you all.

*

On October 9 the telephone rang in London. It was Norah Blunt. 'Am I in time for a PS?'

'Just.'

'We've won the Tidiest Village competition.'

'Good heavens.'

'Walter took me to the presentation. And I've got this great big silver cup sitting here.'
'How about the churchyard?'
'Missed it by just one point.'

Instead of a dedication

My impulse was to write a message at the beginning of this book dedicating it to all the people of Barnwell. But I quickly realized that they might not want it because I've had to leave so many people, and so much information, out, and have probably unintentionally distorted or misrepresented some of what I have put in.

So, just – thank you. Thank you for wholehearted help, hospitality, trust, laughs, and, above all, such friendly interest in what Carry and I were doing.

Paddy

INDEX

After Care 41, 42
Akroyds, the 2
Akroyd, Carry 14, 106
Akroyd, Donald 14
Akroyd, Sheila 14, 94
Ali Baba and the Forty Thieves 117
Allens, the 1, 171
Allen, Florence Elizabeth 59
Allen, Frankie 20
Allen, Georgie 59
Allen, Gerry 24, 56, 57, 58, 59, 113, 114, 122, 157, 158, 159
Allen, Gordon 53, 56, 58, 59, 168, 171
Allen, Liz 20, 56, 57, 59
Allen, Marilyn 58, 102, 139
Allen, Steven 19
Allen, Thelma 59, 105, 118, 137
Allen, Winnie 58, 92, 168
All Saints' chancel – *see* Chancel
All Saints' Church 44, 75, 76
All Saints' Estate 76
Almshouses, the (Latham Cottages) 10, 27, 43, 91, 92, 93, 97 (*entrance arch, illustration*)
Amies & Son, Peterborough 110
Aosta 71, 72
Armston 55, 137
Ashby, Jack 69
Ashton 143, 144
Aylesbury 72

Babbs, the 2
Babb, Emma 62, 63, 65, 66, 67 (*illustration*), 68, 71, 74, 76, 98, 110, 116, 117, 121, 125, 130, 131, 136
Babb, Phil 66
Baillie, Mrs 20

Baillie, William 20, 39, 120
Bairnwell 45
Barber, Dulan 65, 66, 75, 76, 109, 111, 112, 116, 127, 131, 132, 160, 161, 162, 172
Barnwell All Saints 44
Barnwell Broiderers 22, 90
Barnwell Castle 10, 33, 34, 76, 148, 149, 152, 153
Barnwell Cricket Club 29, 114, 157, 159
Barnwell Entertainers 22, 71, 73, 104, 126
Barnwell Estate (*also* Barnwell Manor Estate, Barnwell Castle Estate) 30, 51, 52, 53, 54, 154, 159
Barnwell Manor 2, 8, 10, 18, 21, 33, 39, 42, 53, 76, 78, 87, 96, 105, 148, 149, 150, *150* (*terrace, illustration*), *151*, 152, *152* (*silver garden, illustration*), 153, 154, 155
Barnwell Roosters 51
Barnwell St Andrew 44, 45
Barnwell School 5, 9, 10, 14, 41, 71, 73, 104, 106, 140, 154, 155, 156, 157, *157* (*illustration*), 159
Barnwell Station 7, 69, 150, 166
Barnwell Wold 49
Barton Seagrave 50, 51, 71
Batleys, the 2, 30
Batley, Christine 70
Batley, Kathleen 29, 30, 31, 71, 75, 96, 120, 127
Batley, Marion 70
Batley, Sidney 29, 30, 85
Beesley, Norman 133, 165
Bell, Thomas 33, 44, 91, 155

177

Benefice of Barnwell with Thurning
    & Luddington 119, 173
Beorna-Wielle 45
Bernewell 45
Berridges, the 2
Berridges' Farm (see also Castle
    Farm) 30, 35, 171
Berridge, Elizabeth 104, 105, 118,
    156
Berridge, Colonel Fred 87
Berridge, Oliver 95
Berridge, Simon 26, 87
Beswick, Edith 106
Bigley, William 154
Birmingham 72
Blacks, the 2, 105, 106, 145
Black, Andrew 106
Black, David 106
Black, Geoffrey 2, 106
Black, Jason 85
Black, Michael 2, 85, 106, 108, 109
Black, Richard 2, 105, 106, 109
Borrett, Bletsoe 75
Borrett, Virtue 75
Blunts, the 2
Blunt, Jack 43, 44, 139
Blunt, Norah 3, 4, 5, 22, 23
    (illustration), 25, 31, 41, 43,
    44, 48, 75, 80, 112, 119, 125,
    126, 127, 136, 138, 139, 140,
    158, 165, 169, 173
Booker, Sharon 162, 163, 164
Booker, Ted 159
Boughton House 149, 153
Bowling, Barb 106, 110
Bowling, Dan 8, 61, 62, 69, 70, 81,
    82, 85, 91, 106, 107, 108, 109,
    110, 162
Bowling, Frank 9, 65, 162
Bradford 69
'Bridge Book', the 83, 84
Bright Pitts Farm 75
Brook Lane, Brookside 27
Broome, Agnes 45, 46, 47, 111,
    120, 140, 151
Browns, the 2, 73
Brown, David 9, 10, 12, 13, 17, 36,
    94, 105, 119, 122, 143
Brown, Emma 12

Brown, Judith 10, 12, 13, 28, 105,
    118, 119, 143
Brown, Rachel 13, 143
Buccleuch and Queensberry, Dukes
    of 149
Buccleuch and Queensberry, 5th
    Duke of 154
Buccleuch and Queensberry, 7th
    Duke of (Earl of Dalkeith) 21,
    53, 76, 150
Buckingham Palace 161
Burchell, Shirley 94, 95, 120
Burnham, Hazel 70
Burnses, the 2, 121
Burns, Emma 40
Burns, Mick 39, 40, 41, 42, 89, 90,
    109, 110, 121, 126, 172
Burns, Susan 39, 40, 41, 148
Burrowses, the 2, 29
Burrows, Andrew 19, 72, 101, 145
Burrows, Donna 19, 29
Burrows, Dot 162
Burrows, Karen 70
Burrows, Lewis 10
Burrows, Marilyn 19, 28, 29, 30,
    31, 101, 118, 119
Burrows, Nigel 28, 29, 31, 101,
    108, 114
Burrows, Stewart 108, 145, 158,
    162
Burrows, Trina 19, 101, 137
Bus service 15
Bustins, the 2, 5, 18, 21, 101, 119,
    128, 162
Bustin, Anne 2, 3, 18, 20, 21, 86,
    102, 103, 130
Bustin, Peter 2, 3, 4, 83, 84, 85, 86,
    92, 94, 95, 96, 100, 102, 119,
    120, 127, 128, 130, 132, 173
Carter, Gary 35
Carter, John 35, 52
Castle Farm 1, 26, 52, 87, 98
Chalmers, Betty 130, 151, 153
Chancel, the (All Saints' chancel)
    24, 44, 45, 77 (monuments,
    illustration), 78, 79 (monk's
    grave, illustration), 80, 82
    (Corisande Ludlow's grave,
    illustration), 93, 120

Chancel Terrace 27, 35, 44, 52, 121, 130, 144, 146
Chapmans, the 75
Chapman, Bob 158
Chelsea Flower Show 64
Chunky 39, 59, 112
Church (St Andrew's) 8, 10, 18, 20, 28, 30, 44, 70, 76, 84, 86, 87, 87 *(churchyard, illustration)*, 88, 89, 89 *(reredos, illustration)*, 90, 91, 95, 96, 99, 120, 128, 129 *(illustration)*, 141, 142, 151, 154, 161, 171
Church choir 31, 94
Church Festival 160, 161
Church Hill, Church Lane, Church Road, Church Street 27
Civil War, the 149
Clare, John 136, 140
Cole, Bill 15
Cole, Dolly 11, 14, 15, 18, 19, 24, 25, 58, 80, 81, 104, 122, 150, 165
Cole, Fred 14, 15, 104, 122
Cooks, the 50, 51
Cook, Jennifer 51
Cook, Norah 50, 51, 128
Cook, Phil 50, 85, 128
Cookson, Catherine 127
Cooper, Colin 51, 53, 98
Coppard, F. 107
Corby 29, 114
Cotterstock 39
County Records Office 83
Country Day 165, 167, 168, 169
Cricket Club 29, 114, 157, 159
Croft, The 132
Crowson, Ernest 45, 69
Crowsons 36, 37, 45, 88, 122
Crump, Joan 24, 41, 81, 165
Crump, Martin 145
Crump, Victor 130, 145
Czarnikow, Horace 52, 53, 154
Dalkeith, Earl of (7th Duke of Buccleuch and Queensberry) 52, 150
Davies, Amanda 26, 142, 145, 146
Davies, Miles 145, 172

Davies, Nigel 113
Davies, Wendy 156
De Bocks, the 2, 52
De Bock, Basje 26, 111, 145
De Bock, Hanneke 26, 32, 52, 127, 142, 145, 146
De Bock, Jeanne 52, 111, 160
De Bock, Werner 52, 125
Doherty, Ellen 57
Duffy, Maureen 131, 172
Dyott Estate 50, 51, 52, 56

East Northamptonshire District Council 24, 80, 81, 124, 164, 165
Elcock, Miriam 7, 167
Elcock, Norman 7, 87, 130, 134, 150, 166, 167, 168 *(illustration)*
Elizabeth I, Queen 84, 149, 151
Elizabeth II, Queen 85, 92, 161, 167
Empty Spinney 78
European Economic Community 48, 172
Exchange and Mart 7

Family Walk 143
Ferguson, Nicola 155
Finedon 122
Folker, Gladys 107
Foot Hill Spinney 49, 99
Fotheringhay 39, 104
Foxes, the 165
Fox, Ian 22, 24, 80, 81, 125, 164, 165
Fox, Jane 49, 50, 155
Fox, Jonathan 143
Fox, Liz 22, 24, 112, 125, 126, 128, 145
Fox Covert 98, 151
Freckles 39, 59, 112
Frend, Mary 132
Frend, William 132, 163, 173
Friars Close Farm 50, 51, 52, 68, 72
Friendly Club 18, 19, 22, 63, 92, 104

Garratts, the 61, 71
Garratt, Agnes 61, 62, 63, 131
Garratt, Eric 31, 61, 62, 63, 64, 65, 66, 70, 71, 109, 110, 131, 151
Gilbert, Margaret 70
Girl Guides 137
Girls' Brigade 3, 136, 137, 138
Glapthorne 158
Gliszczynskis, the 52
Gliszczynski, Jan 52
Gliszczynski, Peter 130
Glitter, Gary 109
Gloucester, Prince Henry, Duke of 33, 34, 53, 55, 78, 93, 148, 150, 151, 153, 159
Gloucester, Prince Richard, Duke of 2, 85, 150, 151
Gloucester, Prince William of 150, 151, 167
Gloucester, Princess Alice, Duchess of 2, 33, 39, 53, 86, 130, 142, 148, 151, 152, 153, 154, 155, 161, 168
Gloucester, Princess Birgitte, Duchess of 2, 167
Graley, Audra 130
Grant, Julie 105
Greenham Common 111
Greenwood, Constance 92
Grenfell, Joyce 117
Grimes, Flo 151
Groom, Bill 27, 28, 31, 63, 64, 144
Groome, Ethel 93
Gunns, the 38, 69, 74, 121
Gunn, Derek 36, 37, 91, 122
Gunn, Eileen 36, 37, 38, 122
Gypsy Lane 79

Hamilton, Barbara 168
Hamilton, Ian 159
Harrisons, the 114, 146
Harrison, Brett 146, 171
Harrison, Kirk 146, 171
Harrison, Melody 171
Harrison, Ralph 112, 113, 162
Harrison, Sylvia 112, 113, 114, 146, 169
Harrison, Tiffany 146, 171
Harvest Festival 172

Hastings 39
Hastings, Bert 146, 161
Hastings, Jean 52, 146, 161, 162
Head, Charles 42, 43, 87, 92, 96
Head, John 42, 96
Head, Margaret 42, 43, 86, 96, 104
Head, Maurice 96, 158
Head, Tracy 96
Helpston 140
Hemington 117
Henry VIII, King 149
Hereward Radio 165
Hobbs, Jack 46
Holly 122
Home Farm, Thurning 51
Horseradish Lane 27, 55, 92
Huntingford, George William 21

International Stores 51
Isham 89, 90

Jack-in-the-Green 140 (illustration), 142
Jeffs, John 37, 38

Keep Fit classes 22
Kettering 56
Kettering Grammar School 73
Kettering High School 73
Kim 92, 93
King's Cliffe 20, 36
Kirks, the 18, 61, 68, 68 (Kirks' & author's cottages, illustration), 71, 75, 169
Kirk, Bert 18, 51, 62, 68, 69, 71, 74, 78, 87, 92, 158
Kirk, Helen (Mrs Grist) 69, 74
Kirk, Pat (Mrs Wiggins) 18, 69, 74
Kirk, Pauline 18, 69, 70, 74
Kirk, Rene 18, 24, 69, 70, 74, 80, 85, 120
Kisbees, the 14
Kisbee, Rhoda 21
Kitchen, Doris Ena (author's mother) 63, 65, 106, 107, 108, 131, 162
Knight, Susan 130

Larkins, Geoffrey 140

180

Larkins, Jessie 130, 140
Larkins, Judy 140
Larkins, Reg 130, 140
Latham Cottages (the Almshouses)
    10, 27, 43, 91, 92, 93, 97
    (entrance arch, illustration)
Latham, Nicholas 27, 36, 91, 154,
    156
Leesons, Elizabeth 35
Leesons, Marion 35, 36, 42, 55, 94,
    136, 138, 139
Leland, John 45, 149
Le Moines, the 34, 148
Le Moine, Berengarius 148, 149
Lilford Hall 164
Lillymans, the 62, 66, 71, 168
Lillyman, Ann 71, 72, 73, 155, 160,
    172
Lillyman, John 71, 72, 73, 98, 103,
    104, 105, 118, 125, 126, 165,
    171, 172
Lillyman, Mark 71, 72, 94, 118
Lillyman, Sarah 71, 141, *141*
    (illustration), 142, 155
Limes, The 76
Litchfields, the 58
Litchfield, Ann 33
Litchfield, Tom 2, 33, 76, 84, 86,
    132, 148
Lloyd George, David 52
London 1, 2, 64, 69, 70, 91, 92,
    106, 109, 162, 173
London Boat Show 29
Long Meadow 50
Lower Farm 4, 46, 47, *47*
    (illustration), 58, 99, 100, 161
Luddington-in-the-Brook 85, 117,
    130
Ludlow, Basil 75
Ludlow, Corisande 75
Lyons icecream 14

Main Road, Main Street 27
Malster, Arthur 37, 45, 69, 88, 94,
    120
Malster, Phyllis 37, 130
Manor, the (see Barnwell Manor)
Marlow, Joyce 64, 65, 70
Marriotts, the 157

Marriott, David 48, 157
Marriott, John 48, 58
Marriott, Margaret 58
Marriott, Mary 46, 47, 48, 49, 61,
    146, 161
Marriott, Percy 4, 47, 48, 158
Marriott, Robert 48, 159
Marriott, Trevor 4, 47, 48, 49, 61,
    133, 134, 135, 157, 158, 159,
    161
May Queen ceremony 140, 141, 142
McGrath, Gioya 53
McGrath, William 53
McIntoshes, the 144
McIntosh, Bobbie 143, 156
McIntosh, Donald 144
McIntosh, James 143, 144
McIntosh, John 143, 144, 155
McIntosh, Kirsty 102, 137, 142, 143
Mee, Arthur 8
Meltons, the 145
Melton, David 145
Melton, Jean 145
Metcalfe, Bill (jnr) 98
Midler 131, 169
Montagu Arms, the 10, 112, *113*
    (illustration), *115*
    (illustration), 116, 162, 169
Montagu, 1st Duke of 149
Montagu, 2nd Duke of 149
Montagu, Sir Edward 149, 154
Montagu family, Earls of Sandwich
    76, 78
Montagu, Henry 78
Montagu, Sir Sidney 78
Montagu of Boughton, 1st Lord 149
Montagu Terrace 3, 24, 27, 28, 42,
    44, 72, 106, 132, 144
Morrison, Sandy 43

Nassington 85
Neave, Betty 136, 137
Nene, River 7, 148
Nene Valley Steam Railway
    Preservation Society 7
Norfolk 30
Northampton 52, 137
Northamptonshire County Cricket
    ground 46

181

Northamptonshire Education Committee 157
Northampton-Peterborough branch railway 46
Northamptonshire Rural Community Council's Tidiest Village/Churchyard Competition 87, 145, 173, 174
North Lodge Farm 33
Northolt 28
Norum, Heather 50, 84, 85
Norum, Per 84
Norway 50, 84
Norwood, William 28
Norwood, Gwendoline (Mrs Groom) 28

Oakleaf Country & Western Band 153
Old smithy 39
Orchard End 49, 125
Orpington 69
Oundle 7, 15, 29, 35, 37, 42, 43, 45, 55, 59, 70, 85, 88, 94, 106, 107, 120, 139, 154, 162, 164
Oundle Bookshop, The 43, 136
Oundle Church 143
Oundle Marina 29
Oundle Market Hall 76
Oundle School 43, 69
Oval, The 46
Owen, Emma 57, 85, 146
Owen, Joe 85, 146

Parish Council 3, 4, 21, 22, 24, 41, 80, 81, 89, 90, 112, 132, 134, 157, 164
Parish News 83, 86, 90, 93, 95, 119, 128, 132, 145, 165, 173
Parkeses, the 156
Parkes, Anne 73
Parkes, John 73, 155, 156
Parker, Rowland 120
Parochial Church Council 119, 136
Pask, Annie 14, 15, 19, 58, 84
Pask, Walter 14
Perkie-Liza 131, 169
Perkins Engineering 14

Peterborough 55, 104, 107
Peterborough Medieval Society 153
Peterborough Museum 138
Peterborough Operatic Society 94
Playgroup 18, 19, 20, 22, 29
Polebrook 117, 143, 144
Post Office 4, 9, 13, 14, 15, 17, 111, 146, 162, 163
Pratt, Godfrey 165
Pratt, Rosemary 90
Prestons, the 25, 132
Preston, Barbara 24, 132, 133, 134, 135, 172
Preston, John 133
Preston, Ken 24, 132, 133, 134, 135
Preston, Stuart 133
Prince William School, Oundle 20
Pub, the (*see* Montagu Arms, the)
Pudding 131, 169
Pump Field 3
Pywells, the 121
Pywell, Nene 144
Pywell, Paul 144, 145
Pywell, Teresa 144, 155

Ramsey, Abbey of 149
Ramsey, Abbot of 148
Reading Room 21, 22, 90, 104, 143, 144, 166
Rectory 2, 4, 9, 10, 14, 18, 20, 21, 39, 76, 83, 101, 136, 138, 141, 142, 160, 163
Rectory Cottages 89
Reed, Nicola 144
Reed, Roy 143
Reed, Thelma 143
Richardson, Alan 105, 118
Robinson, Dora 20, 26, 38, 38 (*living room, illustration*), 39, 53, 54, 86, 95, 140, 142, 151, 152
Robinson, William 21
Roman villa site 33
Rooster, The 51
Rotary Clubs, local 153
Rural Schools Project 20
Russells, the 75
Russell, Harold 31

182

Russell, Muriel 30
Russian Revolution 53
Rutterford, James 14, 94, 102, 118, 132, 161, 162
Rutterford, Pat 9, 13, 14, 88, 101, 102, 111, 132, 139, 162, 163
Rutterford, Ron 9, 13, 14, 17, 27, 87, 88, 89, 111, 114, 120, 121, 132, 134, 146, 162, 163, 172
Saint Andrew's Church (*see* Church)
Sandringham 42, 159
Sandwich, Earls of 76
Santa 90, 121, 172
Sawtry Church 34
School (*see* Barnwell School)
Scopes, Peggy 89, 90, 91, 161
Scopes, Peter 24, 89, 90, 91, 120
Scopes, Victoria 90, 91
Scotland 70
Scotney, Bob 65, 66, 68, 110, 116, 117, 121, 130, 131, 169
Scotney, Roly 37
Shacklock, Alan 116, 161, 162
Shacklock, Ann 116, 117
Shacklock, Geoffrey 51, 116
Shacklock, Gerald 116
Shacklock, Graham 116
Shacklock, Hazel 51
Shacklock, Jemma 116, 117, 121
Shacklock, Pat 13, 116, 117, 121, 161, 162
Shakespeare, William 73
Shanahan, Angela 137, 138, 139
Sharmans, the 145
Sharman, Andy 116
Sharman, Brian 52, 114, 172
Sharman, Jack 91, 92, 114
Sharman, Joe 114
Sharman, Neil 130, 172
Sharman, Shirley 112, 114, 127, 128, 130, 162
Shepherd, Moira 50
Shepherd, Rory 52
Shop, the 9, 10, 11 (*illustration*), 12, 14, 15, 17, 150
Smith, Andy 105, 156
Smith, Margaret 104, 156
Smith, Matthew 145, 146

South Lodge Farm 158
Southwick 39
Southwick Hall 39
Southwold 95, 132
Spelman, Judith 155, 166
Spelman, Ray 94, 155
Station (*see* Barnwell Station)
Steer, Annie 93
Steer, Jack 93
Stokes, Laura 26, 53
Stone Cottage 14, 79
Stratton, Millicent 36
Stratton, Pam 24, 36, 43, 57
Stratton, William 36
Stricksons, the 75
Strickson, John 75
Stuart-Jervis, Colleen (author's sister) 108, 160
Sunday School 130
Sutcliffe, Herbert 46
Swingler, Florence 63

Tansor 39
Tess 117, 121
The Day After 100, 101, 102
The Times 172
Thomson, Elizabeth (Mrs Cass) 144
Thomson, Mary 127, 144
Thomson, Winifred 92
Thorpe 30, 158
Thrapston 7, 14, 15, 37, 40, 139
Thurning 51, 85, 101, 117
Tinker 63
Toot Hill 49
Top of the Pops 109
Toughs, the 75
Tough, Walter 30
Tudor House 36, 154

Venice 127
Vinson, Ivy 166
Vinson, Victor 166
Vinsons' cottage 166 (*illustration*)

Waite, Jim 35, 54, 54 (*garden, illustration*), 55, 75, 85, 120
Warliker, Nicholas 153
Warner, Dennis 87, 154

Watsons, the 51
Watson, Joyce 76
Watson, Peter 76, 80, 81
Wellingborough 46
Well Lane 79, 162
Wells, Tom 14, 25, 81
Westminster Abbey 90
Whist Drives 22, 41, 42
Wickham, Colonel 52
Wickham, Lady Etheldreda 52
Wiggins, Harvey 75
Wiggins, Nathan 75
Wigsthorpe 24, 81, 82, 99
Wigsthorpe bridleway 24, 25, 80, 81, 132, 134, 172
Wilkins, Roger 36
Wilkins, Sandra 36, 160, 168
Williams, Sandra 80, 81
Wind in the Willows, The 5

Wine Circle 22
Wises, the 35
Wise, Amy 128
Wise, Esther 128
Wise, Graham 24, 35, 80, 81, 101, 105, 145, 156, 164, 165
Wise, Hannah 128, 138
Wise, Juliet 35, 94, 101, 102, 104, 105, 128
Women's Institute 3, 22, 92, 136, 143, 144
Wood, Natalie 3
Woodhouse, Barbara 118
Woolman, Eileen 28, 56
Woolman, Walter 22, 24, 55, 80, 94, 95, 164, 165

Youth Club 22, 29, 72, 101, 105, 132
Youth Fellowship 101

Wendy Davies playing skittles at a local hostelry on a W.I. night out. 1991